Murder in Georgetown

An Academic Mom Mystery

Books by Jacque Rosman

The Academic Mom Mystery Series
Book One: Murder in Georgetown

Coming Soon!
Book Two: Murder Off U Street

Murder in Georgetown

An Academic Mom Mystery

Jacque Rosman

SPEAKING VOLUMES, LLC
NAPLES, FLORIDA
2024

Murder in Georgetown

ISBN 978-1-64540-903-8

To my family,
Mark, Alexa, and Miles

Acknowledgments

Thank you to all who helped me research and prepare for this book: Frank Eldridge ex-FBI, Lane Stone my critique partner, and Laure Levin. I so appreciate the generosity from all.

Prologue

Monday Morning

I trudged up the hill to Lauren's Georgetown Victorian after vowing at her party, "Never again." A brisk wind lifted the tree branches like girls' dresses as I held my thirteen-month-old baby, Noah, and tugged two-year-old Alyssa's hand. I had forgotten the stroller, a gaffe for which I would be put to shame if I stayed home full-time. Because I was employed and my entire identity wasn't wrapped in mothering, I could get away with it—just.

Alyssa whined, "Don't want to walk."

"Come on, Petal." Her face, flushed from the cold air, was like a flower turned up to me. "You were the one who forgot Toto. Can you remember where you put it? Miss Lauren said she couldn't find it."

"With Kitty."

"You put Toto under the bed with Kitty?" This was the fun part of two—the development of imagination. We kept finding stuffed animals around the house in cute poses: a teddy in the highchair; a bunny with a dishtowel wrapped around its neck as a bib; a panda in the couch cushions made to look like a bed.

Suddenly, a scream rent the quiet October morning. Noah burrowed into me, and Alyssa stopped walking. "Mama?"

I waited for the tell-tale laughter that would say the scream was a joke of some kind, and I could start reassuring my children.

The laugh didn't come. Wind rattled the branches above and rustled the remaining leaves. Another scream sounded—louder—but still I saw nothing.

I dipped my hand into my tote to search for my cell in case I had to call for emergency. But I'd tossed it into the bag when Lauren hadn't answered as I'd swept her neighborhood for a parking spot. After pawing around in the rubble of my bag, I broke the news to Noah. "I'm going to have to put you down." I lowered him to the ground, but he hung on without putting his feet on the sidewalk, a ploy that sometimes worked so I would keep holding him. When I plopped him onto his bottom, he wailed, tears sprouting instantly.

I had just wiped the Cheerios off the phone when a heavyset woman ran out of what looked like, at this distance, Lauren's house. I pressed the numbers 9-1-1 and grabbed Noah into my arms. Sheer panic was driving this woman, I realized as she came closer. Her eyes were wide with terror.

"Carmen?" I hadn't recognized Lauren's housekeeper at first, fear had so distorted her features. "What's happened?"

When she got to us, she was gasping with exertion and sobs. I put a hand out to steady her. Her arm was soft, but I could feel her shaking with fear.

"Miss Lauren!" She closed her eyes, and tears squeezed out. "In there." Her finger trembled as she pointed back toward the house. She covered her hand with her mouth.

"Is something wrong with Lauren?" I glanced at Noah and saw that he was riveted on Carmen's face.

Her mouth contorted. "Oh, miss, *si, si.*"

"Mama, why her crying?" Alyssa demanded beside me. It suddenly occurred to me that my children had probably never seen a grown-up cry.

This time Carmen grasped my arm. "Why do God have to take him that way?" Her pronouns seemed to be getting mixed up in her fright.

"Is she—?" I didn't want to use the word "dead" around my children, but I couldn't think of anything less than death that would create such fear in Carmen.

Carmen glanced back at the house in terror. "*Vamanos*! What if—he still there?" She tried to pull me along away from the house.

"Someone—" I stopped again before I said words that I didn't want my children to hear. "Did something to her?" As the trees creaked with another blast of wind, I scooped Alyssa into my other arm, fleeing for the minivan and pressing the send button for 9-1-1.

Chapter One

The Day Before: Sunday Late Afternoon

Stressed out from my baby's crying in the car, I walked into Lauren's party and pasted a smile on my face. Okay, here was my chance to meet grown-ups.

"Sorry, I can't hug you, Cara. I have a cold." Lauren had long, dark hair like me, but whereas I'd only dragged a brush through mine, hers looked like it had been professionally blown out that afternoon. "Remember to take off your shoes." Her tone sounded abrupt. She was more interested in the older man in the entryway behind me. "Tad, I need to talk to you."

"Sure, we can find some time later. Who's this little princess?" The man was talking to my two-year-old in the Snow White costume she now wore constantly. But his grin, flickering like a neon light in his tanning bed-orange skin, was for me. "Tad Gowers."

I was reminded of a former colleague in my last faculty position. I'd been drawn in by the fatherly, reassuring manner and discovered later it was just another style of flirting. At least Tad was being friendly, which was more than I could say for Lauren.

"Hi, big guy," Tad said to Noah, whom I carried in my arms. To his credit, he didn't react to Noah's pink Crocs—his sister's—which Noah insisted on wearing. They turned out to be an instant barometer of a person's conventionality.

Sure enough, Lauren made a face at Noah's choice of footwear. "Pink?"

I noticed that she tripped around in ballet flats while the rest of her guests looked ridiculously self-conscious in socks. And it took some persuading to get Alyssa to part with her ruby slippers.

Lauren's husband Rob, a lean and angular 40-something with hair as curly as my husband's, skittered across the shiny hardwood floors from their living room. "Do you mind about the shoes? We just got these floors done." He gave a quick, fidgety grin, and I pretended to air kiss him back when he loomed close.

My husband Seth gave a hearty, "My man!" hello, and they clapped hands and pulled on each other fingers, a male bonding ritual that seemed to cheer them both up immensely.

"Rob!" Lauren called. "We have guests arriving at the door, and Tad and his wife want a tour. Do you want to organize some other people? And tuck in your shirt."

Rob obediently karate-chopped his long-sleeved polo into his khakis. He was an assistant professor at Georgetown; I had read the guy's study on a new medicine for ADHD in *The Journal of the American Medical Association*, and now he was being relegated to tour director? He didn't even seem embarrassed when he asked, "Do you guys want to see the house?"

"Let me just get Noah settled in first," I said. "He cried his head off all the way here."

Rob eyed my baby. "What's wrong with him?" Rob appeared to have no bedside manner, but that was typical of the psychiatrists I'd interacted with at my various social work jobs throughout the years. And I knew Rob only maintained a small clinical practice; like most professors, his primary job was research and publication.

"Rob!" Lauren gestured that he should get a move on, and he took off after his wife, trying to gain purchase on the slippery floor.

"What's with her?" Seth said in a lowered voice as we walked toward the dining room. "I knew coming here was a mistake."

"It's what your mother wants," I said, "for you and Rob to be best friends, like her and Arlene." Arlene was Rob's mother and her best friend and neighbor.

He shook his head. "We can't leave the house with Noah again." Parenting wimps, we both became undone by Noah's relentless crying in the car.

"We can't just stay home with these kids." I began with my usual complaint. "You have a whole office full of people to keep you company. I work at an outpost—" An off-campus program of a school of social work, which, despite its location near the nation's capital, was tantamount to academic Siberia. "I need to talk to some grown-ups."

Another couple passed us bearing plates, and Seth and I scrunched our lips into smiles and pretended to become engrossed in the décor. I challenged my mother-in-law's penchant for beige, but seeing it here in all its subtle variations—cream, taupe, and champagne—against the richly painted walls—mauve, hunter green, dark mustard—made me want to revise my taste. Seth was contemporary all the way. I had adopted the style, as well, having had none before I met him.

I thought I'd liked our place—open, spacious, bright colors—but now it seemed like a Gymboree playroom in contrast to this dark elegance with mahogany floors, curving antique furniture, and heavy drapes. Strategically placed lamps threw out soft lighting, even at four in the afternoon.

"Where are the paintings?" Seth asked.

I hadn't noticed, my eyes fighting to take in all the statuettes, patterns, and flowers, but my husband had zeroed in on the bare walls right away. Seth's hobby was collecting conceptual art. I didn't like most of his pieces individually, but they kept us awash in primary colors, which was helpful for combating grey October days like these.

A leprechaun of a man with a bristly red beard and freckles smeared across his face, scuttled up to us, a small plate in his hand. His mouth full, he said, "I'm Griffin Sewell." His hand, when he shook mine, was as freckled as his face. "That's my wife over there." He pointed. "Jodie didn't used to be so heavy, but she's on this thyroid medication now, made her gain thirty pounds."

Aghast, I struggled to respond and came up with, "Do you have children?" I regretted the question when he answered.

"I'm trying to get Jodie pregnant. It's tough with the thyroid medication. She doesn't get her period regularly, and you don't know if she's pregnant or not."

I hoped my face was blank, not revealing the inner horror I was experiencing at this level of detail. If I had been alone with him, I would have wondered about sexual harassment, but he included my husband in the conversation. Griffin honestly didn't seem to know better.

Seth practically ran off to introduce himself to what we called a Dysthymic Dad, a depressed-looking man with a balding head.

"Can you take care of Alyssa, and get her some food?" I called after Seth.

Good luck: her range was so narrow—a certain brand of strawberry yogurt and pepperoni. I scanned the serving dishes arrayed on the dining room table. Seeing paella, I gave in to the temptation and put Noah down so I could grab one of the small China plates. Noah shrieked so loudly that the pacifier dropped out of his mouth. That boy was total oral gratification—if it wasn't the breast, it was the pacifier.

Noah turned up the volume on his cries, and tears sprouted from his eyes. Regretfully, I returned the dish and scooped him up, sticking the pacifier back in. He turned to give me a wounded expression, and I marveled at the amount of tears he could generate in such a short time.

Lauren breezed through on her way to the kitchen, appraising the food on the table. "Did you make the paella?" I asked, trying to engage her in conversation rather than having to talk to Griffin, who was spooning something mayonnaise-drenched into his mouth. *Maybe Lauren is just shy*, I thought, *and that's why she comes off so badly*. I needed to give her a chance.

"Carmen, my housekeeper, did." Lauren didn't stop, heading into the kitchen.

Griffin veered after her. "Bad news." Before the door swung shut, I heard him say, "The release date got delayed, needs more testing,"

Noah wouldn't let me put him down, so I couldn't eat. The dining room was empty; people I didn't know had moved into the living area to sit with their plates. My husband was with a bunch of dads in the family room, watching football. I didn't really have a choice but to eavesdrop. Jiggling Noah in my arms, I moved closer to listen to the rest of the conversation.

"Always a lot of money in the extended release," Griffin said.

Extended-release formulations were sometimes offered for medications that left the system quickly, like stimulants, so people could maintain their benefits throughout the day.

"I need it *now*."

"How bad can it be?" I strained to hear Griffin over the sound of a T.V. playing in the kitchen. "You live here."

"You've obviously never had to do a renovation." Lauren's voice dropped as if she were talking through gritted teeth.

I scooted away as Griffin, still clutching his plate, emerged through the door as if she had booted him out. Lauren stayed behind to bark orders at a woman who answered softly in a Spanish accent. Now she was going to turn her ire on the person who must be Carmen. Displacement was the clinical term.

Lauren's voice rose. "And turn this damn thing down." She had obviously pushed the T.V. remote as the sound of a news announcer got cut off mid-word. "I'm so sick of hearing about that intern. Can't they leave it alone already?"

It was Chandra Levy all over again: a missing congressional intern who'd supposedly been having an affair with her boss. The national news shows, as well as the local media, were drooling as hard as Noah at the prospect of a new version of an old story.

I pushed open the door to the kitchen and said, "Everything okay in here?" I looked over at the short heavyset Latina with the long braid down her back—Carmen, I assumed—but she was chopping a red pepper, and I couldn't catch her eye.

"We're fine," Lauren snapped.

"Is there anything you'd like me to help with?" The offer was unrealistic since I couldn't put Noah down, but it was a way to try to relieve Lauren from the stress she seemed to feel from hosting this party.

"No, thank you," she said stiffly.

Hoping my point was taken, I retreated from the kitchen.

Hitching Noah to my other hip, I sidled up to Griffin, who shoveled saffron rice on his plate from a serving bowl at the table. "What do you do, Griffin?"

He mumbled through a mouthful. "Chemist for B.X. Martin."

A pharmaceutical firm. Not on the level of Eli Lilly or Merck, but a definite player. What was he doing giving information about the timing of a new medication roll-out? I hoped I'd not been witness to insider trading. With all that and the mayonnaise, it was time to get away.

Casting around, I spied a woman with thick, glossy long hair walking toward the dining table to refresh her plate. The baby balanced on her hip had obviously inherited her mother's hair. On the woman, it was like a shampoo commercial; on a child that young, it was frightening. But the woman looked friendly enough and said, "Hi, I'm Meredith. How do you know Lauren and Rob?" She placed some carrot sticks on a plate as a little blonde girl who looked Alyssa's age sidled up to her.

I was about to answer when Alyssa came up, waggling her soft toy. "Mommy, play. Talk Toto." All her stuffed animals were named Toto after she'd watched *The Wizard of Oz*. And no, she wasn't scared of the witch or the flying monkeys.

"We know Rob because his mother and my mother-in-law are good friends in Miami, where they live," I said. "But they only became close recently, so Rob and Seth never knew each other. Then we all got married about the same time and moved to this area."

"Small world," Meredith said, batting her thick hair behind her shoulder.

"How about you?" I asked.

"I sublet from Lauren, see clients a couple of evenings a week."

"You're a therapist, too? What's your background?"

"Social work."

"Same here," I said, delighted. I would probably not become friends with Lauren, but maybe Meredith was a possibility, even though, like most mothers of young children, she was about ten years younger than me.

Seeing Lauren rushing by, frowning at the food, Meredith said, "Your house is so beautiful, Lauren. You did a great job with the renovation."

Lauren sighed in response. "But if we have a baby, I don't know what we'd use for a playroom. I don't want the living room to become a play area. I hate that."

I flashed to our living room—the giant, plastic play yard and the landfill of toys within it—as Meredith's face lit up. "You're going to have a baby?"

"I'm not pregnant now, God no." Lauren put a hand on her flat stomach and laughed.

By the depth of that frown line on her face, Lauren would have to get a move-on. I could say such things since I'd given birth to Noah at forty-two.

"And if I have one—it'll only be the one. I don't get along with my brother and can't deal with the sibling rivalry."

When Lauren walked off for more introductions, I said, "Whoever said two children was three times harder was right." I'd never had such unrelenting stress, even when going through a Ph.D. program.

"Oh, I don't think it's that bad having two," said Meredith. "We're planning on four."

I goggled my eyes at her in disbelief. When I saw mothers with that many children, I wondered how they did it and felt inferior. But the better question was *why* they would do it. Then I saw that Meredith's baby gazed vacantly from her perch on Meredith's hip. If I had one that stayed still for even thirty seconds at a time, it wouldn't be as bad. Right now, Noah had his feet planted on my hip bone like he was going to rappel off my side. My arm muscles labored to keep him in place.

"Where would you buy if you moved?" Meredith asked.

"I love the Georgetown area," said Lauren. "I mean, I wouldn't want to be stuck in the nasty suburbs."

That's where we lived, near Landmark Mall, a section of Alexandria so unfashionable it had no Starbucks for miles around. Seth and I would occasionally wonder why we lived in an industrial area, and then we would remember: so I could have what's called the million-dollar commute—our town home was essentially on the nether regions of the industrial park where my office was housed.

"We were just talking about your psychotherapy practice," Meredith said.

At that, Lauren produced a card out of her dress slacks and handed me one. "Check out my website."

I murmured something agreeable and slipped the card into my bag. It was awfully hard to imagine Lauren with clients. Her frown deepened as Carmen, laden with plates, headed toward the dining room table. Lauren charged over to her. "Not those!"

At that point, Meredith's face had creased into a smile for somebody behind me. I turned to see a woman who was clearly Tad Gower's wife. At least fifteen years younger than her husband, she looked totally glam next to Meredith's natural, fresh-scrubbed look. I had done my usual five-minute lashing of makeup in the car, the only time I had my hands available to do so as Noah was strapped, screaming, in his seat.

Noah began to probe at my shirt. Griffin magically reappeared and ogled Noah's obvious groping. "It starts early, doesn't it?" he commented.

I'd become quite casual about exposing my breasts. Even as an infant, Noah wouldn't stand for the discreet blanket draped over his head as he nursed. But in front of Griffin—no. I wrestled with Noah as he thrashed, trying to pop a breast out.

"I know how it feels, buddy." Most people pretended this wasn't going on, but Griffin watched avidly. "Get used to it. They're always trying to keep you away."

With a tight smile, I cast around for Rob or Lauren to get permission to go upstairs. Griffin was following me. "Do you think women's breasts get bigger when breastfeeding, or is that just an old wives' tale?"

Alyssa glanced up and saw me walking away. "Mommy!" she wailed and, abandoning her artwork, ran after me. I could see the crayons being stepped on by an unsuspecting guest and smashed into the precious hardwood floors. I didn't want to shout across the room to get Seth's attention, conscious of not wanting to be like Lauren—all controlling. But you'd think he'd notice Noah's growing sounds of distress.

Lauren had. She dashed toward me, blinking against the noise. "What's wrong with him?"

"Can I take him upstairs to breastfeed?"

"He's still breastfeeding?"

A wave of heat coursed through me—hormones, Noah crying and needy, but still wanting to repel off my body, the crayons on the floor, the embarrassment. I fumbled to get the pacifier into Noah's mouth, but he wasn't having the rubber substitute.

"He's still sucking a binky?" Lauren went on. "Isn't he over a year old? He'll end up with braces."

"So, can I go upstairs?" I said over Noah's wails.

"Rob, can you show her upstairs?" When he didn't instantly appear, she hollered, "Rob!"

"I can just go up myself," I said.

"You don't know where to go. You haven't been on the tour."

Rob hurried over. "Show her upstairs," Lauren ordered. "And while you're up there, you might want to check your messages. Your voicemail is full again. New patients are calling. If you miss out because you haven't returned the calls —"

Now, in the middle of the party, she ordered him to go through his voicemail?

As Noah blissfully snuffled against my breast, Alyssa quickly tired of the guest room with its drawn drapes and heavy furniture. "Where's Kitty?"

"He's hiding, lovey—very shy."

"Going to find Kitty." She moved toward the door and the master bedroom where she had been told that he lurked under the bed.

"Alyssa, no." My command didn't even register, and she slipped out into the hallway. I tried to pull Noah off to go after her, but he protested, and I sat back, weary. Ever since Noah was born, it seemed that one of my children was unhappy because I was trying to take care of the other one.

Since everyone had been made to take off their shoes, I didn't hear footsteps until voices murmured outside. Lauren was speaking, "You said they did this kind of thing."

"I didn't say they did, you decided they did. That is different." A man spoke with a Russian accent. I had seen who must have been his wife downstairs, growling her "r's", and a little girl with one of those boyish, European short haircuts.

"I might have to rethink being your sponsor. And what would the government think about your connection to—" Lauren broke off. "Alyssa, what are you doing up here? Where's your mommy?"

I bolted up and pulled my shirt down, although my bra was still uncomfortably hitched over one breast. Honestly, there was no dignity with children. Over Noah's rising cry at being deprived, I said to Lauren in the hallway, "I'm sorry, Alyssa followed me up here. She's obsessed with your cat."

When we had all been ushered downstairs, the phone rang, and Lauren darted back up, Noah scooting after her. My "come back here" was taken as an invitation to be chased. As he rounded the stairs, I lost sight of him. When I reached the top, I heard murmuring from behind the door of the master bedroom. *Lauren*? This voice was light, girlish.

I'd been around the block more than a few times. This sounded like a woman talking to a boyfriend. But that didn't seem possible.

Noah was at the dark end of the hallway. When he giggled at me lunging for him, Lauren went silent and ripped open the door. Her voice was shrewish once more. "I told you it wasn't child-proofed up here."

Reaching the bottom of the stairs with us again, she spotted Rob standing with Seth at the dining room table, munching on hamburgers. She shrieked, "What are you doing eating red meat?" Give the guy a break, I thought, and that was before she said, "You know, aren't for you."

Tension thrummed in the air. I thought, good, he's finally going to snap. Tell her he's a grown man and can eat what he wants.

But no. He meekly placed the hamburger on the plate. His Adam's apple bobbed as he swallowed.

Seth and I sneaked a glance at each other. You didn't have to be married to know what we were thinking. It was time to leave, never to return. Little did we know how soon I'd be back—and what I'd find.

Chapter Two

Monday Afternoon

I dove at my ringing phone, tripping over a Wiggles truck. I tried to keep the toys tidy in Pottery Barn-inspired baskets, but Noah just flipped them over. Seth and I had missed each other's calls throughout the day; the police department where I'd spent the long afternoon had been a cell phone dead zone, and I was desperate to talk to him.

"Hi, Cara," my mother-in-law, Barbara, screamed into the phone from her townhome in Miami. "You never answer."

I winced, moving my ear away. It was true—I didn't want to encourage her. Seth already talked to her once a day. I just couldn't be added to her list of regular contacts. Nobody ever talks about tough love for grandmothers, but sometimes it's got to be done.

"Can you believe it? Lauren—dead?" Barbara sounded like she was enjoying this way too much, considering Lauren was the daughter-in-law of her best friend.

"You've already heard?" The stress of the day was as if a balloon had been blown up in my chest, and I was trying to breathe around it.

"Arlene called me, sobbing." Barbara paused dramatically. "Rob waits all this time to get married and then his wife is killed. What a shock. And you were just with them last night. Is Seth there? I tried to reach him at work and on his cell phone, but he doesn't answer."

"You know how busy he's been lately." He was the lead government attorney on a big case, involving Enron-type executives.

Barbara failed to understand the concept of "work." She would ask Seth each time she visited, "Are you going to work today?" as if it was an optional exercise. And because my schedule as an assistant professor of social work was flexible, it fed into her confusion about whether I had a job.

Seth had told his mother he was too busy to take her calls during work hours, but that didn't stop her from trying. As if she read my thoughts, she said, "I know usually he doesn't like me to call him, but this was an emergency. Arlene wanted me to find out some names of good defense attorneys. She wants to hire someone for Rob."

"Why does he need an attorney?"

"Everyone knows the husband is the first one they suspect."

"I don't know about that," I said. "The police were still questioning Carmen, the housekeeper, when we left."

"She was the one who found the body," said Barbara. Obviously, Arlene, Rob's mother, had filled her in. "And you were at Lauren's house, too? The children—putting them in danger like that."

I sat on the couch and leaned back, exhaustion sweeping over me. "It's not like I knew we'd encounter a murder scene when I drove to Georgetown this morning."

"Do you think the maid did it?"

I remembered again Carmen's features distorted in terror. Could that have been at the realization that she had killed someone? She certainly had a good motive—the way Lauren had hounded her about putting out the wrong plates at the party, not chopping the red pepper the right way, etc.

"She didn't have blood on her," I said. "And she was scared, like maybe she was afraid that someone was going to come after her, too." Had she seen anyone? I had asked her, as we waited for the police to arrive. She shook her head, but I wasn't sure how well she understood English.

"You didn't leave the babies with her, did you? I could just see you running up to the house, wanting to see what you could do."

"Of course not." I wouldn't admit to Barbara that I *had* wanted to do something.

What if Carmen had been mistaken and Lauren had only needed mouth-to-mouth resuscitation or some other basic first aid I might have remembered from one or another mandatory training? But I was a mother, and my children would always come first, especially over a woman I hadn't even liked.

"The detectives said there was nothing I could have done." But neither Sergeant Jenkins—a middle-aged white man with the square haircut of law enforcement—nor Sergeant Reynolds—a very pregnant African American woman—would tell me much else. It was definitely the "we're the ones asking the questions around here" routine. And they hadn't been interested in my suspicions, even when I mentioned the conversations I'd overheard. They only looked at me the way I did when I waited for Alyssa to finish one of her long, non-linear stories, and they hadn't written anything down.

"She died of a head wound," Barbara announced now. "A blunt object of some kind."

I was the second person on the scene, had spent all day at the police department, and my mother-in-law knew more than I did. "They didn't find the murder weapon?" I asked.

"Not when I last talked to Arlene. I just shudder to think what might have happened to those children. And then you had to drag them to the police department. Did they get anything to eat?"

I gripped the phone harder, felt like throwing it across the room. My frustration tolerance was depleted. For Noah, the Homicide division was more fun than the library or bookstore; instead of shelves, he hid behind the cubicles and giggled as I chased him. "They ate some snacks out of the vending machines, and they drank a week's worth of juice." I was constantly warned by their doctor that all juice had to be diluted into mostly water, only totaling six ounces a day. As a parent, it was impossible to keep up with the dietary requirements.

"Why didn't you get the nanny?" Barbara said. "Why did you drag the babies over there?"

"You mean Rosa?" I could hardly refer to her as a nanny since she only worked for me part-time as I crammed my full-time job into the corners of my life. "The detectives wanted me to go straight to the police department to give my statement. I was going to get her later when I taught, but then I had to cancel my class."

When I phoned Rosa to tell her I couldn't come get her, I filled her in on the police station and Carmen. "She speaks no English," I had told Rosa.

"I call her," Rosa had said, anticipating my request.

"Would you?" Now I just had to get Carmen's number.

"Did you wash their hands?" Barbara's nasal voice broke into my thoughts.

"Yes," I sighed. "I washed their hands."

"Where are they now?"

"Sleeping in the minivan."

"I could never hear them when they were in there."

"I can hear them. The doors are open." That was the good thing about our town home. You could leave sleeping children alone in the garage in the car with the doors open to the basement space where Barbara stayed when she visited.

"They passed out immediately when we drove away from the police station," I told her.

Barbara cackled in glee, loving a good nap. "Well, I've booked my ticket. I'm coming out."

"You just left," I couldn't help but say.

"I know, two weeks, and I miss 'em like crazy. But the main reason—I owe Arlene. When Seth's dad died, she was the only one who stuck with me, and she can't fly out there alone because of her health. Who else does she have?"

"How will you take care of her?" I asked. Barbara was the one who had ripped the toilet roll dispenser out of the wall, using it as a handrail to get off the toilet. She could barely walk up a flight of stairs, although she had no uncontrolled malady other than never moving more than she possibly could.

Barbara avoided my question. "All those years, Arlene was heartbroken, lonely, aching." She drew out the drama of the words. "For grandbabies to hold. I knew just how she felt. And then finally, finally, her son gets married. If only they'd had kids. Then he'd have someone to keep him company. They'd been married a couple of years already. Lauren hardly worked; he made plenty of money. Why the wait?"

Before I could answer that Lauren didn't exactly strike me as "mother of the year" material, a familiar sound reached my ears—the wails of my children in concert. "Sorry, Barbara, the kids—they're crying." I punched the "end" button on the call and ran downstairs.

* * *

When Rob walked into our house that evening, his face wore a grey pallor that matched silver strands on his head I hadn't noticed the night before. He stumbled on one of the stairs leading from the front door to the living room. His head twisted to take in the amoeba shapes of the outsized acrylic painting hanging in the entryway. Seth reached out a hand to steady Rob. He didn't want anyone touching his artwork.

With Noah in his usual place in my arms, I said, "I'm so sorry, Rob. What a shock. I can't even begin to know what you're going through."

I was conscious of the counseling dictum: don't say "I understand" because you can never understand another person's experience, especially something this horrifying. I couldn't even imagine. I didn't want to imagine.

Rob nodded. His eyes couldn't seem to focus, as if he were searching for an explanation for his wife's murder. The cheesy antics of the *Wiggles* on the T.V. that Alyssa watched from her Sesame Street couch was a bizarre background to his apparent grief.

"Rob, please—sit down," I said. "Can I get you something to drink?"

"Just water." He perched on the armrest of the couch with his head in his hands.

"I'll get it." Seth practically bounded after me. My feet sank into the exercise mat we placed underneath the stairs. Noah had walked for ten months, but this was to protect him from potential falls. Seth hissed, "What do I say to him?"

"There's not much you can say. Just listen and avoid platitudes. Remember, you're the Master Communicator."

Seth grinned, always gratified when I referred to him by his honorary title. He'd been trained by a professional (me). "Don't say, 'You're better off without her?'"

"Seth," I chided. "Just keep him talking about it."

"He probably wants to forget."

I shifted Noah to my other arm. "He can't forget. The images will be going through his mind."

He grimaced. "My mom begged me to take care of Rob for Arlene."

"You had to," I said.

He put his arms around me for a hug, and we laughed when Noah pushed him away. I was all his.

Seth called to the living room, "Rob!" He clapped his hands in a hearty gesture that was all wrong for the occasion. "Let's get some takeout. Pizza, Chinese, Thai?"

"Not pizza," I whispered, and then in response to Seth's quizzical look, I said, "Tomato sauce—blood?" I gave a sharp shake of my head. Rob had viewed Lauren's body.

Not surprisingly, Rob said, "Nothing, I can't eat."

Wiggles over, Alyssa toddled toward me and in a parody of a two-year-old, said, "I want, I want, I want—"

"What do you want, Alyssa?" I asked.

"Milk."

As I placed the cup in the microwave to heat up the milk, I heard Seth talking to Rob in the living room. "As soon as my mom told me, I started making some phone calls, finding out the best defense attorneys. I know the big firms. You want Chase Frankers, and David Synder's the guy."

Alyssa clutched the edge of the counter like a swimmer who would drown if she didn't get her milk in the next minute.

"But you may not need anyone," Seth continued. "Why don't you wait and see?"

I handed Alyssa the sippy cup, warm to the touch, but she slapped it away with a "No!" The discontent of the two-year-old. Alyssa had been a delightful baby, but then her brother was born, and she turned two. As we say in research, confounded variables might have accounted for the change.

I heard Rob saying, "They want to take my statement tomorrow. Isn't the husband always the prime suspect?"

"But you were at work," Seth said.

"I was in my office with the door closed dictating. No one saw me between nine when I came in and when the police called."

"The police will ask around. Someone must have noticed you," Seth said.

When Rob looked dubious, it struck me then, like cold water dousing my head, that maybe Rob knew no one could vouch for him because he was back at his house murdering Lauren.

* * *

The idea of having a murderer over for dinner soon receded in the face of my hunger. As I'd driven back from the police station, I'd scooped up animal crackers from the van floor, which swam in as many assorted items as my bag. But I could no longer do the single woman stretches of not eating, and I was breastfeeding.

The noise of the children during dinner was loud enough to keep Rob from getting lost in his thoughts. I tried to bond with him by asking when he would go up for tenure.

"Maybe four years." He shrugged, twisting the Pad Thai noodles we had ordered with his fork. "But I should be okay with the Zemeron trial behind me."

Mental health was my area, so I kept up with the medications that were prescribed for the various disorders. Zemeron was a drug being touted as a new treatment for adult attention-deficit/hyperactivity disorder.

"You got great results." I turned to Seth to explain. "Usually, in clinical trials, the researchers can only hope that a medication is better than a placebo pill on, in this case, ADHD symptoms. It's very rare that a new medication would be better than something already on the market."

Seth nodded while forking in noodles.

"When are you coming out with the follow-up findings?" I asked Rob as I scraped the last of the orange sauce off my plate.

"We're crunching the numbers right now."

Whenever people said that I knew they didn't run their own statistical analysis. Statistics only took seconds to "crunch" on any computer program once the right buttons were pushed.

Remembering what I'd overheard Griffin reveal, I said, "Is there an extended release coming out?"

Rob looked at me with surprise. I couldn't read whether it was because I knew at all, or whether he was in on the possible insider trading scheme with his wife. Why wouldn't he be? Then I thought of the flirtatious tone of Lauren's voice on the phone. Maybe she had been involved with someone else on this.

He swallowed his mouthful of food and slugged at the water glass. When he set it back down, he said, "There is, as a matter of fact, but the FDA hasn't granted approval yet."

Soon any conversation was impossible, and dinner deteriorated, as it usually did, with Noah climbing on my head. At least Alyssa's fingers, slick from pepperoni grease, couldn't stain the black yoga pants I had worn all day. Our dog, a geriatric Maltese wearing diapers, had lost a lot of his faculties, but not his sense of smell. He scavenged the floor for grains of rice, crumbs, and other bits that fell from the children's mouths and plates. My best childrearing advice is to get a dog, otherwise you have to vacuum after every meal.

* * *

After I'd sprinkled Noah's crib with pacifiers like flowers at a wedding, so he would always have one at the ready, I came downstairs blinking at the light. On the living room couch, Seth looked desperate to have me join him and Rob, offering me up as the professional who could help. Of course, he hadn't been so desperate as to take on the bedtime routine himself. Most days, putting the children down felt like climbing a mountain after hiking all day, but this time it was like facing Everest. When I had asked Seth to do it as a special request, he had said, "But they want you."

"Maybe we can watch a little T.V.—the national news?" Rob said. "I need some distraction."

"Sure," Seth said, grabbing up the remote.

The avuncular tone of the newscaster announced, "Washington D.C. police conduct yet another search tonight of Congressman Kutchin's Georgetown apartment, but did they find anything tying him to the missing intern, Kristin Stockhauser?"

I glanced over at Rob, gauging his reaction. After all, the intern may have been murdered. Perhaps the topic was too close to home right now. I couldn't read his blank expression as he watched the street view scene where police-issue cars flashed their lights outside a high-rise condo building. "Are you okay?" I asked.

When he nodded, I turned my attention to the camera view sweeping from the street to a window that presumably belonged to Kutchin's condo. An almost tirelessly attractive blonde reported, "The third search of Congressman Kutchin's apartment, this one involves black lights that can pick up DNA even if blood has been washed away."

My interest quickened. "Do you think they'll find anything?"

"He did it. He had to," said Seth.

"Of course," I agreed. "What's the probability of a woman being a victim of random violence when she's also having an affair with a congressman?" Guiltily, I stole a glance at Rob. Should we really be having this conversation about spouses murdering people? I jumped up. "Let me get you some herbal tea. Calm the nerves."

"And I'll do the dishes," said Seth, also springing to his feet.

He was still banging around in the kitchen when I handed Rob a steaming cup and sat down next to him on the couch.

"Who would kill Lauren?" he said. "She was the nicest person."

I had long experience at keeping my facial expression neutral no matter what people told me in counseling sessions. Nicest person?

"There were so many people at our house last night, you didn't get much of a chance to talk. But you two had a lot in common," Rob said. "You were both therapists. You had the mothers-in-law you could complain about." His lips twitched in a smile of reminiscence.

He and Seth had bonded during the house tour at the party. Rob had confided that Seth's dad had inspired him to pursue a residency in research psychiatry, even though his mother wanted him to go into the highest-paying specialties possible: radiology or anesthesiology. But while they were talking in the guest room, Lauren had stormed in. "I've been looking all over for you." And then she'd dragged Rob off.

"She just wanted to help people." The steam from Rob's tea now wafted in his face as he held the cup to his mouth. "That's why Lauren became a therapist."

"What kind of clients did she see?" I asked.

He sipped. "ADHD mostly—sometimes co-morbid depression or anxiety." Putting down the cup, he looked around the living room but wasn't taking in the life-sized abstracts on the walls.

"So, ADHD was her specialty, too?"

Rob squinted against the heat of the tea as he gulped at it. "Lauren and I shared patients. They would call to get medication from me, and I would refer them to her for testing."

So, that was the business model and why Lauren had shrieked at him about his voicemail. He obviously took his own appointments when he should have probably hired an answering service.

"You required your clients to go through psychological testing before you prescribed anything?" Not that I disagreed with having a thorough assessment. Some general practitioners, for instance, now prescribed stimulants to children based on a ten-minute interview with their parents. However, psychological testing was an expensive endeavor, requiring more than a day of filling out questionnaires and costing thousands of dollars. Insurance companies may or may not reimburse, and certainly not for the full amount. Testing was more commonly carried out with children so parents could ensure that they got needed services at school. Not so much for adults.

I took a tentative sip of Herbal Wind Down, which was described as Syrian chamomile with a scent of peaches and almonds. "How about any of your wife's clients? Do you think it was any of them?" I spoke euphemistically, not wanting to say "kill" or "murder," but he understood what I meant.

"Depressed and anxious people aren't usually homicidal."

"Even the men?" After another drink of my tea, I decided that despite its appealing ingredients, Herbal Wind Down tasted like dishwater.

"We saw more women than men," he said.

That was typical—more women than men sought help. "People with ADHD can be pretty impulsive," I remarked.

"She didn't mention anyone she was worried about."

"Did you talk to her today?"

"I feel bad because I didn't call her back. Maybe if I had, I could have—" He let the sentence dangle. The mind tried to grapple with grief by twisting events around, thinking what one could have done to prevent death. Only in this way was there any sense of control over what had happened.

I reached for my dog Miffy, who was trying to get on the couch. When he nestled against me, I stroked his soft fur for comfort. My fingers tangled in the snarls of hair. He'd received short shrift since the birth of my children, and there was no time for grooming.

After a while, I said, "The police kept Carmen a long time today. And their questions for me mainly revolved around her."

Rob set his cup down on the tray we kept on the ottoman-cum-coffee table. "It's hard to believe Carmen would do something like that, otherwise, we'd never have hired her. She was mature—we liked that. The last person we had, she said her cousin dropped her off, but it turned out to be a boyfriend. We couldn't have that, somebody who lied."

"Carmen seemed like a nice person. And she didn't get mad when Lauren—" I paused. How to put it—*laid into her*?

He frowned. "Lauren was nervous about putting on a party, her first one since the renovation. I think that's why she was a bit hard on Carmen."

"That was unusual?"

"I mean, she always told Carmen what she wanted. Lauren was particular about the house."

"Where does Carmen live? How did she get into Georgetown?" I was used to Rosa, our babysitter, who didn't drive.

Rob's gaze was focused on a picture of amateur-looking squares hanging on the wall. No, Alyssa hadn't drawn it—one of my husband's latest acquisitions. I was used to people making comments about Seth's art, but I didn't think Rob was really seeing anything beyond the horror in his mind. "South Arlington," he finally came up with. "She has a car." His eyes were still trained on the flat geometrics of the painting as he talked. "Lauren insisted on that. She wanted someone who could go to the grocery store and run errands, make a sit-down dinner every night because she didn't have time for all that."

"How much was Lauren working?"

"About ten clients a week, although she wanted to build her practice. And with the renovation, there was always a big mess to clean up—dust, plaster." He shrugged. "I didn't think we needed someone every day. Not until we had a baby anyway."

"So, you were thinking of having a baby?"

"Sure –" He grimaced, and I thought he would cry then. As I told some of the rare students who were phobic about clients' tears: that's how you know you've done a good job— when someone cried. Rob grabbed up his cup and went through the motions of drinking from it, even though it was empty, and successfully swallowed the emotion back down. "It had to be random, someone looking for something to steal to support a drug habit."

"Did the police say anything was missing?"

"They had me look around. The only thing was my mother's silver. She gave it to us as part of our wedding present. The police thought maybe Carmen had disturbed whoever it was when she came today. The back door was unlocked, and Lauren would never have done that. She was very safety conscious."

"Do you think Carmen needs a lawyer?" I asked.

He shrugged. "I tried calling her to find out what happened, but her voicemail keeps rolling over."

"Maybe the police kept her because they thought she'd be a flight risk. Where's she from?"

"El Salvador."

"She was undocumented?"

"Lauren said she was working on getting her green card and hiring a lawyer."

"What about a husband, boyfriend, son—does anyone live with Carmen? She sounds like a good person, but maybe a male relative thought there might be something worth stealing at your house."

"She has children—a teenage boy and a girl, about eleven. I never met them. I think the father is still in El Salvador. She's never talked about a boyfriend, but that doesn't mean she doesn't have one." His gaze focused on mine for the second time. "That's a good angle. I'll have to ask the police about it tomorrow."

Walking in from the kitchen, Seth said, "She reads a lot of mysteries." He smirked when I threw him a look. Seth regarded my penchant for mysteries as incredibly low brow, although was impressed with how many I read and how often I solved the crimes early in the story.

I turned back to Rob. "You're welcome to stay tonight."

"I was going to go home—" His sentence fell off.

Seth waved a hand, dismissing that idea. "Isn't it still a crime scene?"

"The police said they were finished," Rob said.

I didn't want to get into the bloodstains, so I said, "You know, they don't clean up the fingerprint powder after they leave. There'll be soot all over everything."

"I'll make up the spare bedroom," Seth said, "and Cara can show you where it is when you're finished talking."

That settled, he retreated upstairs after kissing me good night.

"What about your cat?" I said to Rob, suddenly remembering the kitty Alyssa had been obsessed with.

The way Rob's eyes suddenly rolled around, it was as though Lauren was still alive and berating him for forgetting the cat. "It was Lauren's before we got together. I don't think he likes men. Or maybe he was jealous of me for taking her away."

"Don't worry about it," I said. "The cat should be fine tonight. Tomorrow I can go over there and feed him." I hesitated, thinking quickly. What did I have to do the next day, and how much did I want to get involved?

I decided to take the plunge. "I could even call one of those crime scene cleaners, meet them out there. You don't want to have to deal with that."

"I can't ask you to do that. My mother's coming in tomorrow. She'll make some calls."

"I've had experience with that kind of thing from my social work jobs. I'm sure it won't be easy for your mother to face either. She'd have to show the cleaners in and hang around to pay them. Anyway, I need to get Alyssa's soft toy. She left it at your house. That's why we went over there this morning."

I had offered several good excuses for why I had to go back to their house. But my main reason—here in front of me was a genuine mystery. I could find out if the police had looked beyond the obvious.

Chapter Three

Tuesday Morning

When I clomped in late for the three-hour faculty meeting the next day, one of the associate professors, Beverly, said, "Oh, you young girls and your high heels." This was why I loved my job. My colleagues were all fifteen to twenty years older than me and still called me "the baby." I looked ten years younger than my stated age, and I directly attributed this to not having to dress up every day and be present at eight a.m. Neither did I stay home all day with children and have no reason to get out of sweatpants.

"The traffic." I made my usual lame joke about why I was late when all I had to do was bypass a drainage ditch to get to the campus.

After the meeting dragged to a close, Joan Divers, one of our myriad associate deans who had come up from Richmond for the day, followed me back to my office as we'd scheduled. My office had no window, but that made me feel even more sequestered from the noise, demands, complaints, and tedious tasks that had to be done repeatedly, such as putting on Noah's socks and shoes after he'd yanked them off.

Over her glasses, Joan surveyed the stacks of papers splayed onto the floor, the books pulled from shelves. "What happened in here?"

"I brought my children over." Seth had forbidden my owning a printer at home. I produced so much paper with all my articles, writing, and grading that our printers were always breaking down, and he was right—then it became his job to fix them. "Noah's like Curious George Goes to the Office."

The joke was lost on Joan. "How old are the kids now?"

"Two and thirteen months."

"Seems like Noah was just born."

"Not to me."

"Hard work?"

I gestured to the fallen stacks. "Let me put it this way, I come to work to relax."

"I have two cats, and that's bad enough. One of them has been to a pet psychic, and the other's on Prozac."

My office was so small, Joan was forced to sit on the other side of the desk from me, which I'm sure galled her to no end. Joan liked a good hierarchy despite the so-called collaborative nature of our field.

She started with a speech. "As you know, I've been hired as the associate dean for assessment and strategic planning, and I'm still trying to define my role, but one of my responsibilities, clearly, is assessment of the faculty. I'm going to meet with all the faculty individually, and I'm starting with the junior members."

As she carried on in that vein, my gaze took in my computer. Noah had sat at my desk like a little king on a throne, banging on the keyboard. Predictably, he had screamed and thrashed when I carried him potato-sack style out of the office. I itched to deal with the strange error message Noah had managed to produce on my screen.

"When were you planning to go up for third-year review?" she asked.

The third-year review was a way to get feedback to know you were on track for tenure. "Fall," I bleated.

"That means putting your record together this summer." She peered over her spectacles at me. "You haven't been here that long."

"When I was hired, the dean said I could go up in three years. Remember, I was already an assistant professor in Texas for two years."

"But you didn't want to get tenure there. You chose to come to us, and we're much better." She allowed a small smile. "Of course, your scholarship record is fine—no problem there."

"Isn't that what counts?" That was the prevailing wisdom in academia.

"Not here. You've got to be rated "excellent" in two areas and at least "very good" in the other. Your teaching is okay, not great."

"That's because I don't give out all A's. And I teach research— that's never popular."

"But your service record—you're not on any University committees. You know, we have vacancies in the Faculty Senate and the University Council. Think how good it would look if you filled the position on one of those committees and, say, became an alternate for the other."

"I live two hours away from Richmond," I protested. "If a meeting is two hours, that would mean six hours of my time, almost a full day. And," I added, "the dean says if we work up here, we don't have to go to University committees."

She bristled. "He's never mentioned that to me, and I'm his associate dean." Our dean was an ostrich about conflict and would usually agree with whomever he was with at the time. "Anyway, you should get your butt down to Richmond more often."

My turn to bristle at her word choice of "butt."

She went on, "It would be good if people down there saw you because they're the ones who'll be voting on your tenure. We didn't want you to move up here in the first place."

Ah, the things you do for love. When Seth and I got married, Washington D.C. was the logical place for him to transfer, so I made the move, as well—from Richmond to the off-campus program in Alexandria.

"And what about your community service? That's part of our strategic plan."

"You have my self-assessment in front of you." Which had taken more time to fill out than to write an actual article. "Look at the list of agencies where I tried to do my adolescent girls' coping groups." Social work was in trouble if more agencies couldn't take advantage of free services that were offered to them.

She nodded and peered at my C.V some more. "What about national conferences—you haven't made a presentation in two years. Do you have something accepted for this year?"

"My children are too young to leave them at this stage." How on earth would Seth manage? He had even called in the babysitter the one time I fell ill after he came home from work.

"One of these days you're going to have to break the ties. Might as well do it sooner rather than later. And I bet they'll manage just fine without you."

I tried to be patient. The woman was one of my bosses, after all, and she didn't have children. But she taught the same Mental Disorders class I did. Didn't she recall anything about the critical importance of early attachment?

* * *

How had I ever found Lauren's house beautiful? In cold daylight without the warm light of the lamps, a draft blew in through the windows, furniture hulked in corners, and heavy wood weighed down the silence. Even the view outside failed to charm. The Victorians that lined the streets were like haunted houses after Lauren had been killed in hers. I'd eagerly escaped from my two guests, Barbara and Arlene, who had arrived earlier that afternoon. But now, in the presence of

Lauren's death, I longed for the light, color, and yes, even the noise I had left behind.

I avoided the fireplace area where Lauren was supposed to have died and averted my eyes until I got to the stairway, where the fingerprint dust ended abruptly, like a woman who doesn't know how to blend foundation into her neck. When my footsteps bounded up the stairs, I belatedly remembered Lauren's dictum about no shoes in the house. So stern were her admonishments that I almost turned back to leave them at the doorway. Then I realized with renewed shock that she was gone. Here, her death was so much more immediate and personal than when I had talked to Rob about it.

The master bedroom, luxuriant before in pale green and ivory silks and satins, now also looked dark and oppressive. I peered underneath the bed where the black furry mound of the cat and the pink soft toy shared the space. Toto was comforting against my chest as I clutched him and looked around.

A phone, pad, and pen rested on the night table next to the bed. Moving closer, I noticed letters indented into the surface of the paper. Maybe the police had already noticed this and taken off the first sheet. I ripped off the next two and pocketed them. I lifted the phone receiver and scrolled through the recent calls. Amidst the usual one-eight hundred sales calls, my own cell phone number startled me. I *had* called Lauren to say we were running late and my difficulty finding a spot. She hadn't picked up. Had the murderer been here and heard the ringing phone? Shuddering, I continued to scroll.

In between my cell phone number and the call I'd made from the house asking to come rescue Toto, was sandwiched the number "Harrigan Builders." The company in charge of her renovation, a subcontractor, just a sales call? I copied down the number on a piece of paper from the pad.

The night before, a "no caller ID" popped up at seven, which is when I'd roughly estimated I'd heard Lauren. Of course, she could have been talking on her cell. It made me think of this morning when I had tried both her home and cell numbers while I was circling, late for the assigned time. What if that was the case for the "No Caller ID?" as well. He had called Lauren's cell phone, but he couldn't get her there, and took the risk of trying her home number. I had no basis for any of this except her voice tone, but I was pretty good at reading these things. At the same time, modern life was full of these annoying calls, as common as gnats. It could just as well have been a random telemarketer.

I jumped when my own cell phone went off. I answered, and a sea lion groan washed over the line. My mother-in-law's voice blasted in my ear. "Noah keeps throwing the cars I got him and hitting Daddy's paintings. I can't get him to stop."

I glanced at the clock on the matching nightstand at the other end of the bed. I'd been gone a little over an hour. "Hours," Barbara had told me. "Take your time."

"Between the two of you, you can't handle him?" I said.

"Arlene went down to take a nap. She's exhausted. And I am, too."

"The cleaning people aren't even here yet," I said.

"Noah doesn't listen."

"No, he doesn't." I felt validated. I wasn't a total wimp for not being able to handle him. "I can call Rosa."

"God, no. She won't stop talking."

I paused. This was the first I'd heard. "Well, I can't come back right now."

"Why are you doing all this for Rob anyway?"

"Arlene's your best friend."

"Arlene's my friend, yes, but that doesn't blind me to the fact that Rob's just like his father—cheap."

Gosh, Barbara was cranky when she went without a nap.

She went on. "And once the *Cinderella* DVD ended, I didn't know how to put on the T.V. And Seth wants me to make chicken, too."

"Forget the chicken," I said.

"Good. I hate chicken. Don't tell him I said that."

Why she wasn't allowed to have an opinion separate from him, I wasn't sure. "I'll call Rosa," I announced. "I can't get home any time soon." While I was in the area, I decided to stop at the police department and see if they had a Victim Services unit. There, I could maybe find out what was happening in the case. Perhaps I could even volunteer to evaluate the Victim Services program and boost my community service record while I was at it.

After hanging up the phone, I hurried to the closet. "Rob will need some clothes," Arlene had said. "He's wearing the same thing he wore yesterday. And we don't know when he can go back to the house. Lauren used to choose his clothes, put his outfits together."

Man, oh, man. Was there no end to the control? I agreed to grab some clothes. "But I can't promise they'll be coordinated. I'm not used to putting together men's outfits. Seth buys his own clothes *and* dresses himself." I paused for maximum shock value. "*And* he takes his clothes to the dry cleaners *and* does his own laundry."

Arlene and Barbara had gasped in unison.

In the master closet, I packed some basics—underwear, socks from the drawers—and then this is how I rationalized what I did next: the police were not being thorough. Obviously, their investigation had stopped at the first floor. They were so convinced that it was either Carmen or a random crime. But what about Lauren's pharmaceutical drug insider trading and the Russians? With that, I searched all the drawers—his and hers—and underneath the mattress. The closet was legit anyway—I pulled some slacks and shirts down and then just happened to browse . . . okay, *search* Lauren's side of the closet, which dominated the space.

Nothing of interest there. I still had some time—maybe five to ten minutes before the cleaners arrived. I plunged into the study and rummaged through the desk and shelves. I found no paper trail for stocks Lauren had bought, although that could all be handled on-line nowadays, or she could have squirreled them away in a safety deposit box. From what I could tell, Rob and Lauren's bank accounts, which they had held jointly, were healthy in balance. Rob's retirement stock seemed to be going down, but wasn't that the case all over? I didn't even read my own retirement funds. It was like jumping on a scale every day—a path to frustration and obsession.

As I was checking the kitchen and the junk drawer for random paperwork, I called Rosa, getting her to understand that I wanted her to babysit even though I wasn't there. "The thing is," I said. "You'll have to walk there yourself." It took ten minutes from Rosa's apartment building, and she was as wide around as she was tall. The exercise wouldn't be a bad thing.

"Oh, miss, it's too cold. Can't Miss Barbara come get me?"

"No, because I have the car."

Rosa changed the subject, and I knew she wasn't coming. "I talk to Carmen. *Aiy*, it is so sad. The police questioned her for hours and kept saying she did it. She was the last person to see him." I knew Rosa confused her pronouns, just as Carmen had done at the scene. "And she scared, miss. She was crying, and it made me cry." Rosa's voice grew husky with tears. "Her English—no good. I tell her, you must take classes, you must study. Is that not right, miss?"

Right now, Carmen seemed to have worse problems than not speaking the language. And that was made even more apparent when Rosa said, "She have two children. They go into foster care if she arrested. I say no, that can't happen. Is that true, miss?"

"I'm afraid so," I told her reluctantly. "Unless she can have them stay with a relative."

"She have no one. Everyone in El Salvador. "Oh, miss, is terrible. She cry. I cry." Rosa's voice broke. "No, I must not cry. The *policia* say she will be deported. Mr. Rob won't call her back. She afraid he's mad and won't want her to work there no more. No money for children, no money for lawyer. Please, miss, you social worker, you must help."

Chapter Four

Tuesday Evening

"Don't you want to find out who killed Lauren?" I asked Seth, who had just reacted badly to my not having made the chicken for dinner. To emphasize the tension between us, a soda bottle rattled down the steps to the living room. One of what we called Noah's "projects." He would get each bottle of soda from the pantry and toss it into the living room. Did we mind? Not in the least—it kept him amused.

"You promised your mom you would help Rob," I said.

"We've done that." Seth heaved his briefcase onto a kitchen barstool. "He stayed with us last night, and I referred him to a good lawyer. His mother is staying here now. You arranged for the clean-up of the scene. Isn't that enough?"

"Rob's coming over for dinner tonight, too," I added. "I just didn't think I'd be stuck in traffic that long coming back."

Seth slapped the mail onto the counter. "Now you see what I put up with every day. For an attorney leading a sixty-five-million-dollar case, I should be staying late like the other attorneys on the team, going in on weekends. But I'm not. I come home early every night just so I can help you out."

After he'd finished his little speech, I announced, "The cat's here, as well." I ran my hand over the snags on my sweater from her claws.

The cleaning people had forbidden the cat; it was against their policy to have pets in the house while they worked. I'd left with the cat yowling in her carrier, which sounded a lot like Alyssa in one of her moods, as the cleaners—a man and a woman—had gone in wearing full Haz-Mat suits.

"I don't have the time for this, and neither do you." Seth started pawing through the mail, the usual bills and circulars. Nothing fun came in the mail anymore.

"It's just so unfair that the police are focusing on Carmen," I said.

He ignored me, studying an address and then thrusting the envelope into a pile.

As I spoke, Alyssa tugged on my hand. "Mommy, play."

"Hi, buddy," Seth said to Noah, as he marched by, struggling to hold a full bottle of soda. Noah didn't look his way, intent on his task.

Alyssa still pulled on me. "Why don't you go find Kitty?" I suggested.

She hung on my hand. "You go."

"You can do it yourself. See if she's still under the bed and tell Daddy."

"No!" Her face crumpled. "Mommy, you hurt my hurt feelings."

"Oh, I'm so sorry." Charmed by her cute phrasing, I pulled her into my arms. To Seth, I said, "I met with the director of Victim Services when I was up Rob's way. Carmen is still the main suspect, but she had some interesting information about Rob."

Seth was reading a flyer advertising an art opening in New York. I had wondered how I was going to explain what I planned to do next, but now I was mad for his ignoring me. "I'm meeting Tad Gowers tomorrow," I announced.

Seth rolled his eyes and slapped down the envelope. "That old guy at the party, the historic preservationist? Uncle Tad—he's so full of crap." A tight smirk creased the corners of his mouth, which meant he was really pissed.

"I want to find out about his connection to Lauren." I told him about the indentations I'd found on the nightstand. Alyssa and I had scribbled in the numbers, and I had dialed.

"Attorney's office," the young woman had sung over the phone.

"What kind of attorney?" I had asked.

"Family law, divorce, civil matters," she'd trilled.

"I wonder who wrote the number down—Lauren or Rob?" I said now. Seth knew my theory about Lauren's possible affair after I'd overheard her lovey-dovey tone on the phone at the party. He had dismissed it, believing I was jumping to conclusions.

"Tad seems the type," I said, although that didn't explain Lauren's phone conversation. Tad was still at the party at that point.

"You're taking this too far. Rob's paying a lawyer for this. *And* there's the police."

"Remember what happened with the Chandra Levy case? The D.C. police really bungled that one."

Noah, having finished his project, tried to clamber up my leg like a monkey. Alyssa clutched on harder, knowing that she would soon be displaced.

"And remember what Joan told me?" I said, grunting at my state as a human jungle gym. "If I want to get tenure, I need to do more community service."

"How is solving a murder considered community service? Isn't that usually being on some board?"

"Social work is very broad. I can count it as advocacy work." But he was right, I would need to find a way to document my efforts. The *Journal of Helping Reflections*? Maybe I could write an article for that.

"I don't want you dragging the kids all over the place to talk to suspects or whatever."

"I'm going alone." I paused and took the plunge. "I'm meeting him for lunch."

He grabbed up the discarded mail and stomped over to the garbage can. "You won't come into D.C. to have lunch with me. You said you don't want to pay for babysitting for that. And now you're going to go in and meet that old guy?" The garbage lid banged down for emphasis.

"It's not like I'm interested in him. Plus, he's married."

"I'm sure that never stopped him before."

Noah started to wail, tears sprouting magically, like in a cartoon. Now I know why they say, "Boys don't cry." Because it's so loud when they do.

"Can Dad hold you?" I asked Noah.

The phone rang, and Seth said, "Is it that guy?"

I shook my head, feeling guilty even though I hadn't done anything wrong. Had I?

Seth peered at the Caller ID, then thrust it at me. A series of consonants spewed off the side of the screen.

"Oh, that's the Russians. I tried to phone them earlier, as well as Jodie Sewell. See, that Tad Gowers wasn't the only one I contacted." I smiled at Seth, who winced at Noah's screaming as he hoisted him into his arms. I said "hello" into the phone, amazed that Noah's clamor hadn't roused Barbara and Arlene from their naps.

* * *

"Shouldn't they be going to bed?" asked Seth after we'd finished the pizza we'd had delivered. This was code for: *Cara, start the nighttime routine, so I can watch the news.*

"Those kids need a good scrubbing," said Barbara, pushing herself away from the table. A mound of napkins towered on top of her plate. "They didn't have a bath last night either and that was after spending all day at the police department."

I realized the baths-before-bedtime was the typical routine for most families, but I already looked at thirty minutes to get the kids ready for bed. Wrangling Noah into p.j.'s could take up to ten minutes alone—and then there were the stories, the songs, and the cuddles for each of them. As to baths, I looked for those lulls during the day when the children seemed to be at a loss for something to do. That's when I'd plop them in the tub, which was good for a half-hour's amusement.

But since Barbara was so hot on it now, I said, "Could you do me a big favor and get the baths started? I just want a quick word with Rob."

Arlene patted her hair into place, which was one of those reddish, old lady styles that never moved. "Rob, shouldn't we be getting back? You must be exhausted." Rob had met the cleaners after they finished to pay them and inspect the work. He had deemed it acceptable to return to the house that night.

Arlene had re-applied her lipstick since dinner, being one of those women who never revealed her natural lip color. Her strategy was to draw attention away from rather wide thighs by emphasizing her upper half with dark lipstick, brightly colored tops, and flashy necklaces. I wondered why Barbara had not learned any of Arlene's fashion tips. The all-black tracksuit Barbara wore wasn't some grief thing about Lauren. She always dressed this way.

"You must be exhausted," Barbara said. "I'm exhausted and haven't gone through what you've been through."

"I'm kind of wired, actually," Rob said. "I don't think I'll sleep."

He and I watched from the kitchen as Barbara gripped the banister and made her way up the stairs, placing a foot on each step and heavily putting the other one down after it. It was as careful and laborious a process as if she were rock climbing.

Arlene grabbed a sponge and made as if to wipe off the counter. It looked like she wanted to hang around and hear what I had to say to Rob.

"Oh, you don't have to do anymore," I said to her. "I'll get it later." Or not. The pizza box still lay on the counter with a half-eaten slice inside it. You would suspect one of the children, but no, Barbara was the culprit. I was used to her returning food with bite marks to the common stockpile.

"Maybe we can go downstairs?" I suggested to Rob in a low tone, so Arlene couldn't hear.

As we started out of the kitchen, Arlene said, "Where are you going?"

"Mom, we're trying to have a private conversation."

"What could be private at this point? We've been talking about this all night." How Rob could do no wrong, so he couldn't possibly have killed his wife. How it had to be the housekeeper, Carmen.

"Mom, please," Rob said in the same way I now said, "Alyssa, please" to make her stop whining for stuff she didn't want anyway.

And just like with Alyssa, the statement proved ineffectual because Arlene went on. "Is it something about the house? Did they damage it when they were cleaning? Rob, are you having second thoughts about going back there? We can always go to a hotel."

"Cara was at the police department today," Rob said. "I want to hear what she found out."

"What's the big game?" Arlene spread her arms wide. "Why can't we all know about this?"

I didn't think he'd want his mother learning what I'd discovered. I had met with the director of Victim Services, Anita Ware—the only kind of woman police would tolerate, one dressed in skinny jeans and high heels. Anita and I had bonded as professional women and mothers.

Downstairs, Rob and I weren't able to sit down since Arlene's and Barbara's suitcases took up every available surface, so we remained standing.

"I hate to tell you this, Rob," I started out, somewhat ominously. "Your alibi's not checking out."

He shifted his weight and stared at what appeared to be a piece of leather hanging on the wall. The art pieces were increasingly strange in the downstairs family room as my veto power extended only to our bedroom and the living room floor.

"The police didn't say anything when they questioned me," he said.

I folded my arms in front of me. "The cell phone records came back after they took your statement."

"So, they'll probably have me in again? More hours for my lawyer to bill." He seemed more concerned about the money involved than anything else.

"You were near a medical office building connected to George Washington Hospital."

"But not anywhere near my house."

"Then why did you lie to the police?" I leaned in and found myself whispering in case Arlene went so far as to eavesdrop.

"It wasn't any of their business where I was."

"Did you tell your lawyer?"

"Yes, but he said they wouldn't pull the cell phone records, that police weren't usually that thorough."

"So, why were you in that area?"

He shook his head, and I scanned through the possibilities. Was he sick, getting treatment, psychotherapy? Despite his being a psychiatrist, there was still the stigma of seeking mental health treatment.

Suddenly, he blurted out. "I was going for fertility treatment. We really wanted to have children."

"Lauren did?"

"I wanted them more than she did, but she'd come around. Then, after all that, to find out I couldn't. We thought it would be her age."

Lauren would have been furious with him for being unable to have children. Even his eating red meat had provoked her to no end. But she was the one who had died, not him. Had she lunged at him, and he pushed back in self-defense? A jury might not blame him. I started to say that when an unfamiliar ringtone sounded upstairs.

"Rob!" Arlene shrieked. "It's your cell phone. Shall I get it?"

"No!" He bounded up the stairs, and I followed.

Arlene handed him the phone. "It's the police." She was as bad as Barbara, who couldn't walk until our phone rang and then watch her move!

I went into the kitchen and started to wash the countertop. Of course, I listened to Rob's side of the conversation but not as blatantly as Arlene, who stood before him, staring up. Actually, he did more listening than talking.

When he finally hung up, he said, "Carmen's been arrested for Lauren's murder. She was trying to board a plane to El Salvador when they caught her."

Chapter Five

Wednesday Morning

In Gymboree class, I was breastfeeding on the floor against the wall behind a multi-colored tube. Barbara sat nearby on a chair that she'd dragged into the playroom and plopped down on. In the classes, Noah enjoyed himself about twenty-five percent of the time, easily mastering the activity of the day—climbing up and down slides, throwing balls through hoops, and so forth—while the other children sat there like blobs. The other seventy-five percent of the time, Noah spent breastfeeding like this, overwhelmed by all the color and noise.

Alyssa liked Noah's Gymboree play classes a lot more than she had her own. She was one of those unadventurous girls who had to be prodded to crawl through a tunnel, and she hadn't walked until fifteen months. Now she sang along lustily with the song, her face bright red with enthusiasm, clapping her hands to the traditional nursery rhymes being sung to Gymboree-inspired lyrics.

"Look how cute Alyssa is in circle time. Can you sit with her?" I felt bad that I wasn't with her and thought Barbara should act as my representative.

"I can see her from here." Barbara clapped her hands to the offbeat. "I love the Snow-White costume. You just let her wear it?"

"Sure—why not?"

Before taking Barbara along for Gymboree, I'd gone to the gym with the children where I'd told Rosa that Carmen had been arrested. "Oh, miss, how could this happen?" Rosa had said.

"She was trying to leave. It made her look guilty." I towered over Rosa as I spoke to her outside the nursery door.

"She no do such thing, and the children. What will happen to her children? Miss, you social worker, you can find out what happen to the children."

"I'll try."

"Please, miss, Carmen so worried. In the meantime, I pray. I wake up at five every day and pray for everybody. I pray for you, Noah, Alyssa, and now I pray for Carmen, too, and her children."

Bored and frustrated from being trapped with Noah frantically nursing in a corner, I tried to make conversation with Barbara. Our only real commonality was the children. "What do you think about the disappearance of Kristin Stockhauser?"

She stopped clapping. "I haven't really been paying much attention. You know, I don't watch those news shows."

"That congressional intern, who was having an affair with her boss?" I prompted.

"The one with the long, blonde hair? Isn't she beautiful?"

Kristin Stockhauser's look was the anti-Washington D.C. Maybe she'd fit in in New Jersey, California, or Texas, but not here. She had Barbie-doll, bleached hair, a dark tan, gold jewelry, and tended toward white Liberace-like pantsuits. Her makeup was so heavy you couldn't imagine what she might look like in the morning, although you could be guaranteed she would prance about in matching cami attire.

"Congressman Kutchin's good-looking, too," she said, and I made a face. "But sleazy. He must have been having an affair with her, and he should know better. Did I tell you about the time I met JFK?"

"Yes, a few times." When my mother-in-law had visited the Capitol at age 15, looking about 30, JFK had supposedly approached. He had conversed with her for a few minutes until her aunt appeared. If nothing else, the incident convinced me of the level of JFK's sex addiction.

"Do you think Kutchin killed her?" I asked.

"He had to—who else could it have been?" Her painted-on eyebrows shot up to her hairline. "Do you think this Kristin was going to tell his wife?"

"That's the speculation—she might have been applying pressure in some way. It might have been the end of his career, his marriage." Noah flipped around to get to my other breast, and I pulled my shirt down as much as I could. "But Kutchin has an alibi. He was back in Odessa, Texas that weekend with his wife when Kristin went missing. But there's ways around that—he has money, he could have hired someone to do it."

"Who was the last person to see her?" she asked.

"Good question," I said, as if to my students. "I saw on the T.V. reports that Kristin went out with two other Congressional interns on Friday after work. They remember her saying she didn't have plans for the weekend. But if she was seeing a married man, she wouldn't necessarily talk about that. There's no way of knowing whether she made it back later to her apartment because by the time her parents reported her missing—she hadn't talked to them in a week—the surveillance tape at her apartment was erased."

"Oh, that poor girl. And her parents—that's just so sad." She shook her head. "Doesn't anyone at her building remember seeing her? The neighbors, the concierge?"

"I think it was a nice apartment in D.C., but I don't think it had a concierge."

After a while, Barbara said, "If she was at a bar drinking, maybe some weirdo slipped her one of those date rape drugs."

I made the same argument I had made to Sgt. Reynolds—what was the probability of someone having an extramarital affair with a public figure and the same person also being the victim of a random crime?

"Well, D.C. is a very dangerous city," Barbara commented.

I pointed out that Miami had its fair share of crime, too.

"Are we still going to Georgetown today?" she asked.

"Yes, I'll drop you off, but then I'm meeting with this Tad Gowers alone. Right?"

"Of course. I'll have the best time just being in Georgetown, wandering around, exploring." She smiled at Alyssa watching the bubbles the facilitator blew above the group of babies.

"Is Seth still mad about the lunch with Tad Gowers?" she asked. "I don't know why you tell him everything. Men always feel threatened by that kind of thing. They can't understand that women can be friends with men."

"I don't want to be friends with Tad Gowers."

"Ooh, I don't know why not." She might have wriggled in her seat. Googling him that morning, Barbara had seen his picture in the *The Washington Post* metro section and said, "Yum. You can tell when they work out." She cupped her hands in a "tight buns" gesture.

"I want to find out what happened to Lauren," I said, stroking Noah's hair off his forehead. His eyes met mine, and I smiled down at him.

"Now that I don't understand," she said. "They've arrested the maid. Isn't it over?"

"I'm not convinced they've got the right person."

"I'm not saying a word to Arlene about this. She thinks you're just out to get Rob, and we so wanted him and Seth to be friends."

How could I explain myself to Barbara? She and I were from such fundamentally different species. I had even been unable to convince Seth of my reasons: the injustice to Carmen; my personal involvement—having just met Lauren the night before and then turning up at her house to find that she was dead.

"And you're so busy already with the kids and your work. How are you going to fit this in, too?"

"Well, I may be able to justify this for work." Barbara's eyes glazed over as I told her about the community service requirement for tenure. But when I said, "Maybe I just need something that isn't work or the kids," she jumped in.

"That's exactly what you need," said Barbara. "When Seth was young, I had the nanny, so I could go out to lunch with my friends and have my nails and hair done."

Usually, I would file one of these frivolous comments to tell Seth, but he was still miffed about my upcoming meeting with Tad Gowers.

* * *

White tablecloths and wine glasses, even at lunch. Tad Gowers and I sat at a two-top table that put us too close to each other. He showed off his teeth in frequent smiles, and his skin looked a few shades dark for Fall. I was surprised at the level of my relief that I didn't have to do this anymore—make small talk with strange men.

Our waiter recited some dishes in an indefinable European accent, but this was one of those pretentious menus I could read through. The dishes were no better than what I used to call Seth's "boring pasta" that he ate when he was single.

The waiter didn't write anything down, which made me nervous. When he left, I said to Tad, "I was shocked to hear about Lauren even though I didn't know her well. I was there that day, you know."

"I thought it was the housekeeper who found the body."

"I came right after her and called the police."

"This city." He shook his head. "We've got to get tough on crime." He expanded upon the theme, and I checked out. Now that I knew a lot of psychotherapeutic techniques, I'd lost the ability to listen.

Finally, I broke in. "It must have been a shock for you. After all, you knew her much better than I did."

He shrugged. "Not that well."

"Really? I saw you two having what looked like a serious conversation."

"To be honest, I don't remember. The number of people I talk to every day. The phone calls, the e-mails—"

I played on his sense of self-importance. "I know, that's why I'm glad you could fit me in." He put the beams back on me, but they dimmed when I said, "Do you know if Lauren had any enemies?"

The waiter, with supreme boredom, filled our glasses with a tinkling wash of water. When he drifted off once more, Tad said, "It was random. I love this city. I must love it to do the job I do, but I have no illusions. We still have a serious drug problem here. Not as bad as Baltimore, but serious. And where you have drugs, you have crime. Lauren was just another unfortunate victim of that."

He flicked on the smile again when the waiter dealt out our plates. Tad pierced a french fry and said, "Now what were you mentioning on the phone? You volunteer somewhere?" In his world, this was what wives must do.

"No, I work—" I awkwardly added the obligatory phrase, "—outside the home."

"What do you do?"

"I'm a professor."

"You don't look like a professor."

The flirting slightly gratified me. I thought I'd lost my touch; you don't get many admiring looks when you have a baby attached to you, no matter how much breast you show. "I designed a prevention program to help teen girls build their coping skills. I have a curriculum, students to implement it, and money to test it, but I haven't gotten any sites to agree to it."

"We need more programs like yours—get to the kids *before* they're in trouble." He pulled out his wallet, gave me a card. To reciprocate, I had to go through the awkward rendition of crossing off all the information on mine that had to do with the main campus in Richmond address where I had taught before. I'd transferred to the Northern Virginia campus before Alyssa was born and still hadn't received my new business cards. University bureaucracy.

"Give me a call or drop me an e-mail, and I'll give you a couple of people to contact. Give them my name and say you're a sociologist."

"Social worker."

He pointed a finger at me. "Right, I'll get it yet."

I slipped his card in my purse. "How did you become part of the Historical Preservation Commission anyway?"

"How did you know?" He positively preened and was eager to go on. "I started as a real estate agent. Commercial property only, no residential." It sounded as if that was supposed to make a difference. "I was around for a while, took on some of the development projects in the P Street area, built connections in the rezoning office, and then got the attention of the mayor's office." He shrugged, like "no big deal." "Ended up getting appointed to the Board of the Historical Preservation Office. Eventually, I became chair."

"And what does the Board do?"

"We approve any changes D.C. residents want to make on their homes, make sure that the historical structures and façades stay close to the original. There's a government office that handles routine matters, so anything more involved or controversial goes to us."

"You must know all the laws and codes for historic buildings in D.C. Sounds complicated."

He smiled, pleased. "Not when you've been doing it for a while."

"And how did you meet Lauren?"

"We're neighbors," he said and leaned back as our dishes arrived.

My pasta with shrimp was not worth the price but preferable to eating the same lunch every day—yogurt with grape nuts or a peanut butter and jam sandwich. And to be served lunch, even if by a waiter who conveyed it was all beneath him, was something I hadn't experienced since one of my mother's infrequent visits. Most of all, I was glad I could stay in my seat rather than jumping up and down and running back and forth. And that I had my hands to myself, rather than holding Noah in my lap or having him breastfeed as I shoveled in food with the hand that wasn't supporting him.

I decided to come right out with it. "So, you and Lauren didn't have something going?"

He threw back his head and laughed. When he'd recovered from his mirth, he raised an eyebrow. I could see him practicing that in a mirror. "Are you trying to find out if I have affairs?"

I smiled to soften my words. "I'm more interested in finding out if Lauren had an affair."

"What makes you think she did?"

"I believe she contacted a divorce attorney." I didn't know that for a fact, but it seemed more likely that she had done so rather than Rob. She acted like she hated him.

We both turned at a honk from the street. There was my minivan with Barbara waving and smiling from the front seat. Once, when I was a teenager, my father picked me up from a party and *actually came to the door and asked for me*. This was reminiscent, and I wanted to hide under the tablecloth now.

"Someone you know?" he said.

"My mother-in-law. Do you have one of those?"

Barbara was valeting the car. She never bothered with street parking because that meant walking.

Once inside, my mother-in-law, dressed in one of her all-black sweatsuit affairs, limped over to our table, screaming "hi" so loudly other diners turned to stare.

Tad stood up as she approached. Still seated, I murmured introductions, conscious of everyone looking at us; now our scornful waiter had arrived, too.

Barbara sat and peered at Tad's plate. "What did you get?"

"The steak sandwich and fries."

"Can I have a fry?"

"By all means."

So much for getting Tad to confide in me with Barbara plopping herself down in the middle of our lunch, wanting to taste our meals, and making frequent references to "my son, the lawyer."

"I'm thinking of moving to this area," she said to him as she polished off Tad's sandwich ("Are you going to eat that?" she'd said). "Could you be my real estate agent?"

"I only do commercial, but I could recommend someone. Where do you live now?"

"Near Coral Gables." That was just pretentious name dropping because Kendall, where she lived, was nothing like Coral Gables. Although the streets were lined with palm trees, they didn't hide the commercial shopping malls. And it was so far inland that, by the time you fought an hour's worth of traffic to get to the beach, clouds had rolled in, and it was storming. But Barbara never went to the beach, so it didn't matter to her that she lived in a congested Miami suburb.

Chapter Six

Wednesday Afternoon

When we were back in the minivan, Barbara studied my business card, seemingly oblivious to my annoyance with her. Since I'd given a card to Tad, she had wanted one, too.

She peered at it. "You don't go by Jacobs? Then no one can tell you're married."

My hand flew to my mouth. "Oh, horrors!"

The sarcasm was wasted. The traffic light changed, and she stuck the card in the console, then stomped on the gas. My seatbelt strained against my neck. She was driving because she wanted to become more familiar with the area. Fair enough, I understood that unless you negotiated them, you didn't really take in your surroundings. But if this lead-foot driving—heavy on the gas, then the brake, with no in-between—kept up, I was going to vomit my noodles.

I tried to explain that I had built a reputation in my field, had published articles, and even a book with another on the way—all in my single person's name. How could I suddenly convert and build a new name?

The explanation did nothing to lift the incomprehension from her eyes.

By the end of the conversation, I was even more irritated with her. "Why did you show up at the restaurant? I told you to wait until I called when we were done."

"I tried calling, but you didn't pick up. I went shopping and bought three pairs of shoes. By then I was tired of walking around. Plus, I wanted to see if Tad" —She stroked his name with her voice as if she were saying *Klonopin*—"was as good-looking in person as he was in his picture."

I wrinkled my nose. "I don't think he's that great. Too old."

"Not for me!" In her delight, she swerved into the next lane.

"Wait 'til Seth hears about this," I said as we lurched to another stop.

"Go ahead, tell him." She put all her weight on the gas pedal, and off we went as if we could race on traffic-clogged M Street. "I'm not interested in having a new man anyway. That Tad Gowers looks like he'd want to boss you around."

"You told Tad you wanted to move here. I thought you'd decided it was too cold. Remember when I dropped you off in front of the Pancake House last winter? You said you were going to die as you walked to the door."

"I have nothing left in Miami," she announced dramatically. I had to turn my head to roll my eyes and found myself staring into the hostile, round-moon face of the driver in the car next to us.

"Arlene's gone for me now," Barbara continued. "She won't even return my calls. The only thing I have left in life is my grandbabies."

"I thought you were going to buy a condo on Biscayne Bay now that prices are coming down in Miami."

"I don't want to be stuck out there all alone, just sitting and looking out at the water."

Holding back my laughter—I didn't think a Miami condo on the beach had ever been explained quite that way—I said, "Did you tell Arlene you had nothing to do with me suspecting Rob?"

"I left a message and told her that. And that it doesn't matter anyhow. They arrested Rob's girl trying to leave the country. Why would she have done that if she wasn't guilty?"

"Grieving sometimes takes strange forms. It comes out as anger. You and Arlene have been friends for so long, I'm sure this isn't the end."

She pressed down on the horn. "I can't believe the drivers around here."

That was so rich coming from her, I was speechless.

"Of course, nothing can be worse than the ones in Miami," Barbara added. The sad bulldog expression returned. "Arlene might move here now to be with Rob since Lauren died. To help him deal with it."

I think there was probably a reason that Rob, like Seth, didn't live in Miami. And that was to be far away from their mothers.

"It couldn't have been easy for Lauren either, being with someone like Rob," she said.

"What do you mean?" My attention was riveted on her now, and she enjoyed it, dragging it out.

"Rob's not the perfect person, like Arlene would have you believe." Barbara wasn't completely insensitive to vibes because she said, "I know you think I'm bad, the way I am about Seth, but Arlene has me beat. You should see her house. It's like a mausoleum. She's never thrown out any of his baby clothes."

"There's medication for that," I said.

"I've told her—she won't take it."

"What's the deal with Rob?" I said, trying to bring her back.

"He was cheap. Like father, like son. Once, when Howard was threatening to leave Arlene, I said to her, 'Maybe you'll be better off without him. Then he'll have to pay you alimony and child support, and you can spend your money any way you want to.' Until he met Lauren, Rob always lived in crummy apartments. She finally got him to move into a nice place."

Was that so bad? I could have been charged with the same offense before I met Seth.

"Rob had the money—his dad's trust fund, his income—but he wouldn't spend it."

"He must have spent a lot on the renovation."

"Good for Lauren." Then her face went into the characteristic bulldog, poor-me expression. "And I never even got to see it. I so enjoyed Arlene telling me about every little detail." Her cell phone rang, and she fumbled in her purse.

"Do you know what company she used for the renovation?" I asked.

She was too fixated on the ringing phone to pay attention.

"You can't talk on a cell phone while driving in D.C.," I said. "It's illegal."

She ignored me and screamed "Hello!" into the phone. We swerved into the next lane and got honked at again. "Oh, hi, Arlene!" She listened for a moment, then said, "We just happen to be up near your neck of the woods. We ate lunch at Café Milano. Cara and me." She paused, apparently listening. "Is it okay if she comes, too?"

I shook my head violently. "I can just drop you off," I said.

She ended the call. "That was Arlene. She's gotten some bad news. She wants me to come over."

"I can drop you off," I repeated. "She probably doesn't want me around, and that's fine with me."

"Then how do I get back?"

I relented to sticking around but only if I drove home, and not her. "What was the name of the company that did the renovation on their house?" I asked again.

"An Irish name. What was it?" She rubbed her fingertips together, trying to summon it.

"Harrigan Builders?"

She snapped her fingers and looked at me, the minivan now hogging two lanes. An annoyed horn blared.

* * *

"Lauren was pregnant," Arlene said as soon as she opened the door to us. She and Barbara fell into each other's arms in mutual hysteria.

"I'm so sorry," I said to Arlene. "I know how much having grandchildren meant to you."

She sought my arms then, and I marveled at how short she was. It must have been the force of her personality, but I had thought of her as taller. She shook with sobs. I had not seen her cry for Lauren; this was clearly worse for her.

But, I wondered, was it Rob's child?

He talked to his mother daily, but how much had he confided in her? How much, if anything, did she know about his fertility treatment? I tried to think of Seth in that position. He didn't tell his mother personal stuff, and he was more there for her than she was for him. It had always been that way. I had no idea if that dynamic translated to Rob and his mother, but it was hard to differentiate between Arlene and Barbara at times.

"Does Rob know?" I asked.

"He was the one who told me," Arlene said into a shredded tissue. "I told him not to go to work, to take some time off, but you know how he is. Just like his father. I think that's what eventually killed his father; he worked himself to death. Anyway, the detectives called him at work and told him."

Rob might be the father if the fertility treatments had worked, but it was also possible that the baby wasn't his. I already knew that a medical examiner wouldn't, without cause, perform a test on the fetus to make sure it matched the husband's DNA. "How far along was she?" I asked.

"Early—about eight weeks."

Had Lauren even realized she was pregnant? She had denied it when Meredith had asked at the party that Sunday night.

"How did Rob sound when he told you?" Barbara asked.

"He must have been devastated, but he doesn't wear his heart on his sleeve like I do. His father was the same. He wouldn't have known an emotion if it smacked him in the face. I know how important it was for Rob to have children, though. This is another loss all over again." Her speech dissolved into sobs. She hung on to Barbara, who, despite her solidity, was not meant to be leaned on. She was supposed to be the invalid, remember?

I raced over before they toppled en masse, guiding Arlene to the couch, where she said, "I was holding it together pretty well, I thought—until now."

"That's natural," Barbara said. "You weren't that attached to Lauren. Let's face it—she made it difficult to like her. We were more shocked than anything else. Someone that young, and the way it happened—so violently. But most of your grief was for Rob at that point, that he had lost the woman he had chosen to marry."

Pretty well articulated, I had to admit.

"But now, it's an entirely different story," Barbara went on. "You've wanted to be a grandmother for so long."

Arlene nodded, her chin wobbling with new tears. "Barbara, can you stay with me?"

Barbara made a face over Arlene's bubble of hair, like "Help me!" But, come on, this was Barbara's stated motive in coming back here: "I need to take care of Arlene." So here was her chance to show her stuff.

Plus, my strangulation fantasy of Barbara had still not faded. I couldn't yet forgive her for inserting herself into my lunch with Tad Gowers.

"Barbara, you need to be with your friend," I said.

"But what about those grandbabies? You need my help," Barbara insisted.

"Don't worry, I'll manage. But I have to get back. The babysitter's expecting me." I leaned over and patted Arlene's shoulder.

"Can Rob write you a script for Klonopin, or can he bring you some samples?" Barbara asked Arlene. "I know you don't like to take anything, but after what you've been through?"

Arlene shook her head, and Barbara looked at me as if I was supposed to argue her case.

"No, she should let the feelings come through, Barbara, instead of numbing them," I said.

"Just to get through the night, just to sleep."

"She has you here with her, doesn't she?" I said and left, still wondering whose baby it was.

Chapter Seven

Wednesday Afternoon

When Jodie Sewell answered the door, she stared at me without recognition as if she didn't remember we'd arranged this. At the party, she'd shared with me Instagram photos on her knitting site. Learning she had completed hundreds of cute and clever beasts, all species, and was running out of space at her house, I offered to organize donations to the children's advocacy center and perhaps other youth organizations. Mainly, I wanted to question Griffin, but it didn't look terrible on my CV to do a few community projects here and there.

To be fair, Jodie's reaction at the door could have been the sight of me standing with two squalling children, one in each arm. "Cara Knight."

"I know." Jodie's expression didn't change.

"I'm sorry. They fell asleep on the way here and woke up badly."

I staggered forward when she ushered me in and flopped with a groan into the nearest seat—one of those wicker chairs that look like scooped-out mushrooms and have no function indoors. Noah was grappling, frantic as a young animal for its survival, to seek out the breast. I didn't know what I would do for Alyssa, who was at the point of no return; she wouldn't stop crying, no matter what soothing words I uttered or how I stroked her blonde curls.

I understood how she felt, unraveled by the last thirty minutes of Noah screaming as we battled traffic on US 1, a stark, wide highway that better belonged in Texas with its line of commercial centers and old-school motels ("Air-Conditioned" and "Color T.V."). I'd called Seth, so he could share my pain, but he refused to stay on the phone.

He couldn't stand the noise, even at a distance. I had opened the windows to let the screaming out, but it didn't lessen the intensity. And I had made a tactical error; I had brought no food. Forgetting snacks with children was akin to going to Tyson's Corner without makeup to try on clothes.

Just as I'd driven up to the Sewell's rancher and said, "Okay, guys, here we are," I looked back, and Noah and Alyssa were both asleep.

Now the annoyance sounded in my voice. "Your husband said he collected all the Disney videos. Maybe you have *Lady and the Tramp?*" My parents had yet to find that one in the garage sales they frequented. I hated to take over the woman's house, but she didn't have the social skills or the mothering experience to do what was needed. "Maybe that will calm Alyssa down," I explained.

"I guess I better get used to this," Jodie said. "I'm pregnant."

Right now, having a baby didn't seem cause for celebration, but I forced the right word out. "Congratulations."

"Did the prenatal vitamins give you diarrhea?" she asked.

Trying to find solace, Alyssa shifted, her elbow jabbing my liver. I winced. "Um, no."

"They're really upsetting my stomach."

"Gosh." Before Jodie could reveal more detail about her pregnancy, I said, "How about that video?"

The living room was testament to Jodie's talents. Knit animals of all types—elephants, giraffes, monkeys—squashed into the shelves of a built-in bookcase. And someone, I guessed Griffin, had saved all his books from childhood.

"Alyssa," I cajoled. "Look who's peeking at us. See the monkey. It's George."

"Not George," she said, shaking her head.

Jodie returned with unfortunate news. "I don't know where Griffin put *Lady and the Tramp*."

On cue, the front door opened, and Griffin walked in. After viewing the row of children's books that shared space with the knit creations, Griffin appeared to me now as Willy Wonka with the pointy beard and elfin face.

"Where's *Lady and the Tramp*?" Jodie said by way of greeting.

"I love that movie!" Griffin said. "Are we watching it?"

"If we can find it," she said.

"Hi, Griffin," I called from the wicker chair. He didn't respond to the usual social interchange or seem bothered by Alyssa's crying. The kids were lying across me in the wicker chair, so he didn't seem to know breastfeeding was occurring right before him; otherwise, he wouldn't have let it pass without a comment or leer. Instead, he disappeared into the house's nether regions.

Jodie's stare made me realize that conversation was up to me. I said how nice it would be for victims at the children's advocacy center to receive a special homemade stuffed animal when they were interviewed about abuse. I could organize a collection, and if Jodie knew other knitters who did cute creations like hers, we could include theirs. Maybe it would give them exposure.

As I spoke, I tried to ignore Alyssa, who kept whining and sniveling in my face. To her, "Mama, Mama, Mama," I kept saying, "I'm here, Alyssa," until I wanted to say, "That's my name—don't wear it out."

When I had finished brokering the knit animal deal, I said, "You know, we don't have to watch *Lady and the Tramp*. Anything Disney will do, or we could turn on the T.V.—PBS Kids?"

"He doesn't need an excuse to see *Lady and the Tramp*. What am I going to do when I have a baby? Then I'll have two kids on my hands." She smiled for the first time.

I had picked this time to come over for two reasons: Jodie had said Griffin got home around four p.m., and Seth wasn't due until six-thirty. The late afternoon hours could become a bottomless pit. The kids were cranky and tired, and so was I. Even though I wanted Griffin in on the conversation, I had to start somewhere. "Wasn't it a shock about Lauren?"

To Jodie's blank face, I asked, "You didn't know she was dead? I mentioned it on the phone."

"You did?"

I wanted to smack my head with my hand. Wow, she really couldn't track social cues, and the phone must have made it even harder on her.

She got up and called, "Griffin, get in here!"

Red-faced with irritation at being disturbed in the middle of what must have been an exhaustive search, he popped back in. "I still can't find it. What did you do with it? You know that's my favorite Disney movie."

"Tell him," Jodie said to me, "about Lauren dying."

Now that I finally had them, I forced him to put on the T.V., which meant leaving the wicker chair with children in both arms and heading into a railway-style, drafty extension that served as a family and all-purpose craft room. "It wasn't natural causes," I said and explained the circumstances. I even went into Lauren's pregnancy. I wanted Griffin to feel like he could confide, too.

Griffin, sitting a little too close to me on the couch, had gone from red-faced to pale, and I decided to start probing. "You seemed like you knew her pretty well," I told him. "I heard you talking to her, something about stocks."

His skin color changed to red again. "Jodie, could you bring out some chips, something to snack on? That's what you're supposed to do when people come over, you know."

She scowled. "Well, geez, you aren't helping at all."

"I was trying to find the movie that you lost."

"I didn't lose it. And now that I'm pregnant, you're supposed to be waiting on me hand and foot." She crossed her arms against her chest.

"And you're supposed to be getting exercise. The doctor said you weren't supposed to gain more than twenty-five to thirty pounds, and you already started with an extra fifty."

When Jodie harrumphed out of the room, he stalled for a while, dithering with an uneven pile of CDs stacked on the carpet near the TV. "I love this one," he said. "*Dumbo*!"

When he slid it into the DVD player, Alyssa turned to me. "Gismey, Mommy!" It was so cute the way she said Disney that Seth and I had adopted the turn of phrase for ourselves. I couldn't see ever wanting to correct her.

Returning to the couch, Griffin said, "What were you doing— eavesdropping on Lauren and me?"

"Not at all. I was just holding my baby." What could be more innocent? "You were talking pretty loudly about having information on your company."

While Griffin watched elephant antics on the screen, I repeated what I had heard of his and Lauren's conversation, ending with, "Lauren had money. Why did she need to do this?"

He shrugged. "That was her husband's money. Always would be. She signed a prenup."

I kicked myself internally. I had never even asked Rob about a prenup—duh! "Why, was Lauren planning to leave him?"

He twitched another shrug. "We didn't get into that. She wanted money of her own. That's all I knew."

Jodie came in with a plate of chips and a creamy-looking dip with clumpy green chunks that turned my stomach.

"Honey, don't you think you should get dinner started?" he said.

She set the bowl down on a worn ottoman, saying, "All we're having is leftover spaghetti. I just have to cook the noodles and heat the sauce."

"I'm not staying much longer," I said. "Go ahead and start your dinner. We'll be out of your way in a few minutes."

After Jodie left the room again, I asked, "How did this deal start?"

"Well, she knew I was a chemist for B.X. Martin, and we started talking about my job and what I worked on." I could see he'd been flattered by her attention. "Then somehow we talked about how much I made—that it wasn't enough to pay off my student loans and buy a house, have a kid, all that." He scooped a chip into the dip, and I had to turn my head. "Lauren said she'd help me."

Just so he wouldn't open his mouth again when he talked, I supplied, "If you told her about something that was coming out soon from B.X. Martin that would make stock prices rise."

He nodded grimly and finally swallowed the mouthful he'd been working on. "It was the extended-release version of Zemeron."

"So, you were going to tell Lauren when the best time was to buy stock to take advantage of its release," I prompted.

"I wouldn't have done it," he said, "but my bosses hung me out to dry right before that. Made me look like a fool defending one of our drugs." His face reddened again.

"What do you mean by 'hung out to dry?'" Another technique I taught my students: ask for clarification when people speak in generalities.

When he flapped his hand in dismissal, not wanting to get into it, I said, "What went wrong with this new drug?"

"Well, you know the hoopla about antidepressants making people suicidal. The extended-release seemed a little worse on that front compared to the placebo pill. Although no one *died* or anything," he said.

"And Lauren didn't take this well," I guessed.

"Nooo. At her party, she threatened to write an anonymous letter to my boss and tell him I was spreading information about the drug."

"But she couldn't do that—she would have been in trouble, too."

"Not as bad as me."

I hadn't felt a hint of alarm for my safety or my children's coming here. But without Lauren in the picture, Griffin no longer had the threat of losing his job hanging over his head. Wasn't that a motive in itself? Had he been the one to bash Lauren over the head?

I said, "Don't worry, they've already arrested the housekeeper." Although I'd revealed a lot of detail, I kept back the fact of Carmen's arrest to keep up the pressure.

"They have? Who-o-o." He exhaled stale onion breath in my direction.

"But just in case the police ask, you must be prepared to answer. Where were you on Monday morning?"

"I was at my job. We're on a time clock, so we punch in."

"So, you have proof that you weren't near Lauren?"

"Of course." He glared at me as he plowed another chip into the mound of dip.

Chapter Eight

Thursday Morning

It was such a cold, dreary day that we were the only ones at Fort Ward Park when Masha and her daughter Daria pulled up. Alyssa and Daria ran to each other like lovers with arms outstretched from their time together at Lauren's party. I would have preferred if Alyssa had shown more affinity toward Meredith's two-year-old. Partly toward that end, I had arranged to meet with Meredith and her children next week. The other part was to supposedly see the office that Meredith sublet from Lauren. I'd claimed I was interested in maybe seeing clients in private practice again. To seal the deal, I said I was helping Rob by packing Lauren's office. Right before calling her, I had emailed Rob to do just that.

A cold wind blasted now, and leaves from the surrounding trees swirled in the air. Masha zipped her coat up higher. "Brrr," she said, rolling all the r's.

"You must be used to this from Belarus," I said. She wasn't Russian, as I had assumed, but from Belarus.

She shook her head. "I was always cold there."

"Cute jacket," I said, chucking my chin at Daria's get-up—a pink, quilted affair with a faux leopard-print fur collar and matching cuffs.

"Macy's on discount, twenty dollars. I got one in a different color for next year as well." She was obviously thrilled with U.S. prices. The styles in Belarus were probably still in the early eighties.

Alyssa wore a gender-neutral navy blue—she hadn't entered her princess stage when I had bought it for her big at twelve months. It was a bit incongruous with the Snow-White costume, but it had cost less than a fast-food meal, and it still fit her at two. I wasn't sure Noah would fit into it next year. They were such different species size-wise.

Noah was barefoot, which was ridiculous. I had forced him into his jacket and a striped hat that framed his beautiful face, but he adamantly refused socks or shoes. I marveled as he walked over the bark surface of the playground without even wincing.

"He will get very sick," Masha warned. "You need to put on the socks, the shoes."

In defense of my parenting, I had research on my side. "Studies have shown that being cold doesn't make people sick."

No one believes me when I tell them this. Masha flashed me a dubious glance and then watched in skeptical silence as Noah reached one of the plastic play structures twisting out of the ground and began to climb.

I needed to gain her trust before discussing the conversation I had overheard at Lauren's house. I was used to speaking about uncomfortable topics as a social worker ("You'll have to go into foster care while your mother figures things out") and educator ("You get a zero on this assignment because you plagiarized"). But just the thought of saying, "So, what are your ties to the Russian Mafia?" or "Were you organizing a hit on Rob for Lauren?" made my insides heat up despite the cold.

Preschool was always a hot topic, and Masha and I had both tried to get our children into different Montessori schools. Please, graduate school entry was more straightforward than the process we had gone through with Alyssa. We never even got close to the rock star teacher whom everyone fawned over. After Alyssa was rejected, I tried to apply to other schools with two-year-old classes, but they all had waiting lists. Hence, I missed out on a whole year of preschool for her. The D.C. Metro area preschool rat race.

I was as out of the mothering scene as Masha, a foreigner. I felt a sudden spurt of jealousy for Meredith, who had told me at Lauren's house that her daughter was enrolled in the Jewish Community Center preschool three mornings a week. What I wouldn't give for such non-T.V.-related time as that for Alyssa. Meredith was connected to a network of other mothers, while I held a full-time job but seemed to spend as much time at home as a full-time parent. I didn't know any other mothers except for brief, chance encounters with other parents at Gymboree, who vanished after the forty-five-minute class was over.

Burying my mothering resentments, I edged around to the topic of Lauren. "How did you find out what happened to her?" After breaking the news to Griffin and Jodie, I had established that Masha knew about Lauren's death when we talked on the phone. I wasn't keen on doing another death notification.

"My husband saw the article in the *The Washington Post*. We couldn't believe it. America is so violent—that is one problem about living here, the crime."

Seth told me the night of the party, he'd talked politics in Russia with Masha and her husband Misha (if you could believe the matching names!) while I was secreted away, breastfeeding. "They're in complete denial," he said. When he'd mentioned acid thrown in the face of one of the president's political enemies, they said, "No, no, that was a Botox operation gone wrong." The poisoning death of another: "That was the botulism." I had agreed with Seth that these weren't topics to bring up with Masha when I had her alone.

Instead, I said, "You know they arrested the housekeeper?"

"My husband saw that in the paper, as well. That was the Spanish woman helping in the kitchen?"

A gust of wind blew through the yoga pants I wore to the gym before meeting Masha. The gym had saved my sanity this past year; I could rid myself of stress and have childcare at the same time. And now, all this running around and investigating was proving a bonus by providing places to take the kids and fill our days. With the cold weather of winter descending and outside options closing, the prospects had become even narrower until then.

But this part wasn't as much fun—thinking about how to casually work the conversation around to visas. Masha had mentioned that she would not reapply at the Montessori school because her husband's position with the World Bank was ending. "Can you try to get a visa to stay on?" I asked.

"They want my husband to come back."

"The Belarusian government?"

She nodded and turned away as another wintry blast assaulted us. Her eyes watered from the wind.

"Was Lauren involved in your trying to get a visa?"

"Nothing like that." She avoided my gaze and watched her daughter, who was following mine up the slide, giggling.

"Lauren said she was sponsoring you."

"She told you that?" she said in a fierce tone. "It's a lie."

"Why would she lie?"

"Because we can't stay here. After nine-eleven, they are very strict with the visas."

"Maybe she was going to work some channels." My heart was beating as I pushed this. Masha was getting upset, and my natural inclination was to help people feel better—that was my profession—and to back off. "But Lauren wasn't really the type to do anything without something in return, was she? What did she ask of you?"

"No more of these questions. I thought we were going to have our kids play together. I didn't know I would be interrogated like a criminal." She stalked away toward Daria. "Come on, we go."

I couldn't understand what the little girl said, but the whining tone was unmistakable. Masha made a sound akin to a shush but with a harsher sibilant tone. I would have obeyed, but it didn't impact Daria's whining one whit as she trailed after her mother.

* * *

In the afternoon, I picked up Rosa to care for my kids, so I could visit another child, Carmen's daughter Sylvia. I'd made some phone calls, using the school's contacts at the County Child Protective Services, and found the foster home where Carmen's children had been placed. I had arranged a visit, saying that I was helping to get their mother freed.

The foster home was a cinder-block ranch house in Springfield, a municipality that bordered ours. A girl with shaggy bangs and untied shoes gaped at me when she opened the door.

"Where's your mom?" I asked.

"She ain't my mom." The girl scratched her head.

"Your foster mom," I guessed, and she ran back into the house.

A woman with short black and gray hair walked to the door, carrying an enormous baby, and tried to smile. "I'm Sarah Robinson."

After I'd given my name, she ushered me inside to the living room, where occasional farm animals decorated the otherwise barren walls: a rooster crowed above the T.V., a pair of pigs cavorted behind a wooden kitchen table, and a needle stitch cow gamboled across from my eye view.

A little boy—maybe kindergarten-age—skidded into the room. "We're not getting another one, are we?" he asked. "You said no more kids."

"Now, Zachary, we need to help people, don't we?" said the woman.

He had to be her natural son, balking at more foster children. Could you blame the lad?

I made my introduction, saying I had a professional and personal interest in acting as an advocate for the children's mother.

"You were supposed to meet with Orlando, too, right?" When I nodded, Mrs. Robinson said. "The caseworker was supposed to let everyone know. He ran away last night." Her eyes searched mine for some sense of outrage.

I could only summon an "Oh, dear."

"I agreed to take both Orlando and Sylvia. I didn't have to. You can see I don't have the space." Mrs. Robinson hitched the baby into a new position and, dragging her fingers through her hair, said, "They don't like splitting up sibling pairs. And then what does he do—runs away?" She sighed. "Oh, well, I guess you can talk to Sylvia anyway."

As Mrs. Robinson led me down the hallway. I smelled it first—the stench as foul as a porta-potty—and then I saw it—the alien plastic creature, the Diaper Genie, standing next to the crib and changing table in what had to be the baby's room. We were at least a year away from throwing out our own Diaper Genie, so vile we kept it in the garage.

Sarah Robinson opened another door where a form lay on the bottom mattress of a bunk bed set. "Sylvia, this lady's here to talk to you."

All I could see at first was long hair.

"This lady's trying to help your mama. Why are you lying there, sulking?"

I cringed. "Maybe we can just talk alone," I suggested.

When the foster mother left, Sylvia sat up. Her shoulders were hunched so she could fit underneath the top bunk. Her stomach flopped over pink sweatpants. I drew up a toddler chair across from the bunk bed and sat.

"How can you help my mom?" Sylvia asked. "That's what everyone says—that they're here to help—"

"And it doesn't feel like it to you?"

Her eyes filled with tears.

"Well, I'm talking to a lot of people who were involved with Miss Lauren, the woman who died, and the police officers to try to get them to see there might be other suspects." The overhead light made the room too bright, illuminating crayon marks on the walls.

"My mom would never do anything like this. Never, no matter how bad anyone treated her. She goes to church and prays all the time. She always tells us to do good. She never hits us."

"People have mistreated her before?"

She nodded. "My dad—he used to beat her. That's one reason we moved here. But I wished we stayed in El Salvador."

"You really miss living there." Along with the bunk bed, two twin beds were lined up, taking up most of the room. It was more like a dormitory than a bedroom.

My statement produced more tears. When she had wiped her eyes, I asked, "What did your mom say about Miss Lauren?"

"Sometimes she was upset because Miss Lauren yelled at her. My mom would do nice things like cook for her, and Miss Lauren would just make her take it home. That was okay because it was more for me." For the first time, her mouth curved upward in a slight smile. "But that was mean. You don't do that when someone cooks for you."

"Did you ever meet Miss Lauren?"

"One time, my mom brought me over there when I was home sick from school, but Miss Lauren made us leave because she didn't want to catch my germs." Sylvia fiddled with the brown Afghan blanket that covered her bed. "But that meant my mom didn't get paid for that day. If she was that mean to my mom, she might have been mean to other people, too, and they might have killed her."

"That's a very good point, Sylvia. You know, you're very smart."

She shook her head. "No, I'm not. My grades are bad."

"Did you have to start a new school when you moved here?"

She nodded, and I made a mental note to see what kind of support the caseworker was arranging for Sylvia. She would be an easy child to overlook.

"Another reason I know my mom didn't kill Miss Lauren—she needed that job. Before that, she could only get part-time cleaning offices at night."

Poor kid, an eleven-year-old worrying about how much money her mother made. My heart squeezed in sympathy. Her brother didn't seem particularly supportive, and now he was gone; her mother was in jail, and now she was stuck with a bunch of strangers in this bleak foster home, stinking of dirty diapers. "Did you know your brother was planning to run away?" I asked.

"I heard him on the phone. He said he was too old to have some person who wasn't his mom telling him what to do. I said, 'Mom wouldn't want you to leave me. She'd want you to take care of me.'"

"Do you know where he is?"

"Probably at one of his friends." Before I could ask, she said, "But I don't know where they live."

"What about school?" I wondered aloud.

"Orlando's no good at school. We came here when he was nine already. I learned English before him, so he flunked two grades. I never flunked."

"Good for you." I smiled.

"How long do I have to stay here?"

I shifted on my toddler seat. "You're right that Lauren might have made other people mad. I'm looking into everything I can to find something that will free your mother."

Leaving the foster home, I walked past black gasoline stains on the driveway to my usual disastrous parking job against the curb. I replayed the brief flare of hope in Sylvia's eyes at my parting words, but then it was snuffed out. "What can *you* do?" she had asked.

I'd repeated to Seth all the same excuses for why I was going to visit Carmen's children in foster care—that I'd wanted to help Rob, that I was doing it for community service—but seeing Sylvia gave me the most important reason: she and her brother needed to be with their mom. I had to get her out of jail and back home with them.

Chapter Nine

Monday Morning

In Carmen's public defender's office, I wondered how people could keep showing up for work day after day, year after year, in such depressing surroundings. Warren Brown, a tall man my age, folded himself into a chair across from me. I'd established my credibility last week when I called, that I was both a social worker and professor at Virginia University and had been on the scene of the murder with Carmen. I had information he could use in his defense.

Warren Brown turned over a fresh page of legal pad paper and said, "I've got twenty minutes. I forgot about a meeting with a judge at ten o'clock."

Okay, not impressive, but I started in. First, I told him about Griffin—the insider information Lauren had used and how Lauren had threatened his job.

"Gotcha," Warren said when I'd finished. The phrase didn't work to convey he understood. He sat back in his chair with his arms folded behind his head, feet on the desk so I could see where he had worn away the bottom of his shoe.

I then told him about the conversation I'd overheard with the Belarusian couple and how Masha had reacted when I suggested a connection.

"Gotcha," he said, nodding.

I told him about Rob—how he'd lied about his alibi, that either he or Lauren were considering divorce, and that she was pregnant, although he was undergoing fertility treatment.

The continuous "gotchas" made it sound like Warren already guessed what I would say, so I needn't belabor it.

The phone rang, and he picked up the line. He wore a wedding ring, and it sounded like perhaps it was his wife. "You want me to barbecue tonight? It's forty degrees out there . . . Fine. Look, I'm in the middle of a meeting." That didn't stop her from talking non-stop for the next minute as he didn't say a word.

When he finally hung up without apology, I said, "My husband and I have the same conversations about what we're going to have for dinner." I forced Seth to go down that road with me every day.

Of course, we had the "talk" before marriage about equal responsibility. I didn't want to play the traditional wife role; even with the kids, I wanted equal partnership. There was no way to get that with children. I saw that now. The mother would always do more. But I could make Seth have the dinner conversation every day.

My effort at bonding with Warren Brown seemed to go nowhere, so I returned to the topic at hand. "You know, Carmen might have valuable information about a possible affair Lauren was having. As the housekeeper, she might be the only person to know."

He didn't look like he was registering, maybe thinking about his upcoming judge's meeting, so I decided to get more explicit. "You know, she would change the sheets, notice if Lauren did them herself, if condom wrappers were left behind."

"I thought you said you were friends with the husband."

"His mother is best friends with my husband's mother, but I hadn't met Rob until Sunday night, and my husband only met him once before that."

"Gotcha," he said, finally taking his feet off the desk. "Well, let me tell you how I work my cases. I find the best way is not to overthink it, and I just argue from the heart. When I go in there, I'm not sure what will come out of my mouth."

"You're not going to write anything down?"

He tapped his finger to his head. "I always remember what's important."

"Even my name?"

He scribbled something down on a blank sheet of legal paper, which I was supposed to believe was my name. I had all the faith in the world that he wouldn't lose that sheet. *Right.*

***

Later that afternoon, the kids and I drove to Woodley Park. In Lauren's office, obligatory boxes of tissues dotted the room along a low sofa that a client could really sink into and then look damn foolish trying to struggle out of. An abstract painted in soothing blues hung above the sofa. Seth would call the painting "pretty," which was not a compliment from him.

Meredith and I gazed out at the treetop views of Rock Creek Park from the office window as I told her about my arrival at the scene of Lauren's death, all the way to Carmen's arrest, leaving out the sleuthing bits in the middle.

"You're a therapist," I said at the end of my recital. "What's your assessment of Carmen? Does she seem like the type to murder someone? After all, she has kids." I didn't mention going to see Carmen's daughter. Meredith wouldn't understand why I had done it. The only person who fully understood was Rosa.

"She's probably had a tough life, been through a lot," she said. "You don't know what might have made her snap."

"The police didn't find the weapon, so the case is circumstantial, but she was found trying to leave the country."

"What does that tell you?" she said and popped her gum.

"Maybe she was afraid of being arrested, not that she necessarily did it."

I lunged at Noah as he nearly toppled a receptacle of push pins, paper clips, and pens from Lauren's desk onto his head. I could just imagine that stuff scattered across the floor.

"What did you think about Lauren and Rob's relationship?" I asked.

"I'd never get away with talking to my husband like that," she answered with a smile.

"Exactly," I agreed and marveled at the docility of Meredith's baby as she placed her in the latest style stroller, one of those three-hundred-dollar numbers. "She just lets you put her in?"

"Sure." Meredith reached into her bag and opened a jar of baby squash. Her baby opened her mouth like a little bird's beak.

I remembered how Alyssa would never do that for a teaspoon of any baby food, no matter how much Barbara tried to ram it in her mouth.

Meredith loaded up the spoon. "Lauren was kind of inspiring that way—she just said what she thought. Very honest. But I know a lot of people found her intimidating." She smiled as her baby gummed the orange goo.

There was no good defense against a statement like that. If you said, "Oh, I wasn't intimidated by her," you sounded like you were protesting too much.

"I mean, it's sad and everything—but I wasn't good friends with Lauren." Meredith flipped her hair behind her shoulder in an adolescent gesture.

"Oh, I thought you were," I said.

Opening her mouth in that unconscious way parents had when feeding their young, she said, "We had the therapist thing in common, of course. But we obviously had to work at different times to share the office, so I hardly saw her." Her outstretched arm took in the view outside the window. "Look at this place—she let me sublet for only ten dollars an hour, and I can work when my husband's home to take care of the kids." She dropped her arm, and her gaze returned to me. "That sounds kind of selfish, doesn't it, when she's dead?"

I gave an ambiguous smile, which she could interpret any way she wanted, and looked around, pointing at a stack of empty boxes in the corner of the room. "Are those for me?" The therapist who handled the sublets had said she'd leave them.

I asked the kids if they wanted to play with them. So uninterested they didn't even acknowledge me. My sister and I, at their ages, could amuse ourselves for hours with a single empty box.

I started first with the cabinet. Wouldn't it make sense that Lauren hid her secrets there rather than at home where her husband could find them?

When I tried to pull the top drawer out, it lodged in place, locked. Client files were supposed to be kept secure. But if I knew how this worked, the key wouldn't be far.

"Want bears, want big kitty, want baby horses." Alyssa tugged at the leg of my pants, eager for the zoo.

"Okay, just a few minutes more, darling. Then we'll go," I said.

Lauren's desk was well-organized, mainly containing blank testing booklets and packets. In the center drawer were the usual office supplies—paper clips, pens, an eraser, and, *aha,* a tiny set of keys.

"How about playing with Emily?" Why wasn't Alyssa drawn to Meredith's two-year-old? Mind you, Emily wasn't much interested in Alyssa either, absorbed in taking a sheet of recycled paper at a time out of a box, wadding it up, and then chucking it at the trash can. Sitting on the carpet against the wall with her baby in her lap, her mother cheered at each toss, whether Emily made it or not.

Noah smiled behind his pacifier and went to join Emily's game. He liked anything to do with throwing.

I opened the first drawer. Client records were lined up in manila files. I was not interested in looking at names, wanting to preserve confidentiality. Instead, I thrust my hand to the bottom of the drawer and felt around. The space below where the hanging folders hovered made an excellent hiding place.

Finding nothing, I hefted the hanging folders in my arms and practically spilled them into the empty box I'd placed next to the cabinet. I disentangled one of the hanging folders from my sweater as Alyssa pushed on my leg toward the doorway.

"Do you want to draw another picture?" I cajoled. "They have special pens here. Can I have a picture of a big kitty and a baby horse? Maybe even a bear?"

She shook her head, and her mouth pulled down.

Noah had lost interest in making baskets and was now pulling self-help and psychology books off a bottom shelf.

"Those are Lauren's," Meredith commented, watching him.

"Noah, did you see where I got the box from?" I asked. "Are you strong enough to lift one of those and put the books in there?"

I waited, expecting the usual non-compliance, and exhaled in relief when he jogged off. I turned my attention to the second drawer, unlocking it.

With my back to him, I could hear hardback books being hurled into the box and Meredith urging, "Gentle, gentle."

As my gaze swept past the contents of the files to see what hi-jinks Noah was getting up to, my eyes were snagged by a name I recognized.

It was a name that anyone in D.C. would recognize, perhaps much of the U.S. Kristin Stockhauser—the missing congressional intern.

Meredith's phone rang. "Have you got him?" she asked, indicating my son.

While Meredith's attention was diverted to her phone, I justified opening Lauren's file on the grounds that the police weren't covering their bases and had arrested the wrong person. What if the real killer went on to kill again?

It looked like Kristin and Lauren had only met once for an appointment that had taken place—I did a quick calculation—about three weeks before she went missing.

I glanced up. Noah had gotten hold of a stapler off the desk and was holding it lengthwise, so easy for the spring to jump up and close his little fingers in it. Diving over, I tore it from his hands. He slammed into my legs, swiping his arm up for the stapler I held aloft, keeping it out of his reach as he roared.

Now standing, Meredith was still on the phone, finger to ear, to block out Noah's yelling. "We'll be there in about fifteen minutes. We're FONZ members, too—" Friends of the National Zoo— "We'll try to park in Lot A. If that's too full, we'll head to Lot C. I'll call you, okay, so we can all park in the same place." She clicked off the phone and said to me. "My friend Danielle's on Wisconsin heading this way."

I was a little surprised at what I considered Meredith's breach of etiquette. Maybe this was the difference in the ten years between us. I had called Meredith and initiated the get-together—her getting me in the office and the zoo as the main event. I didn't expect her to invite other people.

"I've got to get this stuff packed up." I gestured around me.

"I don't know why you're doing this," Meredith said. "You weren't good friends with her either."

I pulled Noah into my arms to get him to calm down. "It's for my mother-in-law. She's best friends with Rob's mother."

Meredith's face looked tight with displeasure. "I told Danielle fifteen minutes." She looked down at her daughter and must have read some signal. "Emily, do you need to go potty?" When she nodded, Meredith said, "Do you want me to take Alyssa with us? Maybe it'll get her interested."

I had shared with Meredith my toilet training woes. I doubted this would be the thing that motivated Alyssa, but their bathroom excursion would buy me time.

Before the door closed behind them, I returned to the file, Noah still in my arms. Drool dripped from his mouth onto his shirt as he worked his pacifier.

Apparently, Kristin Stockhauser had initially gone to "Dr. Abell" (Rob) to get a prescription for Zemeron, and he had referred her to Lauren for testing. That was the business plan the Abells had going, apparently. The client information notes confirmed that, yes, Kristin and her much older boss were having an affair. Lauren had noted that this seemed indicative of some impulsivity and lack of judgment. She also wrote that Kristin claimed that "he was going to tell his wife." Such a stereotypic line, and either way, there was no happy ending: he'd ruin his marriage or break his girlfriend's heart.

Hearing the footsteps of children running down the hallway toward me, I closed the file, jammed it back into the hanging folder where it had come from, and scooped up a bunch of folders, hefting them into the box to show I'd made progress.

***

When we arrived at the zoo, I was shocked to find how many other mothers Meredith had invited. I would have felt left out if I wasn't muddling over what I'd seen.

This was not random. The biggest news show debate was the disappearance of Congressman Kutchin's intern. Kristin Stockhauser had seen Lauren, and now Lauren had been killed. What had Lauren done with her knowledge of their affair? Had she kept quiet and said nothing, observing confidentiality as she was supposed to do as part of her professional ethical code? Or had she contacted the congressman, and tried to blackmail him? She seemed desperate for money of her own.

Since Noah acted like the stroller seat was lined with hot coals, I struggled to keep up with Meredith's entourage, holding him in one arm while pushing the double stroller with Alyssa in it. The moms talked about recipes and nap schedules. They were all racing home at some point to do the afternoon nap. The conversation turned to the annual vacation at "the beach" every year. At least three of the women present and their families went on vacation together. The prospect of being stuck with that many people made me feel claustrophobic. Meredith was undoubtedly an extrovert, while I was the classic introvert, the usual type to become a professor.

"Ma'am, oh, Ma'am!"

I turned at the voice.

"Is this yours?" A kind stranger had picked up the pacifier. If I lost the only pacifier between the zoo and home, there would be no recovery.

Noah screamed and pointed backward. "Shoe, Mama, Noah shoe." I had no time to appreciate the sudden appearance of verbal skills I hadn't known he had. I considered just leaving the shoe. If I was going to carry Noah all the way, was there any need for shoes? I didn't think I could lean over with him again to retrieve fallen objects.

Noah had been out of Robeez, those soft leather shoes, for months. At eleven months, he went through a pair every thirty days. They had even let me return them for a new pair the first time, agreeing that no baby could wear them out like that. After the second pair, I realized it wasn't the shoes. Other children wore Robeez for years. One of the mothers had mentioned that her two-year-old traipsed in Robeez's through the cobblestone villages of Italy.

By this time, I was so far behind the other women, that I didn't even look like I was in the same party. This was my punishment for not letting Barbara come along. "The zoo? I love the zoo!" she had said upon finding out our plans.

"Barbara, let's be realistic. You're not going to be able to keep up. I hardly know Meredith, and this is a chance for her daughter and Alyssa to bond." I still felt guilty that I had ruined Alyssa's budding friendship with Daria.

It suddenly seemed pointless to follow everyone from lions to monkeys to the disappointingly yellow-furred Pandas that my children had little interest in looking at. They only wanted to eat three bags of popcorn and cry for more.

Chapter Ten

Wednesday Afternoon

"You barely knew the woman, and you were clearing out her office?" A couple of days later, Sgt. Reynolds sat across the table from me at the McDonald's near Metro Center. Looking bigger than she had when I first met her, she had finally agreed to talk with me.

"I was trying to help Rob, her husband." A paper cup of coffee was in my hands.

"That's what you call helping? Sounds like you're trying to convict him of murder."

While we'd stood in line for sullen teens to take our orders, I'd told her that Rob lied about his alibi. I also suggested that learning his wife was pregnant with another man's child might be a motive.

At the table, she shrugged out of her navy-blue quilted jacket and peeled back the paper cushioning her hamburger. "I'm eating for two."

"Go ahead."

She bit into the burger, which squirted out grease, mayonnaise, and special sauce.

Inside my boots, I curled my toes in revulsion. I kept my fingers around the cup of coffee I'd ordered to avoid the sticky table as I launched into my discovery of Lauren's file.

When I finished, Sgt. Reynolds said, "The name just jumped out at you."

I had the grace to blush at her flat, knowing tone, but kept going. "She was pregnant, maybe with someone else. She wanted to get away from her husband, but there was a prenup in place. She wanted money for herself."

Through with my recitation, I returned my eyes to Sgt. Reynolds, who chuckled without smiling. "You sure know how to spin 'em."

She took a large bite while staring at me, which unnerved me, but I plowed forward anyway. "Lauren might have done something as serious as insider training." I reminded Sgt. Reynolds of what I had overheard between Lauren and Griffin Sewell and fleshed it out with what he'd admitted, emphasizing that I didn't necessarily want to get him in trouble, unless, of course, he had murdered her. After all, if she exposed their scheme, he could get in serious trouble, beyond losing his job.

"Financial crimes—not my jurisdiction—but now you're accusing him? First, it's the husband doing her in, then the congressman, now this wimpy guy?"

"The bigger point is that there are many other possibilities beyond the housekeeper, but Griffin said he was at work and punched a time clock. I'm sure there are ways around that that I don't have access to." I swilled coffee rather than spelling out the point that only she had that kind of power.

Sgt. Reynolds, swallowing, got it. "You already had me checking the victim's husband, now this Griffin guy. You want me running all over town? Look at me—I'm six months pregnant and as big as a house." She smoothed her hand over an old-school pregnancy top that blossomed out with her belly.

Now that she'd brought up what else she could do, even in jest, I returned to the connection with the missing intern. "It can't be coincidence that a woman having an affair with a congressman dies—"

"We haven't recovered a body yet," she inserted, her mouth full.

"And then the person who has proof of the affair is killed? Two events with very low probability happening together?"

She put her hamburger down. "Probability? Don't use big words on me, professor."

"Is the FBI involved yet?"

Unknowingly, I had pinched one of her nerves, and her voice sharpened. "That's why we looked so bad last time an intern disappeared. The FBI nosed in, and we lost control of the case. This time, 'No, thank you.'"

Thus scolded, I said, "Okay, so do you want me to go straight to the detectives on the Kristin Stockhauser case, or will you tell them about the file among Lauren's office things?"

She pointed to herself and punctuated the point by taking another bite. As she chewed, I gazed around the McDonald's to distract myself from pressing her further. A grizzled old man clutching plastic bags shuffled along. A group of tween girls counting out coins argued about what to split.

"I'm liking my case for the housekeeper pretty well," Sgt. Reynolds said. "You know why?"

"Because Carmen discovered the body?"

"That's the start of it."

"Because she tried to leave the country?"

"That didn't help."

The silent treatment probably worked well for her, but she didn't know that as a counselor, I, too, had long practice waiting people out— for them to answer questions, to gather their thoughts, to feel their feelings, to provide their own answers.

Finally, she spoke. "I think the suspect's son might have done it." She pinched a fry. "Did you know she had a son?"

"Yes, he ran away from the foster home. You think she was trying to protect him?"

She tried to play it cool, pointing her fry at me, but I had surprised her with what I knew.

"You're smart, professor. Did anyone ever tell you that?"

I wondered what my evaluations would look like if I talked similarly to my research class. I would be drummed out of social work education, that was for sure. "Is he in a gang?" I asked. "Has he been in trouble with the law before?"

"Car theft, M-Thirteen." Sgt. Reynolds took another bite of her hamburger and watched me.

She seemed to be expecting me to react to the gang involvement, but I had a stint of working with juvenile justice-involved youth. They used to tell me, "Miss, it ain't like that in the gangs, like it is in the movies. It's not like you can't get out. It's up to you what you want to do." Still chewing, Sgt. Reynolds said, "The suspect's son dropped his mom off that day in a friend's car because hers wouldn't start."

"So, you think her son—Orlando—and his friend might have killed Lauren when she caught them stealing? In front of his mother?"

"I'm sure he didn't plan it that way. The boy with him was older. Maybe he pushed this Orlando kid into it to prove himself. Maybe Mom was upstairs cleaning or out back. Then they ran off, and she found the body."

"Then where's the weapon?"

"We recovered the weapon. At Reagan National—one of the dumpsters out back. I don't know what you call a statue, but you can hold it in your hand."

It was my time to be surprised. "A figurine?"

"Yeah, that's the word." She winked. "Good job, Professor."

The news and the caffeine from the coffee quickened my heart rate. "You think Carmen tried to get rid of it before she left the country."

"Or Orlando and his friend went out there to drop it before then. Body tissue and fluid on it matched vic's DNA." She bit again into her burger. She could talk about body tissue and still eat a Big Mac with all its oozing juices. Yum.

She lifted her napkin to her mouth and spoke behind it as she wiped. "Someone tried to scrub it clean."

Who but a housecleaner would have the wherewithal for that?

Sgt. Reynolds reached for her milkshake. "No fingerprints, but you can't completely eliminate trace evidence."

I thought of Lauren's decorative style. "Was it from the house?"

"The victim's husband said he'd never seen it before."

Knowing Rob's level of preoccupation, I wasn't sure if he'd notice. "I can't see Orlando and his mother bringing something like that."

"Maybe Orlando and his friend picked it up from someone's yard right before they entered, realizing they didn't have a weapon. They weren't planning this; it was a crime of opportunity."

I leaned toward her. "Then why don't you arrest Orlando and his friend?"

"No evidence. They have an alibi. A receipt from a McDonald's in South Arlington for that time. But they could have gotten one of their homies to produce it." Taking an enormous bite, she watched me consider.

"Remember, I saw Carmen that morning," I said. "She didn't have blood on her; she seemed genuinely frightened. What evidence do you have against her?"

She put a finger up for me to wait until after she finished swallowing to speak. "Everyone wants DNA evidence now, all those cop shows. Everyone thinks they're an expert."

"I don't watch them. All those beautiful Hollywood types, it's nothing like that." I gulped at my coffee, hoping she wouldn't take offense.

"Then you should know that many cases are tried and convicted on circumstantial evidence. The housekeeper knows the neighborhood. She could have stashed the clothes. Then she tries to leave the country."

"What about fingerprints?"

"A mess of them. Didn't you all have a party the night before? And the back door," she said, forestalling my next question. "The vic's, the husband's—and the housekeeper's."

"Then how did the boys manage to get in?"

"They either walked in with Orlando's mom, or she left the door open, and they came in later."

"Then why did they only steal the silver set?" I asked.

"All they had time for before the vic discovered them. Some pawn shop will call us. Who else would want it?"

The old African American man, obviously homeless, shuffled by with plastic bags rustling. Sgt. Reynolds shot him a look, and he put the motor in his shuffle. It seemed to penetrate through his delusions that she was police, pregnant belly or not.

She called out, "Hey!" to his retreating back. When he didn't turn, she raised her voice and repeated, "Hey!"

I braced myself for the humiliation I thought he was about to suffer.

Instead, she pulled a bill from her pocket. "Here." She reached out her hand with the money.

His eyes, fixated on the bill, lit up. He took it and mumbled without making eye contact with either of us.

I wanted to prompt a "thank you" like I did with Alyssa, but he was beyond social convention. "That was nice of you," I said, surprised, when he'd shuffled away.

"You know the reason I met you here?"

I shook my head obediently.

"Because Sgt. Nelson would have blown you off. I didn't want to meet you at the station. He'd have thought I was wasting time."

Was there really a need to play the good-cop, bad-cop routine, even if I wasn't a suspect? Or did they fall into the role naturally?

Sgt. Reynolds eyed me over her hamburger. "And the main rea-son—so you'll leave this alone."

Chapter Eleven

Friday Morning

Kyle Harrigan roared up in one of those oversized trucks you typically notice bearing down on you through your rear-view mirror. I watched through the blinds as the driver, a tall, husky man with a reddened face, climbed out of his truck. His long-sleeve navy blue shirt did not bear a logo, and neither did his truck. I wondered at the size of his operation.

"Kyle Harrigan," he said by way of greeting when I opened the door. His hand in mine was so rough and dry, I wanted to slather it with petroleum jelly. "You're interested in a new deck?"

I ushered him in wearing Noah on my hip. "Lauren Abell said you'd be able to help me."

He stopped. "You know what happened to her, right?"

"I know, it's so sad, and I'd just met her. That's when I saw the renovation you did on her house. She gave me your name then."

Deep inside were perhaps high school good looks sunken to bloat. I'd envisioned some hunky fella who, after hanging around your house long enough, you couldn't help throwing yourself at. But after seeing him, I crossed him off my mental list of Lauren's boyfriends.

When he walked in, I realized he was taller than Seth, who, at six feet, was my baseline for height. He didn't smile until he saw Alyssa who, as always, was delighted with visitors. The fasteners down the sides of each leg of her jeans for easy diaper changing didn't detract from how cute she looked in them.

"I've got three of them—all boys," Kyle said.

"How old?" I heaved Noah to my other arm. He was giving Kyle that unblinking stare that children do.

Kyle tapped on his phone and showed me a picture. The three boys were attractive, younger versions of him.

As he followed me up the stairs to the living room, he swiveled his head around to take in the life-sized abstracts. "I've never seen anything like this outside of Celebrity Crib."

"It's my husband's doing. I can't take credit for it." My stock response to such compliments.

"He's an artist?"

"A collector."

"Wow. I've been coming into people's houses for twenty years, and this is the first place I've seen where a man decides how a place is going to look."

"Pretty much," I admitted.

Kyle took the call when his cell phone rang, so I used the opportunity to pick up toys. It was so much more motivating to clean when someone had already arrived.

After he had pocketed his phone, I showed him to the back of the house, where doors on the second floor led to nowhere. The view looked out onto the same industrial block that housed my office and the parking lot that cars treat as a shortcut from Edsall to Van Dorn Roads. The view was even worse now that the leaves had all blown off the trees and nothing blocked it. Truck beds rattled over speed bumps.

I would have thought better of him had he said, "Are you sure you want a deck here?" Instead, he dragged us through technical questions I'd not considered. I was flustered until I noticed he didn't seem interested in my replies. I sensed his grief, as palpable as a slap. Even though I taught assessment and diagnosis, intuition could not be taught.

"You miss her?" I said gently.

For the first time, he really looked at me. "What?"

"Lauren. You're upset about her death."

He stared out into the parking lot, then said without making eye contact, "Well, sure, she was one of my customers for a long time."

"Kyle, I know about you and her."

He rubbed his hand over his mouth, and his beard rasped.

When he didn't say anything, I continued. "The relationship you two had."

"Lady, I don't know what you're talking about." He turned his phone up and checked the time. "And I've got to be going. I have another appointment in D.C."

He covered the space from the back of the house to the front faster than I could with Noah in my arms. My heart was beating and not just from the exertion. I was used to being kind and empathic, not aggressive and pushy. "I don't care that you two were having an affair," I said as he was about to open the front door.

He turned, and his face twisted. Why was I baiting a beefy builder when only me and my children were here? But then I realized it wasn't anger that distorted his face; it was sadness. He yanked on the knob. I was losing him. "She might have been carrying your baby."

A word got swallowed around a lump in his throat. "How do you—" He started again and cleared his throat. "How do you know it was mine?" He dropped his hand from the knob and turned.

"Lauren must have told you about Rob's fertility treatment."

The color in his face deepened until I worried what would happen if he had heart problems. "We tried to be careful," he said.

I searched for what Lauren had seen in him. As if he knew what was running through my mind, he offered, "She said I talked to her, told her my feelings. Her husband never did that."

"Come back in," I said. "Let's sit down." I didn't say what I was thinking: sure, it's easy for a man to share in the courting stage. Then he settles down, and the talking's over.

"I wanted to treat her good," Kyle went on. "Her husband was such a—jerk."

"Rob?" I stared, wondering if I had transposed his words in my mind.

"He was so cheap and controlling." The latter was a word Kyle must have picked up from psychologist Lauren. "He wouldn't let Lauren have a bank account. He only gave her fifty dollars a week in allowance. Then he'd look at her receipts to check what she bought."

"But didn't she make money from her practice?"

"She didn't have that many patients."

This was such a change in perspective—Rob as the villain, and not Lauren—I felt dizzy. Had she just told Kyle this to play the victim and to gain his sympathy? Or was it actually true?

"You called Lauren the night before she died," I said.

"I had to hear her voice. That was the last time we ever spoke." The color had drained from his face now, leaving it blotchy. "She left a message for me the next morning, said we had to meet."

"Do you know what she wanted to talk about?"

He shook his head, then winced like he had a hangover, and it hurt. "What do you want—money?" he asked.

"You think I'm blackmailing you—no!"

Alyssa looked up at my sharp tone as she pushed a doll stroller with all the stuffed animals heaped in it. All except for Toto. In typical fashion, he was now lying forgotten in the landfill of the play yard.

I lowered my voice. "Don't you want justice for Lauren?"

He shrugged. "The housekeeper was arrested."

"You knew her?" I asked.

"Sure, I was doing the renovation."

"Did Carmen know about—" I let him fill in the blank.

"We never did anything when she was around."

"But she did the wash," I said delicately, not wanting to go into detail about that point either. "And she must have seen how you two were together." That did give Carmen a motive I hadn't considered before. Blackmail featured in a lot of my theories about Lauren, but what if Carmen had also tried it? She had proof about Lauren being with Kyle and went to her with it, said she'd tell Lauren's husband. Maybe they had argued; Lauren had said she'd fire her or tell the police instead. Would that have driven Carmen to murder Lauren?

As I mulled these theories over, I decided to change tactics and go with a softer approach. "I can't imagine what it must be like for you. You're in mourning, but no one can know." His mouth worked, so I continued. "Your wife must see you're going through something."

"I've been drinking more, sure. I just told her it was stress about the business."

My being seated acted as a cue for Noah, and he assumed breast-feeding position. It wasn't appropriate to nurse in front of a man I didn't know, but neither did I want to interrupt the flow of information. If I left the room with Noah, Kyle might realize he shouldn't be telling me all this.

"Excuse me," I said trying to cover Noah with a blanket from the couch.

Kyle didn't seem to know what was going on until Noah indignantly flung off the blanket. Then at the sight, Kyle became even more undone. "That could have been Lauren with our baby."

Well, hopefully, she would have weaned him by thirteen months, but I got the point.

"I always wanted a little girl. Was it a boy or girl?"

"They didn't say; it might have been too early to tell." I pulled the blanket back over Noah. "If Lauren wanted you two to be together, she must have been desperate to make money." Seeing his pleased half-smile, I pushed it. "I overheard a conversation the night of the party at Lauren's house." I mentioned the insider trading without saying that I had questioned Griffin and discovered more.

When I finished, Kyle said, "Lauren was real smart, had a good head for business. Me and her would have made a great team."

From his reaction, I gathered that he had already known about it.

"Did she know that what she was doing was illegal?" I asked.

He shrugged. "Happens all the time. How do you think those Wall Street types made their money?"

"So, did you give her some money for that B.X. Martin stock?"

"It seemed like a sure thing."

"But then the market went down, and they delayed the release of the new antidepressant."

"Now I guess that stock will all go to Rob." He rubbed at his face, and his beard rasped again.

"I overheard something else that night. She was talking to a Russian couple, and it sounded like she was trying to—" I struggled to find the right way to put it. "—get rid of Rob? I know that if she divorced him at this point under the prenup, she wouldn't get any money."

"Whoa." He held his hands up. "That's extreme. I would never be involved in something like that."

"Maybe Lauren would. She really wanted to be with you, right?"

"She would never do anything like that though; she was so nice and sweet."

Huh? So nice and sweet she might have gone to Congressman Kutchin to blackmail him about proof that he was involved with the intern? Lauren may or may not have told Kyle that, but I couldn't. I had already said enough.

"If only I was there Monday morning," he said. "I'd never let anything happen to her."

Chapter Twelve

Monday Morning

I was in the shower. Of course, I knew that I shouldn't do this when my children were around. But surely, I could take one little shower, right? What could happen in the ten minutes it would take me? I tried not to get too hung up on the fact that Seth got to shower every morning (alone) while I typically showered at the gym.

When suds devoured my hair, I could hear Alyssa's voice over the pelting water. "Mom!"

"Can't I be left alone for five minutes?" I shrieked, my voice ricocheting off the shower walls.

She burst in the door, and I squinted at her through the shampoo drizzling down my face. "Mom, look what Noah did!" she said, her face flushed.

"I'll be right out, Alyssa. Now please leave and close the door behind you." I wouldn't shave to speed up the process. It was winter, so I could get away with excess hair, although I didn't feel truly washed without shaving. I already regretted trying to have a shower with the children around. And that was before I came out and saw what had happened.

"Noah, Alyssa, no!" I shouted to them. They were jumping on top of the bed. "Do not step in here."

Our bedroom had an enclave space for a couple of pieces of furniture that had survived my transition from being single to married life. Now one of them—a glass coffee table—was reduced to slivers, only its metal frame exposed. I hadn't seen anything like it outside of an over-the-top action movie where a motorcycle, or better yet, a whole car comes crashing through the window.

"How did this happen?" I asked.

"Me tell," Alyssa said.

"Yes, you tried to tell me, Alyssa." My voice broke. "I'm sorry I didn't listen."

"Bowl." She pointed. A glass bowl lay upended on the floor, the shells that had been inside it, scattered across the carpet. Noah had obviously hurled the bowl into the coffee table. The bowl, miraculously, had survived.

"No! This was very wrong!" I said to Noah who looked unconcerned. A thirteen-month-old committing such acts of destruction? What type of child was he going to become? A budding oppositional defiant disorder? Neither Seth nor I had such a history in our families. And what type of discipline method could I give a thirteen-month-old other than saying a firm "no?" Even Alyssa was too young for time-outs.

My towel fell from where I had wrapped it around me toga style.

"Mommy naked!" Alyssa laughed, delighted. Noah gazed at my breasts and walked transfixed toward them. If there was one thing we knew, it was that he would become a breast man.

"No!" I shrieked as I grappled with the towel, trying to get it around me. "Don't walk in here. There's glass everywhere. Downstairs now!" As I scooped him up, he positioned himself for breastfeeding position. The towel collapsed again, and Alyssa giggled behind me. "Mommy's bum."

My cell phone buzzed as I passed it on the kitchen counter where it was charging. Of all things, I was expecting a call from one of my advisees about going from full to part-time. I picked up the phone as I marched over to the T.V. Alyssa had already watched *Snow White* in its entirety and was still wearing the costume. I had a Ph.D., and I should be doing better than providing this amount of T.V. But if I was going to spend the next forty-five minutes cleaning up glass shards to the tune of the nursery rhyme in my head, "When he was good, he was very, very good; and when he was bad, he was awful," I had earned it.

When I heard loud, shrill laughter over the phone, I was about to put it down, having no patience for nonsense at that point. Then a thick male voice said, "Is this Cara?"

"Kyle?"

"Yeah."

"Where are you?" Now I translated the sounds in the background—a bar at noon.

"I can't take it anymore," he said.

As I stood there naked, Noah started sucking on one of my exposed breasts. This seemed beyond inappropriate, so I tried to put him down.

Kyle must have heard Noah's sound of protest because he said, "Kids, they're the only thing worth living for."

He had thrown me a line. "Tell me about your kids. How old are they again?"

"I've made such a mess."

In the pause, I felt the anguish in his voice.

"I don't want to ruin their lives." He breathed in raggedly. I don't want them to know what I've done."

I imagined the dark bar, the floor smelling of yeast, and smoke from past generations. I listened to the clink of glasses, a couple of men cheering in unison, abrasive female laughter. "You're feeling trapped right now." I sensed Kyle was crying. Women started with tears, but men often went straight into shaking, silent sobs. Perhaps they held back until it got to that point.

"You're in a lot of pain right now." I carried Noah away from the *Maisy* theme song playing on the T.V. It was ruining my delivery.

My heart wrenched at the sound of Kyle's crying, like a truck engine turning over without catching. "I know it doesn't feel like it now, but there are always options."

"Not this time, not now."

"What makes you feel that way?" I sat on one of the kitchen chairs, my flesh suctioning on the red faux leather, while Noah suckled. At least the nipple in his mouth kept him quiet.

"I'm stuck for all this money, and I don't have it."

"What happened?"

I sensed him shaking his head. "They're connected. You know what they'll do to me if I don't pay?"

"Does this have anything to do with Lauren's death?"

"No, nothing like that. He wouldn't do anything like that."

I tried to quell my frustration. Fortunately, I was better at doing that with grown-ups than children. "Who are you talking about when you say 'he?'"

"The woman I love is dead, the business I've built over the last twenty years ruined."

"Is there—who can you call?" Not "is there someone you can call," assume with your language that there *is* someone, I would tell my students.

"No one knows about any of this. Except you," he pointed out.

And except maybe Lauren's murderer. To him, I said, "But I don't know what's going on. Can you tell me?"

His voice was thick, and it wasn't just tears. He was soused. "You can't tell."

"If it has anything to do with Lauren's death, I can't promise that."

He gasped. "I would never put her in danger."

"I know, but if there was money involved, that's a powerful motive." I paused to give him time to answer. When he didn't say anything, I prompted, "What if it leads to exposing her murderer? Wouldn't you want justice?"

"The housekeeper's already in jail," he mumbled.

"I saw Carmen right after she found Lauren's body. She was scared. There was no blood on her. Lauren was involved in something that got her killed. You may be the only one who knows about it."

When he was silent, I said, "I just want justice for Lauren." Talking about justice for Carmen wasn't going to cut it, even though my heart still squeezed when I thought about my conversation with Sylvia, Carmen's daughter.

"I can get justice for Lauren," he finally said.

"If you do something, then you're going to be even worse off. You'll be in trouble, and if you think you feel bad now, imagine how bad you'd feel in jail, without your kids. At least you're free now."

"There's no one I can go to." He sniffed. "If my wife found out how deep I'm in, she'd divorce—" He broke off.

"You're scared about your wife finding out."

"It was her dad's business."

I strained to hear him as he went on. "When he had a heart attack, I took over." He cleared his throat, and his voice grew stronger. "Of course, I've grown the business, and I make more money now than people with college degrees." His voice dropped again. "But let's face it, I wouldn't have had the chance if I didn't have a business to step into. And now I'm going to be in so much debt, the business can't take it."

"What about the people you work with? Is there someone you can talk to there?" Now I was seriously trying to assess his support system.

"They're relying on me. They don't want to hear how much I've screwed up *and* screwed them over. They won't have jobs after this."

"Other relatives—your dad, mom? Do you have brothers or sisters?"

"My dad died a few years back. Liver disease."

That was suggestive of alcoholism and validated my thought that Kyle needed to watch his drinking.

"My mom's so proud of me, and what I've done with this business. I can't let her down like that. And my brothers are screw-ups like my dad. They can't do anything for me. Hell, they can't do nothing for themselves."

More boys in his family tree—the chances of him having a girl with Lauren were slim.

"I can't tell them what's going on. I'm the one who made good. And they love Ann." I gathered that was his wife. "We all went to high school together, and they wouldn't understand. Lauren wasn't our kind of people. She was smart, rich—I still don't know what she saw in me."

Kyle had all the risk factors for suicide: recent loss, drinking, hopelessness, low self-esteem. My priority was not pumping him for information but making sure he would be all right. "What are your plans now?" I asked.

"I just want to be with Lauren. I wish we hadn't waited."

"What do you mean?" When he didn't answer, I had to go to the next place. "Are you thinking of hurting yourself?"

"I don't know what to do."

"Do you own a gun?"

"Sure, a rifle—for hunting."

"Can you give that to someone to hold for you until you're feeling better?"

"Why would I give someone my rifle?" Kyle gave the common re-action.

"I'm worried about you. Can I give you some numbers for after we get off the phone?"

"Like for a counselor or something?"

"You don't have to tell me what's going on if you don't want to, but it sounds scary to be alone with what you're struggling with."

"I'm not crazy."

"I'm not saying you are." I used my standard way to debunk this myth. "I know you're not seeing things or hearing voices."

"One time I thought I saw her."

I wanted to ask if it had been after another day at the bar, but you learn as a professional not to give in to these impulses.

"She was standing there in my kitchen when I went to get some water, but it was like she didn't see me. Her eyes—they were blue—and they weren't in real life. That was the strange part." The choking sound again was like something being ruptured.

I listened, my heart sinking with how bad he felt, until he spoke again.

"There's nothing you can do," he said dully. "There's nothing any-one can do. You can't bring her back."

I eyed the clock. Before I arrived at school for my one o'clock class, I would have to rip Noah off me, get dressed, pile the kids in the car, and pick up Rosa. I couldn't skip my class. I had a great deal of freedom as an academic, but meetings and classes were mandatory. I promised Kyle I would call again after class. At that point, Rosa would still be looking after the kids. I had opened this up by making him come to my house on a pretense and forcing him to talk about Lauren. I owed Kyle now.

* * *

Tuesday afternoon, I had arranged to meet Kyle Harrigan at the local Panera. I'd spent another hour on the phone with him on Monday afternoon to get a promise that he wouldn't leave the bar and shoot himself. By that time, he was drinking coffee, not beer. He'd still insisted he had no one to confide in but did agree to copy down the crisis hotline number and to meet me the next day, so I could ensure he was doing okay.

Panera was the usual afternoon scene: the loudmouth salesman who had set up office, complete with headset; office workers coming in for a late lunch; and mothers desperately trying to amuse young children. I sympathized but tried to sit as far away as possible from the children's high-pitched voices and constant demands; after all, I was trying to escape that very life. And then there were always the people staring with great intensity at their computer screens. I'd assume they were writing a Russian novel or studying for medical school. But then I'd pass by, and they'd be playing solitaire, shopping online, or, at the most, looking for employment. I could see Kyle Harrigan fitting in here and answering his many calls. But, at that point, he was twenty minutes late.

I despised when people used their cell phones in Panera's, so I furtively punched in the numbers for Kyle's mobile phone. I drained the last sip of my caramel latte, as I listened to the ringing phone. The caramel had coagulated at the bottom, and I shuddered at the sweetness. When the message clicked over, a gruff announcement that this was Harrigan Builders, I hung up the phone. My worst fear, of course, was that Kyle had succumbed to the hopelessness that I'd managed to extricate him from the day before.

As I continued to wait for Kyle, I managed to write up some conclusions of the pilot study on the adolescent girls' coping group I had tried as a ruse to talk to Tad Gowers about. I had called the mayor's office and some other D.C. government contacts, as Tad had suggested for implementing the groups, but they had seemed confused as to why I had contacted them. Maybe Tad wasn't as important as he thought he was.

Frustrated that Kyle hadn't yet come or even called, I decided to pursue another angle. As a social worker, perhaps I should have already known how to find a congressman's contact information, but I needn't have been ashamed; an easy search of the Web pulled up the information in a few moments, and I composed an e-mail message:

Dear Congressman Kutchin:

I am an assistant professor at Virginia University School of Social Work and am involved in advocacy work related to Carmen Fernandez whom I believe has been unfairly arrested for the recent murder of a Washington D.C. therapist. It turns out that the therapist, Lauren Abell, may have known Kristen Stockhauser, and I wonder if the therapist's death and Kristen's murder are linked. I would like to talk to you about what you may know about this connection.

Of course, I signed my professional title and gave my work address, but still, if I were on Congressman Kutchin's staff, I would turn it right over to the police, which is what I wanted. If they didn't, it would mean something.

Seeing it was time to retrieve my children, I closed my computer and waited until I was outside before trying Kyle Harrigan again. I put my briefcase behind the front seat. As I dialed Kyle's number, I surveyed the mess on the floor. Dried-up yogurt was glued onto Alyssa's car seat, and a plastic sandwich bag with congealed grease from pepperoni littered the floor along with pages of articles, mismatching socks that Noah had yanked off, scribbled coloring sheets, and stuffed animals.

I was surprised when Kyle answered the phone—if he had stood me up, why not continue to avoid me? Then again, he never seemed to let a ringing phone go by.

"Sorry," he said when I mentioned that I'd been waiting for him at Panera's for the last hour.

"Are you okay?" I climbed into the van. "I was concerned when you didn't come."

"I got tied up with a surveyor in D.C. And I'm doing a lot better now. I'm fine."

"Look, I know you had something going on with Lauren," I said, slamming my door closed.

"Yeah, I told you that."

"More than that. You had a plan to make money, so you could run away together." When there was no answer, I went on. "You've got to come forward. The killer might be part of whatever plan you had. Don't you see—you're the only one who might know that person. If you don't go to the police, I will."

"The police already arrested the housekeeper. They won't care."

"You would just allow an innocent woman to spend the rest of her life in prison?"

"I can't talk right now."

"Then I'll go to the FBI. Anytime you plan illegal activities over the phone across state lines—it's a federal crime called wiretapping." I'd discovered this from Seth.

"I'm not doing nothing like that." Under stress, his grammar had slipped.

"Virginia and D.C.?" I pointed out.

"D.C.'s not a state." His voice sounded slurred.

"Same laws apply."

 At the houseKyle said into the phone, "I gotta go."

"But the other day you were so upset, so worried." The clouds through my front window were like white waves rising in the sky. Although I was surprised at the change in his state of mind, I shouldn't have been. Clients had often been at the end of their ropes one day, and at the next session, canceled their appointment because they were feeling so much better.

"I've figured out a way to make this work," Kyle said. "Like you were talking about, I'll make sure justice is done.'"

Chapter Thirteen

Wednesday Afternoon

I burned up a lot of the afternoon on the Metro getting downtown, but around the Capitol, there were only parking garages at twenty dollars a day. I'd received a reply from Congressman Kutchin's office, and I was to meet with his aide in surprisingly short order on the steps of the Capitol. Finally, I'd been able to rouse a reaction from somebody.

At least the long ride on the Blue Line forced me to be alone with student papers. The natural inclination was to gravitate to the ones that I knew would be good. Having finished those two, it was hard to face the remainder, and I wanted to jump out a window. The windows on the Metro fortunately didn't open.

Casting about for a way to procrastinate, I dialed Sgt. Reynolds again in Homicide. Maybe I'd have better luck there. I'd held off from contacting her after our McDonald's meeting. But on T.V., I hadn't heard anything new on the Kristin Stockhauser case, namely that a link had been discovered between her and the recent murder of a therapist. I wondered whether Sgt. Reynolds had done as she'd said and passed the information along to the detectives on the Kristin Stockhauser case.

I was surprised when a terse male voice answered the phone. I was used to it rolling over to voice mail. Recovering, I identified myself and asked for Sgt. Reynolds.

"She's on leave." He sounded like he was about to hang up.

"What happened?" I asked.

"Bed rest. Had some problems."

"Is she okay?"

"She's had this with all her pregnancies."

Good heavens, how many had there been? "Who's handling her cases?"

"They've been re-assigned."

"I just wanted to know if she had called the detectives in the Kristin Stockhauser case."

"Was she supposed to?" he said.

"She said she would."

"If she said she would, then she did. She's very responsible."

I wasn't getting that vibe off her but okay.

***

Even on an overcast day like this one, the white marble stairs to the Capitol dazzled the eyes. I shivered. My dress coat, though flattering, wasn't all that warm—and even with a scarf, the wind had found its way in.

A non-descript-looking man wearing intellectual glasses and a grey-green suit emerged from a clot of people. "Dr. Knight?"

As he came toward me, I realized Congressman Kutchin's assistant Brad Miller couldn't be more than late twenties. I had expected some-one older.

He shook my hand as he introduced himself. His palm was soft. "How's Starbucks?" he asked. "There's a couple around here."

A funnel of wind from the rows of buildings surrounding the Cap-itol tangled my hair and blew the collar of my coat open. As we walked, Brad smiled in recognition and called greetings to people that seemed to fit into two main categories: those in their twenties like him and old men who, though indistinguishable from each other, I'm sure wielded great power.

"Thank you for getting back to me so quickly." Somehow, I had attained the status of a priority for the congressman's staff. What did that mean?

"We're swamped. Right before Thanksgiving is a busy time for us."

My stomach sank at the prospect of Thanksgiving. Holidays were like weekends, only with more days to figure out how to amuse the children.

"And we have to be careful now that Congressman Kutchin is in the limelight," Brad went on. "His P.R. firm says he has to limit his exposure to the public as much as possible."

I wasn't clear on the whole P.R. thing. Were there really companies that told people what they should have known anyway?

As I ordered at the counter, I wondered if Brad would pay for my latte to cultivate good will. But perhaps I was considered a potential blackmailer, and they had to avoid any appearance of bribery. I handed over my reward card as payment.

At the condiments table, I spanked chocolate powder into the latte and tore up two packets of sweetener. As Brad leaned over to pour cream into his coffee, I noticed that his hair was that blonde that faded into the wasteland between brown and blonde. I hoped that Alyssa's hair wouldn't turn that color as it darkened.

We sat at a table for two, and I took my first sip. The milky espresso burned my tongue. Ah, scalding hot—just the way I liked it.

Brad's phone buzzed, and he grabbed it, frowning with importance. "Excuse me, I need to respond to this."

I hated to tell people, but when they worked their thumbs with such intense concentration, they looked like they were masturbating.

Brad eventually raised his head and smiled. His teeth were the same color as his hair. Could he be any blander?

"You wanted to talk to the congressman?" he asked. "Because he's really busy—chair of the Committee on Health and a member on other working committees. And that's without all the—" He twirled his finger. "Spin surrounding him right now."

I launched into my topic. "A friend of mine, Lauren Abell—" She wasn't really a friend, but Brad wouldn't want to hear the mothers-in-law backstory. "She was murdered."

He gave a tilt of the head that I recognized from teaching. He didn't want to reveal what he knew or didn't.

"I have reason to believe Kristin saw Lauren for either testing or therapy just before she went missing," I said. "Isn't it too much of a coincidence that Lauren ended up dead, too?" He leaned back, tipping on the legs of the chair as I continued. "Kristin revealed she was having an affair with your congressman.

Brad's chair legs landed back down, scraping harshly against the floor. "He loves his wife. They've been married twenty-five years. High school sweethearts."

"Lauren wanted money. She came to the congressman." I leaned my elbows on the table, and it rocked dangerously—one of those wonky-legged affairs. I swooped for my drink before it spilled.

"And what do you want?" Behind him, the espresso machine hissed.

"The woman who's accused of killing Lauren is her housekeeper. The police latched on to her and didn't look at anyone else." My fingertips burning, I put the cup down. "It's sad. Her children have been put into foster care while she's in jail. She didn't do it."

"Then why not go to the police if you think this is so suspicious?" He tore the lid off his Americano and steam gushed out.

"Same reason you didn't turn over my e-mail to the police," I retorted. I had positively pestered the police, to no avail. They were not interested in supposed connections between a murder in Georgetown and a missing intern who was presumed dead at this point.

"How are you going to explain to your students how you violated confidentiality?" he said, a sly uptick to one side of his mouth. "What would your colleagues and dean think?"

He knew just the hot buttons to push. I had peeked at a file that contained confidential information. I'd justified that the risk of loss of life—there had already been two deaths—and the unfairness of Carmen being jailed for an offense she didn't commit overrode confidentiality. But the licensing board might not see it that way.

I forced myself to sound as cocky as him. "When do I get to talk to the congressman?"

Brad rocked back in his chair in an arrogant gesture, and I lunged for my cup again.

"You don't have anything on him," he said. "He won't talk to you."

Chapter Fourteen

Thursday Evening

The students needed little encouragement to walk out together at ten p.m., but that left me alone to lock up. That's okay, I considered myself a brave person. I had once tried on a bathing suit in a department store after a pasta dinner.

Outside in the parking lot, the only sound were my boot heels against asphalt. A black Town Car pulled into the parking lot; its headlights swept over the signs posted *Faculty Only*. I hustled my step as the driver's window slid down to reveal a man with angular facial planes. All I caught was, "Get in."

I broke into an awkward run with my bag and laptop weighing me down. The tail lights of the minivan flashed as I fumbled with my key fob.

The driver climbed out, and a whimper arose from my throat. The limousine door dinged. "You wanted to see the congressman," he growled in a Slavic accent. "Here's your chance."

The back window rolled down, and I recognized Congressman Kutchin from the photos and T.V. news clips.

"Miss Knight, please get in the car." Congressman Kutchin had my name wrong on two counts. I was "Dr." not "Miss," and if I did go by Mrs., it would be Jacobs, but I never corrected people, and especially not him.

I hesitated. "Let me just call my husband. He'll worry if I'm late." Seth might have already been in bed. Putting the children down had that effect on him.

"We'll just be a minute," said the congressman. "Don't you have students? One of them could have stopped and asked you a question on your way out."

You were never supposed to climb in a strange man's car. But was he a stranger if he was a public figure, someone you'd seen on T.V. numerous times? Of course, the reason he'd become so recognized was his suspected involvement in his mistress going missing.

Why would a congressman have a Russian driver? Why did he need a driver at all? His condo, I had learned from the news, was in Foggy Bottom. Although perhaps with the congressman's new-found notoriety, he needed protection.

And wasn't a chat with him what I wanted when I went to Brad? Despite him saying the congressman would never meet with me, here he was.

All these thoughts batted around in my mind, but when Kutchin said, "Come on," and patted the seat beside him, he carried a lot of authority in his voice, and I obeyed, sliding in. The car had a showroom smell to it, and I took in the clean carpet under my boot heels. I made an awkward landing with my over-packed briefcase and purse on the soft black leather seat.

"Is there a drive we can take around here while we talk?" the congressman asked. "How about Old Town?"

I glanced out the window as we pulled away. "That's half an hour away."

"I thought we were in Alexandria," he said.

"We are. It's not all Old Town." I don't know how many times I'd made that point to people.

As we drove out of the parking lot, the congressman cast a dubious eye at the main building sign where a massage therapy school was prominently featured. "You're a professor of sociology?"

"Social work."

"And your connection to Kristin Stockhauser?" he asked.

"Didn't your staff person—Brad—fill you in?"

"I want to hear the story from you," he said.

As we drove past my townhome development, I saw Seth's car parked outside, and the usual number of lights on inside. Yes, I had wanted some excitement, but now home looked wonderfully normal. I turned to answer Kutchin. "I knew Lauren Abell. Did you see it in the news? *Georgetown woman killed in her own home.* Kristin went to see her for psychological testing or maybe therapy."

"Ah, Kristin—she's delightful but a little —" He searched for the word, and the driver muttered something, which I couldn't understand, but made the congressman chuckle. Interesting that the divider was still open, and he was letting his driver hear the whole conversation—and make commentary.

"Enthusiastic," Kutchin landed on. "I don't know if you're aware of the fact that I'm the chair of the Committee on Health."

I tried to look impressed, although I was surprised he hadn't been stripped of this role with all the negative publicity.

"Have you heard of the drug Zemeron?" he asked.

The congressman was on the verge of mansplaining when I cut him off. "An atypical antidepressant being used to treat adult ADHD. Like Wellbutrin but with a different chemical structure."

"She's a smart one," he said to the driver.

When the driver lifted an ironic eyebrow at me through the mirror, I felt like making a face back at him.

"Our committee's looking into it," the congressman said. "A public watch group brought to our attention that it may make people feel suicidal. And we must take that seriously after what we went through with antidepressants and kids."

"I see," I said. "And the therapist who died, Lauren Abell, just happened to be married to the lead investigator on the Zemeron trial?"

This time, only the driver's eyebrow showed in the mirror as he steered behind a stream of cars waiting to cross Edsall and Van Dorn. Perhaps the driver knew more about Kristin Stockhauser than anyone. He could have driven them to trysts. Or worse, the drive had constituted the assignation. The seats looked immaculate, but who knew what might have happened here? I shifted uncomfortably.

"Understand I never met this Dr. Abell," the congressman said.

"But you must have heard of her husband if you looked at the studies," I said.

"Sure, but to be honest, I didn't put the names together," he said.

"And the connection between you and his wife is just a coincidence?" I asked.

His face was in shadow. "There is no connection between me and his wife."

"Through Kristin Stockhauser there is. Your intern went to Lauren for testing and confided personal information."

I was surprised when he chuckled. "That Kristin—she's quite the pistol. She decided, without telling me, you hear, that she would go to doctors in the area complaining about symptoms of ADHD. She wanted to see how easy it would be to get a prescription for Zemeron, and if there'd be mention of side effects."

Side effects seemed a poor word choice. Constipation or grogginess were side effects; suicidality was another realm altogether.

"Then why didn't your staff person tell me that?" I asked.

"He wasn't authorized to say. It's not something we really want to get out. Like I said, Kristin did this on her own, bless her heart."

We finally moved through the light. For once, I hadn't minded the interminable wait. The closer to home I stayed, the better. "And Kristin started her investigation with the lead researcher himself?"

The congressman splayed his hands. "Who better?"

I frowned, trying to puzzle this out. "So, then he referred her to his wife to get a complete psychological work-up for ADHD. As you probably know, that's not standard practice, but it certainly showed that Rob Abell wasn't handing out Zemeron like candy."

Kutchin chuckled, all folksy. "ADHD sure wasn't a stretch for her. That's what all the staff said, that Kristin had ADHD. I'm not a psychiatrist, but she was—high energy." He stroked his tie. "I have a question though, since you're the expert here—isn't ADHD only for kids?"

I wondered if Kutchin was trying to distract me by pandering, but I answered. "About a third of the time, it supposedly continues into adulthood."

"What are the symptoms of ADHD in adults?" he asked as if fascinated.

"Restlessness, impulsivity, difficulty concentrating, lack of organization," I rattled off.

"And I thought it was boys mostly."

These were mainstream facts I spouted. "ADHD is less common in girls, but it also may be under-diagnosed." I brought the focus back around. "Kristin may have been posing as a client, but she confided in Lauren, said she was dating you." I used the politest word I could find. Dating.

He chortled. "What a character—making up stuff to make it seem like she was a real client. Kristin's a little—no, I don't want to speak ill of her, but—"

Kutchin smiled as he said, "She was used to getting what she wanted."

"And that was you?" I asked.

He considered. "Not so much me as a man in my position."

"That must have been flattering. She was a beautiful young woman."

He shrugged, then frowned, "*Is* a beautiful young woman. We've got to keep up hope." He looked out the window as if he could see Kristin in the distance.

All I saw were people running across Edsall Road with plastic grocery bags from the Giant on the corner.

The light turned, and the driver hit the gas pedal hard, pressing me against the back seat. When he braked at the next light, I jerked forward. "How did you find out what your intern was doing?" I asked. "She disappeared after that."

"We went through her computer—after the police were done with it. We found some notes and put it together."

"And then you told the police of your new find? Because maybe it connected to her going missing." As the townhome development of Cameron Station swept by, I felt dizzy with the sudden driving speed, reminiscent of Barbara's. I'd only eaten cheese and crackers before class, not a proper dinner, and now I was being driven by a Slavic man, which was confusing because Masha and her family might have also been connected to Lauren's death.

And now Kutchin, a media obsession for the last two months, was explaining himself to me, saying that, of course, he was cooperating with the police.

Unfortunately, I had no way of confirming this. We were now stuck at a light near the central Alexandria Library. I'd been inside many times, most recently attempting story hour for Noah. We'd had to leave because he was so disruptive. Now, all I wanted was such an ordinary scene.

Kutchin turned to me. "Why didn't you go to the police? Why come to us?"

Again, the police weren't interested. "My concern is more with Lauren Abell." I tried to crack the window, but it wouldn't open. Fear crept in. I was trapped. Was this ride going to end up at the Potomac River, where I'd be thrown in? Had that been Kristin's fate? "Could you open the window, please?" I said to the driver.

His eyes flicked to mine in the rear-view mirror but then returned to the road.

"Oh, let's not open a window." Kutchin leaned forward to address the driver. "I know I'm a big sissy, but I can't get used to the cold up here after Texas."

Feeling a bit panicky, I decided to pose a scenario and force the issue. "Lauren must have come to you. She was desperate for money. She tried to make a deal." I didn't want to make him skittish with the word "blackmail." "Lauren agreed not to go public with the affair."

"Now wait a minute, I categorically deny—"

I raised my voice over his objections. "The affair that Kristen *claimed*." I tried to make it sound like it had nothing to do with him. "Lauren wanted her husband left out of the Zemeron investigation." I felt my way as I spoke, trying to sense the congressman's reaction. I peered at his face, but it was in shadow in the darkness of Duke Street. I kept fishing. "Maybe she wanted the whole investigation dropped." After all, the stock depended on the success of the drug. "Or money."

We were stalled at another light moments after leaving the last one. The driver huffed and puffed in audible impatience. Welcome to the neighborhood.

Congressman Kutchin put a hand up, like stop right there. He had lost the avuncular air. "Miss Knight, I don't like people who won't play fair. You got me to come out here—" He peered up, like this godforsaken place—"Because that's what *you* wanted. Now *I* want whatever evidence you have of Kristin making that allegation to your friend."

"I don't have any."

He harumphed. "This is all on your say-so, huh? No photo on your phone? No clinical file? No copies?"

I struggled to explain. "I did happen to see Kristin's name as I was packing Lauren's things, but I took nothing with me. I'm sure you can figure out how to gain access. All her files are with her husband Rob. He came to collect the boxes that night."

The congressman's head was turned resolutely toward the window.

I perched at the edge of my seat, the belt straining across my shoulder. "Congressman Kutchin, I need to get home. My husband—he's going to be worried sick that I'm not back yet." That is if he wasn't snoring.

He turned to me, his mouth a snarl. "You've wasted my valuable time coming out to your little campus with your lies and attention-seeking."

Whoa. His affect had changed entirely. After turning nasty, Congressman Kutchin stared out the window and sulked petulantly.

I sank into my seat, choosing to disengage from such mercurial tendencies, and watched, anxious, until the driver did a narrow U-turn and headed back the way we'd come on Duke Street.

* * *

At home, I checked on the children first. Relief washed over me seeing their sleeping cherubic forms with wide open mouths. I snapped on the light in our bedroom, but Seth kept sleeping. Usually, that was a good thing since then, I could read and not disturb him.

"Seth," I half-whispered, still cramming a banana in my mouth to stave off the nausea that swam in my stomach.

His eyes blinked open. "What's wrong?" he slurred. Taking in the banana, he frowned.

I refrained from overly dramatic pronouncements like, "I've been kidnapped."

He squinted at me as I explained the evening's events. When I'd finished, he said, "Why did you get in the car?"

"Are you mad at me?" I asked, incredulous.

He sat up and tugged his pillow on his lap. "Why didn't you talk to him in the parking lot? Why did you have to ride off with him?"

"Have you ever heard of blaming the victim?" My voice warbled on the last few words.

He shifted toward me and wrapped me in his arms. "I'm just worried about what could have happened to you. Why didn't you walk out with your students?"

"They're mad at me about the research proposals, so it's weird to tell them I want them to wait while I get my stuff from my office so we can walk out together."

He exhaled. "I'm glad you're okay, but the way he acted, he must have killed that intern; otherwise, why would he have come after you?" He ran his hand through his hair, and it stuck on end.

"The funny thing is, his aide, Brad Miller, told me Kutchin wouldn't contact me. That he was too busy."

"He must have gotten that driver to kill the intern," Seth said. "And then they had you in the car. The same thing could have happened to you."

"And the driver spoke Russian," I pointed out. "I wonder if there's any connection between him and Misha?"

"You've got to stop," he said, putting his head in his hands. "It's getting too dangerous."

I jumped to my feet, too wired to stay in bed. "Sgt. Reynolds—none of them—thought there was anything to what I was saying. But this shows there was. Kutchin must have had something to do with Lauren's death and the intern's."

Seth raised his head. "If he had Lauren killed for having proof of his affair, what could he do to you?"

"But this means Carmen definitely didn't do it." I touched my hand to my chest.

He shook his head. "You don't have any proof Kutchin killed Lauren, and Carmen's got a lawyer to figure all this out for her."

"I told you what her lawyer's like. He's going to wait until he walks into the courtroom to see what emerges out of his mouth. Then he'll say, 'Gotcha.'"

"It's sad about Carmen and her children, but it's not your concern. They have the CPS caseworkers for this. They can't all be bad."

"I'm not saying they are." My stomach gurgled around the banana I'd just downed.

Seth knelt on the mattress, put his hands on my shoulders, and stared into my eyes. "I love how you care; I do. But you've got to care more about your kids and me than strangers' children. You're putting yourself in danger."

Chapter Fifteen

Friday Afternoon

The next day, I had an excellent opportunity to see Rob again when I volunteered to pick up Barbara, who wanted to come back. "Can we talk in private?" I asked when he answered the door.

The children were quickly captivated by new toys Barbara had bought during another Georgetown shopping spree, so I left them with her and Arlene.

The neatness of the study had deteriorated since Lauren's death. Rob had let stacks of mail and papers pile up. He sat behind the desk, presumably to put some distance between us.

A knock sounded, and I jumped. The door to the study swung open, and Arlene peered in. "Cara, honey, do you want something to drink?"

I smiled. "I'm fine, thank you."

"Come on," Rob said. "Mom, not now."

"I was just being a good hostess. You didn't get Cara anything to drink."

"I'm fine," I insisted.

After she closed the door, he shook his head. "I can't wait 'til she goes back home."

"I'm sorry, it must have driven you crazy with Barbara here, as well."

Barbara had been bleating about coming back to our house for some time, but Seth had played the heavy: "You're supposed to be here for Arlene, help her plan the funeral."

Rob made a face. "At least Barbara kept my mom company. Now my mom will want me to spend time with her."

Typical of both Arlene and Barbara—they weren't thinking of what the person in distress needed—after all, Rob was the supposed grieving spouse.

The house creaked. "You don't think anyone will—overhear?" I used that word instead of "eavesdrop."

Rob flapped a dismissive hand. "So, what did you want? If it's to apologize for practically accusing me of hurting Lauren—there's no need."

I smiled sheepishly, knowing I had more accusations in store. "I did pack up Lauren's office for you," I said, trying to smooth the way.

He nodded, brusque. "I appreciate that."

"I'm sorry to talk to you about matters that are—uncomfortable." I came up with. "But you know I'm just interested in discovering the truth since I think Carmen is being unfairly targeted."

He picked up a pen and started tapping it on the edge of the desk. "Does Seth know you're doing all this? He's trying to help. He was the one who gave us the lawyer's name." By "us," he must have been referring to his mother.

My cheeks warmed at the rebuke, but I tried to remain assertive. "Look at it this way, the more I uncover, the more your lawyer is prepared."

He chuckled humorlessly. "Yeah, I guess I don't have to pay for a P.I. now."

I took a deep breath. "There is something else I've uncovered, and there's no easy way to say this. Lauren was having an affair."

His gaze was steady on mine. "Kyle Harrigan? Yes, I know."

"You did?" My voice rose in surprise. "How?"

"I found a condom in her purse."

Ouch. "What led you there?"

"She got a call the night of the party, and I got suspicious."

He *had* registered that phone call. "How were you so sure from the condom?" I asked.

"We were trying to get pregnant. Why else would she have a condom in her purse?" His eye twitched.

"Did you tell anyone?"

"Only my lawyer. I didn't even have a chance to confront Lauren before she—"

The house creaked again, and I lowered my voice. "Does your mother know?"

"She doesn't need to know everything about my life. How did you figure it out?" he asked.

I wasn't about to reveal the lengths I'd gone to discover the information. "I'm a social worker," I said, as if that was my superpower.

He pinched his lower lip as he considered this. "Did you tell the police?"

"Why didn't you tell them?" I said instead of answering.

"I was still wrapping my head around it. Lauren and I never even had a chance to talk."

"Don't worry, it didn't change their mind about Carmen," I said.

"They may never have arrested her if she hadn't tried to leave the country. That was a really stupid move on her part."

As he suddenly stood, the chair squealed in protest at the motion. He rummaged in a stack on his desk and plucked out one document. "Not that I need to prove anything to you, but—" He handed it to me. "Here's the receipt for my medical services the morning Lauren died. Look at the time I paid, and I was there for my appointment an hour and a half before that. So, I couldn't have been here, murdering *her*."

As I verified the details on the bill for service, I said, "Why didn't you just tell the police then? Establish your alibi when they first asked."

"This was personal information. I didn't know if they would use it against me or leak it."

A knock sounded on the door, and Arlene poked her head in again.

"What, Mom?" Rob still hovered over me, scowling.

Arlene seemed to take in our positioning as she said, "Barbara's tired. She doesn't feel well and wants Cara to take her home."

"We'll be down in a minute, Mom."

I waited until her footsteps had receded down the stairs, and Rob had returned to his seat. "There's something else I told the police. You know Misha and Masha—the Russian couple who were there the night of the party? I overheard Lauren talking to the husband upstairs." I repeated their conversation. "What does that sound like to you?"

"They were going to do her a favor in exchange for her sponsoring their visa?"

"Did Lauren ever talk to you about helping them?" I asked.

"No," he admitted.

"Now, this may sound farfetched," I prefaced before giving him the whammy. "It kind of sounds like she was arranging a hit on you."

He surged to his feet again, and the chair spun. "The police have their person. Why are you so determined to pin it on me?" He stomped to the window and gazed out.

I guessed it was easier for him to be mad at me rather than her. "I don't want to pin it on you. I just want to find out the truth."

Canned laughter came from downstairs. Barbara must have cranked up the T.V. and cackled along with the laugh track. She didn't sound so unwell to me.

When he turned back to me, his face was shadowed by the darkening light outside. "You know, Seth and my mother have been friends for fifteen years. Do you want to create a permanent rift between our families?"

This did give me pause. Seth often said, "Thank God for Arlene. At least my mom has someone she can rely on down there." Otherwise, she would lean on him more than she already did.

"And I thought you worked?" Rob went on. "I don't know about you, but as a professor, I'm too busy to be digging up dirt on other people."

"Too busy with the Zemeron study?" I wondered how I would work that in, and Rob had given me the perfect opening. "Have you finished 'crunching the numbers' yet?" I put the phrase in quotes. "What are you learning about its effect on suicidality?"

"Zemeron is effective for treating ADHD symptoms in adults," he said as if lecturing to students.

"Then why is the Committee on Health looking into it? Surely, Griffin told you he was called to testify?"

"He was just there to explain the compound's chemical structure for Zemeron."

After Kutchin's revelations on Monday night, I had researched the Committee on Health's work related to Zemeron. I had read Griffin's train wreck of testimony and didn't blame him for hating his bosses. In response to Kutchin's question about suicidality in people taking Zemeron, Griffin said, "They probably would have felt suicidal anyway. There's no proof it was the medication. People with mental illness want to kill themselves." I could imagine him shrugging. "Their doctors should be monitoring them better. It's not the fault of the medication. And no one actually *died*, have they?"

"So nothing in your data showed that the drug made them feel suicidal?" I asked Rob.

He shook his head. Not at a statistically significant level."

"What about the follow-up data? Same story?"

"I told you we haven't finished crunching the numbers yet." There again was that annoying phrase.

"And could it really be coincidence that Griffin is a chemist at B.X. Martin, and you just happen to win the contract for the study on Zemeron?"

"You probably haven't pulled down any federal grant funding, so you wouldn't know how it works, Cara."

A nasty jab, but he was right—I hadn't had any federal funding, although I had certainly tried.

Time for me to zing him back. "So, I'm sure Lauren arranged this for you with Griffin, just like she bought stock based on his insider information about a new formulation."

The way his eyes moved back and forth like a typewriter carriage, I could tell he was trying to figure out what I was talking about. "How much stock did she buy?"

"So, you haven't found the stock certificate?"

He indicated the mounds of paper on the desk like it was only a matter of time. "And I think you have Lauren to thank for not being called to testify for the Committee on Health."

"Oh, yeah—why is that?"

I told him the missing intern, Kristin Stockhauser, had seen Lauren for testing. "Wouldn't your office have some record of that? Insurance forms, informed consent, intake info?"

"We don't take insurance."

That shouldn't have surprised me. Insurance was an irritant, but if you did without it, you limited your practice to only those who could afford to pay upwards of two hundred and fifty an hour out of pocket. "A record of payment then," I said. "Anyway, I think Lauren might have been blackmailing Congressman Kutchin because she heard from Kristin herself that she was having an affair with him."

The room had darkened with the early night sky, and I couldn't read Rob's reaction. "I suspect one of Lauren's conditions with Kutchin was that you wouldn't testify about the Zemeron study." It sounded like there might have been something hinky with the clinical trial—either Rob had misreported suicidal events in the post-test findings or was stalling on the follow-up findings because they showed a different picture.

"I didn't even get this kind of interrogation from the police. Who do you think you are, Cara? My mom said you were strange, and you really are. Talk about OCD." He laughed snidely.

That was how mental health professionals insulted each other— by tossing out American Psychiatric Association diagnoses. I could have responded in kind: about Rob's mother saving every outfit he ever wore as a young child. Now, *that* was classic OCD! And what did Arlene know about strange? She had her eyebrows permanently painted on like Barbara's.

"Just one last question," I said. "How did Lauren find Harrigan Contractor's anyway? Before your house, he'd done all his work in Northern Virginia, not D.C."

"I was the one who found his company." He had the grace to look chagrined. "I called around, trying to find a good price. He had the lowest bid, beat out all the companies in D.C."

How ironic that Rob had put Lauren and Kyle together. How much of it was revenge on her part at Rob's cheapness that got her involved with Kyle?

* * *

As Barbara, the children, and I drove off in the minivan, she said, "I couldn't sleep on that spare bed another night. It must have been

Rob's before he married Lauren. You know me, I don't like to complain."

I flashed her a glance to check for self-deprecating humor. None.

She sighed dramatically. "Last night was terrible. Sciatic nerve pain. All the way up from the bottom of my feet to the top of my spine. I took something, but then that upset my stomach. Then I had to take two Klonopin." The way she said "Klonopin" was full of lusty regard. I didn't know why she couldn't take Ambien like the rest of us.

I waited patiently until she had finished complaining, then launched into my nighttime saga. Alyssa had come in at one-thirty in the morning, and I'd asked groggily, "Is Noah crying?"

"He dreaming of your nipples." I came awake, amused, and also impressed with her sentence structure. But lost my sense of humor when she ordered "Steps," meaning she wanted to go downstairs.

"No, sleep, still sleep time." Seth could sleep through everything, even the bedroom light on and ringing phones, but not the sound of children. I carried her downstairs and tried to cuddle with her on the couch to avoid disturbing him. But she tickled my ear, then my hair. She kicked her legs like a frog to get free of the blanket I had drawn over, but that also meant I was left without covers. Why did so many parents want to sleep with their children? I wondered.

* * *

Back at the house, Barbara's antics continued so much that I daydreamed about whether I could return her to Rob and Arlene. The children had fallen asleep on the drive, so I wanted to take the opportunity to squeeze in some editing on a manuscript. But Barbara chose that moment to want to check her e-mail on my computer. "I couldn't get on at Rob's house," she said woefully. "And it'll just take me a minute."

Then she couldn't figure out how to get on the Internet, then her e-mail server. I did all that for her to the point of typing in her password, "Bab." Seth had told me her cell phone message also referred to "Bab"—her new single-woman persona.

She kept mistakenly closing her connection, which I had to retrieve. Then she peered through the messages, tapping with fingers that couldn't type, in her excruciatingly slow manner. "I don't know why I check it anyway. It's all junk mail," she said. She looked up at me. "Did you get my invitation to join my Facebook page?"

"Barbara, I need to do some work now," I said in the firm and deliberate tone adults use with children to restrain themselves from screaming. "You'll have to try again when I'm at the office."

"You're going to work now?"

"The children are sleeping. This may be my only chance today."

"I'll only be another minute." Perhaps she sensed that I wanted to yank the laptop from her because she grasped it in her big hands. "Why don't you go off and call those Russians for the invitation to the Shiva? We didn't have an email for them."

Barbara had given me an excellent opportunity to reach out again. I dialed the number a little nervous, given how we'd ended things last time. When Masha picked up, I told her about the Shiva for Lauren at Rob's house.

"Why are you the one calling?" she asked.

"My mother-in-law is helping Rob and his mother organize it. His mother and my mother-in-law are best friends in Miami."

In the frosty silence that followed, I forged on. "You knew Lauren. You were with her the night before she died. I thought you'd want to come."

"And why is it not sooner? The burial—it should have been within a couple of days."

I gently explained that there had been an autopsy, which had delayed things a bit.

She switched to Russian, and a male voice answered in the background.

A deep and accented voice assumed the line. I assumed it was her husband, Misha. "Yes?"

After I repeated my spiel, he said, "We will come. But I will want to talk to you alone."

As I hung up the phone, pondering what he wanted to talk to me about, Barbara announced, "I'm done!" Just that moment, a siren sound of wailing wafted up from downstairs. The children were awake, and I had missed my opportunity to get work done.

As I breastfed Noah for the 30 minutes it usually required to recover from a crying jag, Barbara made box macaroni and cheese for a snack. Predictably, Alyssa wouldn't even taste it, but Noah had three baby bowls full.

Barbara smiled. "I haven't lost my touch."

"Barbara, it was out of a box," I said.

"I make it special."

"Let me guess, you added more butter." She loved to add fat to whatever she could and probably took what she always referred to as a "little taste" as she prepared it.

I watched the clock. In my experience, only waitressing rivaled how slowly time in the afternoon ticked along trying to amuse children. Barbara wanted to "get comfortable," so she changed back into her nightgown.

When Seth called and said he would be a little late, I put back my head and howled, "Noooo!" It was all I could do to make it to six-thirty when he was due.

After I hung up, Barbara went into the kitchen to eat her dinner—we were having leftover meatloaf—and she slipped on a Cheerio. *Womp*, she landed on the floor. Seeing her unable to turn over to support herself on the one knee required to get up was a source of great excitement for the children. We pulled her by the arm, but it was like trying to heave a sofa.

Just then, Seth walked in, calling out, "I've got the paper," trying to make it up to me that he was late. He bought the *Washington Post* on Friday for the weekend section so we could figure out what the heck to do with these kids. Weekends could be excruciating without a plan.

"Seth, help me!" Barbara wailed from the kitchen.

The children danced around as he surveyed his mother on the floor. When he put his hands under her armpits to lift her, she slapped him away. "Why are you tickling me?"

Seth bravely attempted to lift her and staggered back with a surprised look in his eye at how heavy she was.

Eventually, he pulled her up by the arms. When she finally rested in a chair, Barbara said, "This is why I don't want to live alone. If I fall, I can't get back up."

Seth pointed out that if she wasn't so out of shape, she might be able to manage.

After dinner, as I read the Metro section at the kitchen table, I wore the sieve on my head that Alyssa had insisted was my hat. My arms strained to hold Noah in my lap so he could breastfeed, and I could look at the paper without him tearing it to pieces.

I smiled over at Alyssa, who had somehow unearthed the pregnancy indicator stick that had first announced she was coming into the world. Nothing was safe from these children. They found random objects and took them to unexpected places, where I might or might not see them again. Alyssa dug the stick into the Elmo potty we had bought to motivate her. "Mmm, peanut butter," she said, pretending to eat from the stick like a spoon.

I laughed. She didn't even like peanut butter.

When I returned my gaze to the paper, a tiny heading jumped out: *Local man found dead*. Then, the name: *Kyle Harrigan*. The effect was like I had been socked in the chest with a fistful of ice.

"Seth!" I yelled. "Come quick!"

He bounded down the stairs from the bedroom where he'd gone to change out of his suit. His eyes darted to the kids—Alyssa with the Elmo potty, Noah sucking away. "What happened?"

"Look!" I pointed to the article and watched his face as he read.

"It doesn't say how he died," he said. "Sounds like suicide the way it's written."

"Oh, no," I wailed. "He sounded better the last time I talked to him." It hadn't overly surprised me that Kyle's mood had veered from sad to suicidal to seemingly okay in the few contacts I'd had with him. I was used to clients, the vagaries of their moods, and my intense dating experiences. But when Kyle spoke about "getting justice," I had tried to talk him out of it, warned him about the danger of turning the table on someone who might have killed already. Was it suicide, or had he been murdered?

"He has three boys." My eyes filled with tears. Seth leaned over and tried to hug me, but Noah, outraged, pushed him away.

Alyssa, sensing my distress, wandered over. Seeing my tears, her face reddened, and she turned to Seth. "What you do to Mommy?"

I hugged my children and thought of Kyle's boys and their towheaded innocence.

Chapter Sixteen

Monday Morning

This was like déjà vu all over again—contacting the investigator in a case, this time Arlington County. I couldn't waste my paid babysitting, once again, for meetings with police detectives. And I had six hundred pages of student papers to grade. If I could resist the urge to line edit, I could do maybe three at a time. I also had class preps, revisions on a paper I was re-submitting to a journal, and a review of a manuscript I needed to complete for a social work journal.

This time, all I could allow was a phone conversation at work with the investigator, Dalia Spears. My talking on the phone always felt like abandonment to my children, and they would start squawking for attention. I wanted to maintain a certain level of professionalism here.

Detective Spears had a smoky voice, and I imagined over-processed hair and leathered skin. When I outlined what I had learned about Kyle Harrigan, she said, "Do you want me to break his wife's heart? She's already grief-stricken. If I start digging into whether he had an affair and business troubles, it might take me to the same place—he killed himself because of all the pressure."

"Surely, his wife will discover it as bills come due, and she looks into the accounts. Isn't it better for her to be prepared?" I asked.

"Ma'am, do you know anything specific?"

I had to admit I didn't.

"So there might not be anything. You don't know for a fact."

Giving up on that angle, I asked, "Is there a note?"

"Yes, ma'am." Although I know people used the phrase to be polite, I found it impertinent when they overused it, like she did.

"In his writing?" I scanned my office as I talked. The place was a disgrace. I hadn't cleaned up since Noah had pulled everything off the bookshelves and knocked over stacks of paper. I'd been so busy trying to figure out what had happened to Lauren that my work had been squeezed into the corners of my life that weren't taken up by the case and my children, leaving me no time to clean. I'd get to it at the end of the semester, which was only a few weeks away now.

"It's typed on a computer and printed out," Detective Spears said.

"Then anyone could have written it."

Detective Spears's sigh was audible. "This is a nice family, ma'am. I don't want to make their grief any harder for them."

After we hung up, I had to steel myself to make the next call. As it rang, I hoped no one would answer.

When Ann Harrigan picked up, I quickly introduced myself as one of Kyle's customers and offered condolences. "I was friends with one of his other customers, Lauren Abell?" My voice turned up at the end in question.

"She died, too, right? Murdered by her housekeeper—a terrible thing. Kyle was very upset over that. He cared so much about his customers."

"Don't you think it's a little coincidental that Lauren died, and now your husband—"

"My husband committed suicide; did you know that?"

"I didn't." Though I had suspected. "I'm so sorry. He must have been under a lot of stress."

"He handled the business; he said everything was fine, but he was stressed out. A wife can tell."

I swallowed and came out with it. "Before she died, your husband and Lauren had entered into a side business."

I waited out the silence while she digested this news. Finally, she said, "What kind of business?"

"I don't know the details; she didn't tell me. But I think something about it may turn up in his effects when you go through them."

There was a knock at my door, which I ignored. The timing was terrible. "I've been looking into Lauren's death. I don't think it was the housekeeper."

"And you were a friend of Lauren's?"

I took a deep breath. "Yes." Funny, it didn't seem like a lie anymore. I knew Lauren so well now; it was like with clients, even sex offenders didn't seem so bad when you knew them in their totality.

"Are you in law enforcement?" she asked.

"No, I'm a social worker."

The door opened, and Adam, the program director, peeped in. I pointed emphatically to the phone and mouthed that I would talk to him after I was done. The problem with administrators is that they had to be at work for a set number of hours, so they were always wandering around looking for a chat to pass the time. I was on a totally different schedule, trying to cram a work week into small sections of days, and had to pay a babysitter for each hour. At that price, I'd better be productive.

"Then you have no business looking into anything," she said, as Adam wrestled with the keys in my lock.

"I thought you might want to know in case you come across financial irregularities."

Adam walked toward me and handed me my keys. I'd told him before I left them in the lock so I'd know where they were. The last thing I needed when I was about to rush off to collect my children would be to lose time searching through papers to find my keys.

"You must be a very cruel person to call someone out of the blue and tell them lies about a dead husband."

I smarted at that; for a social worker, "cruel" is the very worst quality you can be.

"And let me tell you something, everyone's going through financial troubles right now, but my husband did a great job of running this business, and it's been in the family forty years now. And I've known him since junior high, dated him since high school." She repeated it. "I knew my husband."

Chapter Seventeen

Thursday Evening

As I walked out at ten o'clock after my research class, I pondered the many ways I'd spoon fed my students that night and still they knocked the utensil out of my hand. We had gone over the material on data analysis in class, and I gave them similar questions on the quiz as the ones we'd practiced. But most of them had bombed the quiz anyway.

Heading to my car, I noticed the long shadows on the cement of the parking lot under the streetlight; even pieces of granite had their own shadows. I shifted my gaze upward, but no stars were visible because of the lights and a nearby power plant.

Sensing a sudden presence behind me, I tried to turn, but firm hands encircled my neck. I jerked and wanted to scream, but the man's grip choked off the useless gurgle in my throat. A Slavic voice whispered in my ear. "Stay away from what is not your business."

I became fixated on his foul breath and working out the layers of odors—deep down was stomach acid; a cigarette smoked half an hour ago; garlic eaten the night before; a yeasty smell overlaid all of that, as if he had drunk beer in the afternoon. To get his nerve up to do this?

I tried to ask, "What business?" Kristin Stockhauser and Congressman Kutchin? Masha and Daria and the Russian Mafia? Lauren and Kyle's mystery scheme? But I couldn't talk with his fingers pressing painfully on my trachea.

"You have a nice long neck, Miss Cara. Stop poking around. You don't want it snapped in two." He released me, and my hand flew to my throat. "Don't look around—go!" He shoved me, and gravel bit my palms as I landed. But I relished that I could still feel. I stumbled forward to the van, fear in my throat, knowing he could grab me again. Cars lined the parking lot, just as they always did here, even at ten at night, but no one was around.

* * *

I drove home, my foot shaking so much on the pedals that I lurched up Edsall to our development. When I woke Seth, not surprisingly, he didn't take well to hearing about my attack. "You've put yourself in danger—"

I fell on the sword right away. "I know, I'll stop. I've gone too far, I realize that."

"You've put our kids in danger." He put his head in his hands.

"He didn't mention them." It was unbearable to think I might have put them in harm's way.

"But he knows what you're doing, all about you." His hair stuck out from his head in all directions from sleeping and running his hands through it.

"Someone could have put him up to it, just told him what to say." I moved closer to him on the bed. "The congressman? He called me 'Miss Knight,' just like this guy did."

"Was it Kutchin's driver?"

I looked off, trying to remember the details. As I talked, my eyes focused on the normalcy of the room—the couch sans coffee table, the light glowing warmly on the nightstand, paintings I liked, which were a high priority for the bedroom. "I never saw the person who attacked me. He came from behind and wore a ski mask. He sounded the same as the driver, but that's because of the Slavic accent."

"What about the voice tone?"

"He spoke in a raspy whisper, probably to disguise his voice."

He grabbed my arms. "You've shown how smart you are. You've proven smarter than the police, the lawyer, everyone, but now you've got to let it go."

"I wasn't doing it to prove I was right. I just wanted to find out what happened. It was obvious Carmen wasn't the only suspect here."

"Well, the fact that you threatened someone enough into attacking you means you've touched on something."

I put my hand to my throat, which felt sore. "There's got to be a connection to the Russians—either Masha and her husband or Kutchin's driver."

"I'm going to talk to the FBI agents at work, find out who you can go to." The FBI was involved in Seth's fraud investigations; he always had an agent sitting in on his interviews with suspects. "Write it up for that journal that only social work academics read," he went on, "so you can get your tenure piece out of it. But that's all. It's over." He put his arms around me. "I don't want anything to happen to you. We all need you, Cara. Noah, Alyssa, me—what would we do without you?"

I swallowed as I hugged him back, still feeling the restriction in my throat from the hand that had grasped it.

* * *

Why did I keep getting the women? I thought as I sat in the FBI building at 11 a.m. Seth had worked his channels quickly. First, there was Sgt. Reynolds, then Dalia Spears, was now Agent Bentley in her neat, beige office. I generally did better with men, although I realized their limitations. Somehow, I'd ended up in a profession of women, and in another era, Agent Bentley would have been a sadistic nun.

"Why didn't you come to us sooner? Before this—" She glanced at her notes— "Kyle Harrigan died."

"I didn't have anything concrete. I knew he and Lauren Abell had a plan to make money together, and I surmised it had gotten his business in trouble, but nothing more than that."

"Why did you get involved in the first place?"

When I launched into the story of going to Lauren's house the morning of her death and finding Carmen already there, she eventually put her hand up in a "Stop" gesture. "Are you a stay-at-home mom? I don't mean to offend, but you seem to have a lot of time on your hands."

My face grew hot. "I'm a professor—on faculty at Virginia University."

"Who were the investigating officers at Metro PD?" she asked.

"Sgts. Reynolds and Nelson."

She shrugged as if she didn't know them, and they weren't worth knowing anyway.

"Nothing I said changed their minds about how they saw the case. They only wanted to believe that Carmen—or her son—were responsible."

"So, you decided to take matters into your own hands," Agent Bentley said. "You think you can do better than trained law enforcement?"

"I was attacked," I reminded her. "By someone of Slavic origins."

"I see the police report." She glanced down.

I had called the police the night before after talking to Seth.

She frowned at the paper in front of her. "No witnesses."

"My attacker chose that moment so there would be no witnesses. I think the same person was responsible for Kyle Harrigan's death."

She cleared her throat. "Arlington police seem pretty satisfied his death was a suicide."

"The last time I talked to him, he had resolved to 'get justice for Lauren.' He was involved in something with her, some financial scheme."

The agent narrowed her eyes at me.

"I know it all sounds incredible," I admitted. "But that's why I'm coming to the FBI to make sense of it. My husband is distraught after I was attacked; we have young children. He's an attorney with the Department of Justice and works with FBI on his cases."

"We can't misuse our resources or grant you special consideration because your husband is with the Department of Justice. We'll treat you the same as everybody else that comes in here."

"Really, how often do people come here with a story like this?"

She laughed for the first time. "We hear all sorts of things, including reports of channeling NASA from Mars."

Somehow, she had put me in the same league as people suffering from delusions. So much for help from the FBI.

* * *

The last thing I'd expected that afternoon at work was the call from Ann Harrigan or that I would now be sitting in her living room on opposite sides of a long couch. The house was decorated in a traditional style that had gotten a bit beat up but was immaculate. I flashed to my own house and the toy and paper clutter. The only errant item here was a hockey stick leaning against one of the living room walls. One of her boys must have left it there.

My momma bear impulse was to put it away—on a high shelf. I flashed to what Noah had done with the glass coffee table. What could he achieve with a hockey stick?

Ann Harrigan had a neat, no-nonsense appearance with short hair, gold stud earrings, and jeans. She sat on the other side of the couch from me. Her freckles stood out sharp against white skin. "Orange spots" were what Alyssa called them.

"These terrible men came," she said, twisting one of her earrings. "I'd never seen them before, but they knew Kyle. They said he owed them—" She swallowed. "Five hundred thousand."

I winced at the amount. "Any idea who they were?" As I spoke, I noticed the recliner, complete with cup holders, where Kyle must have spent his time.

"They were white, thuggish, rough. Maybe Northeast accents." Her face crumpled at the memory.

"Not Russian?"

"Definitely not Russian."

I considered. "Maybe it's just New Jersey or New York, but is the building industry here 'connected?'"

She shook her head, emphatic. "I told them he killed himself. They didn't care. He still owed—dead or alive."

I thought aloud. "Then these guys must not have—" I broke off to change my phrasing. "They wanted his money, and it would be easier to get if he was alive."

"They said if I called the police, there would be worse trouble." She covered her face again at the memory. The light from a solid-looking table lamp caught the tiny diamonds embedded in the gold band of her wedding ring.

I didn't want to make things worse for Ann but had to ask. "Have you checked your bank accounts?"

Lowering her hands, she gave me a look of anguish. "He emptied them out. I was married to my husband twenty years. For the first time, I feel like I didn't know him."

Sick at her disappointment and shock, I tried to work out the figures. I wondered whether the bank account money had financed the sale of the Georgetown condos, stock in B.X. Martin, or payment of loan sharks.

She implored, her eyes searching mine, "You've got to tell me what he was involved in. Why were those horrible men here?"

I broke the gaze. Oh, man, I didn't want to be in this position. "I told you he was in business with Lauren. They were also having an affair."

She blinked as if in pain. "When did it start?" she said woodenly.

I shook my head. "I didn't find out until I met Lauren. The next day she died."

"So, you weren't really friends like you said."

"Let's put it this way. I've gotten to know her better after she died than when she was alive."

"Who would do something like that?" she asked. "Who would steal someone's husband?"

"Lauren was trying to get money together to leave her marriage. And I think your husband was part of her plan. Did Kyle ever talk about what he wanted to do with the business?"

She looked toward the mantle where pictures of Kyle with his children in sports-related activities were mounted. They wrung my heart, and I returned my gaze to her as she spoke.

"He wanted to buy houses, renovate himself, and sell at a profit. He would have been good at it, too, but we didn't have the extra money to put a down payment on another property and pay the mortgage on two places."

So, with Lauren's help, he he'd tried to do this on a grand scale with a condo building in Georgetown.

Ann smiled for the first time. "Eventually, he wanted to make us enough money to tear this one down and build us a new home from scratch."

I broached what I was thinking. "Do you think your husband and Lauren could have bought property together?"

"But he couldn't put anything in his name. I would find out."

"Have you gone through his paperwork?"

"I've started to, but his office is a mess. Organization wasn't his strong point." She smiled fondly, though when he was alive, this must have driven her crazy. "Could it have been in her name?" she asked.

"If it were, her husband would be entitled to half of it, and I suspect she wanted to avoid that. I think you should go to the FBI. I've got a contact there." Such as it was.

"Those men said not to go to the police."

"I'm not even talking about reporting the men. There might have been some illegality in what your husband and Lauren were doing." When she bristled, I blamed it all on Lauren. "I'm sure it was all her idea, and she talked him into it." I mentioned that Kyle hadn't denied wire fraud when I brought it up. "He said, 'I'm going to get justice.' I got the idea he wanted to turn the tables on somebody who might have known of their plan or been involved in carrying it off."

"I'm not sorry she's gone," Ann said, standing. "If I had known all this, I might have killed her myself."

Chapter Eighteen

Saturday Night

When we were seated at the Carlyle restaurant in Shirlington, a high-rent configuration of shops, restaurants, and theatres off the highway in Arlington, Seth took my hands. "I'm glad my mom offered to take care of the kids so we could get out. See, isn't it helpful to have her here?"

Seth was never one to hesitate to spend money (hence, the art habit), but even he balked at the double paying—for a babysitter and dinner—when we went out on our infrequent "date nights."

"Do you think Noah calmed down?" I asked Seth, flashing to Noah's sobbing face in the front window, his screams penetrating through the panes, as we pulled out of the driveway.

"Mama, mama," we heard, like the sound of a doll's incessant voice box. A well-dressed couple, obviously out on *their* date night, were seated at the table next to us with a girl in overalls about Noah's age perched in a highchair. On their table, their appetizer plates and breadbasket told me they hadn't yet moved to the main course.

The Carlyle was fairly upscale—we had even seen a U.S. senator there once before his downfall, smiling at everyone and enjoying the attention—and we would never have dared bring our children here.

"We can't escape," I murmured to Seth.

"Mama, mama," the girl said, eyes focused on her mother.

"Why won't she pick her up?" I muttered.

"She doesn't want to get her clothes dirty," Seth said, leaning across the table and gripping my hands like, "We're going to have a good time together, damn it."

I smiled, but nothing I could say didn't involve complaining about the child, talking about our own children, or broaching an even more difficult topic.

The waiter approached, and we ordered our entrees and drinks, worried about taxing Barbara too heavily. She had gone from "Come to Grammy!" in response to Noah's crying to "Shut up, you big baby!" as we walked out the door.

"Mama, mama," the child next to us said. The husband checked his text messages, e-mail, or whatever people were constantly doing on their devices these days.

We had broken our hand clasp to order, but Seth reached for me again when I said, "There's something I wanted to tell you." As I took a deep breath, Seth eyed me warily. "Kyle's wife called. Some strange, thug-types came to her house, saying her husband owed them money."

"And you told her to call the police?"

"The police have just been *so* helpful already." I made my sarcasm clear. "She asked me to come over to talk about it, to tell her what I knew."

He released my hands. "You said you wouldn't do this anymore."

I bit my lip and nodded.

"How would you like it if I said I wouldn't stick to my art budget, just spent what I wanted?"

Even the idea filled me with a surge of panic; he'd take money from our children's college funds and our future travel plans, and we'd be doomed to live near Landmark Mall for the rest of our days just so he could buy *papier mache* phone booths. "I wouldn't like it," I said dutifully.

"What about the kids? Don't you care that they might get hurt?"

"I didn't take them with me."

"These people know where you live. They know you have children."

"These were different men. They weren't Russian." I reached toward him, but he leaned back. "Don't you see," I went on, "this means that Kyle was in debt because of something that involved Lauren."

In response to another bout of "Mama, mama," Seth turned and gave the parents the dirty look he probably wanted to give to me. When he again faced me, he said, "So what now?"

I sipped my water. "Kyle's wife—Ann—is going to look into his things, check his cell phone records and paperwork, see what she can find."

"You like the excitement of all this, don't you?"

More "Mama, mama" resounded as I decided how to answer. If I agreed to one statement, then Seth might lead me down a line of lawyerly questioning where I would have to agree to everything else.

The waiter returned again, and I raised my eyes to him, grateful for the interruption. "I'm sorry, folks, I hate to tell you this, but we're out of ribs." We had both ordered them.

"We're leaving," Seth said.

I shot a surprised glance at him. I was more likely to leave restaurants than he was, but he was already pushing back from the table.

"Aw, man," the waiter said.

I flung him a "Sorry" before scuttling after Seth.

On the street, I shrugged into my coat and caught up to Seth, who was stomping along. I thrust my hands deep into my pockets and said, "I'm sorry, I'm not doing this to make you mad. I've just come so far. It's like writing a book. I couldn't just abandon one when I'd written two-thirds of it."

"You don't know whether it's two-thirds of the way done or not. There may be no ending to this story. Or a bad one, like you or the kids getting hurt."

I stared at his profile, but he wouldn't turn his head. "The police aren't doing a thing. And thank you for arranging the FBI agent, but all I got was a mindless bureaucrat with an edge."

As he continued to march along, I yanked on his arm, making him stop. "Where are we even going?" The cold pinched my ears.

He stared down the length of the road. The outside seating had disappeared with the advent of winter, but the holiday white lights around the trees softened the bare surroundings.

I threw up my hands. "Let's just go home." In therapy terms, this was called a paradox intervention, which would sometimes force people to take the other side of the argument.

"But what do we have there?" he asked.

The children were having their usual scraps for dinner, and Barbara had already made mayonnaise-drenched tuna salad for herself. "An omelet?" I asked.

He made a face. In the years I'd known Seth, he'd never once responded in the affirmative to this suggestion.

"Well, there's a whole line of restaurants here." I gestured at the street. "Except Guapo's. There's no point going without the children."

We dismissed a few lackluster chain restaurants, deciding on a Thai restaurant we had yet to try. As we crossed the cobblestones that lined the two streets of The Village at Shirlington, he said, "You're bored, aren't you? That's why you're doing this."

The night sky was a strange, nuclear brown from the city lights. "Not bored, exactly. Just a lot of this child-rearing stuff is very tedious—putting on Noah's socks, he tears them off, I put them back on again, he cries, tears them off, and so on all day. And I don't see anyone except Roberto, Adam, and my students. It's not exactly the collegial stimulation I was hoping for."

When we reached the opposite sidewalk, he stopped. "Are you bored with *me*?"

His mother and everyone on his family's side thought Noah resembled Seth. Only my mother defended the other side. But right then, Seth did remind me of Noah. I blew out and saw it was cold enough to see my breath. "Not with you. You go to work every day, see lots of people, go to lunch. I hardly see anyone."

The smell of Thai food fanned onto the street. Seth indicated the door to the restaurant. "Shall we?" Despite my average height, I towered over the hostess as she led us to a table in the dimly lit interior. Behind me, Seth must have been double her size. The restaurant wasn't all that busy, which wasn't a great sign, I thought as we sat and received our menus.

I continued the conversation. "All I wanted from Lauren's party was to meet adults and have an activity on the weekend. I didn't know it was going to lead to this." I leaned my head in and lowered my voice. "Remember when you said you had to collect art because that was your passion? If you didn't have that, your soul would wither away?" When he had put it in such dramatic terms, who was I to block his buying "sculptures" that looked like Burger King garbage cans from the nineteen-seventies? I explained to Seth that it was the same for me in getting justice for Carmen. The only way I could do that was to find out who had murdered Lauren.

We looked up when the hostess returned in her new role as our waitress. "You ready?" she asked with a smile.

I hadn't opened the menu, but I couldn't go wrong with Tom Yum soup and green curry chicken. Seth ordered his usual Pad Thai. When

I mentioned his always having the same thing, he pointed out that the same quality made him never tire of me. *Touché.*

Seth moved his chopsticks to the side and reached for my hands across the tabletop. "I know it's been stressful since Noah was born."

"He's impossible," I agreed. "The crying in the car, the constant holding. When's it going to let up?"

"One thing I like about all this is that you've been taking more time away."

He had touched on the one nerve. "I feel guilty for that," I admitted, "like I should only get babysitting when I'm working, nothing else."

He squeezed my hands for emphasis. "You need the time away. Noah has to separate, learn to comfort himself without constantly being at the breast. He's almost fourteen months now. It's time."

I nodded, agreeing. "But how? He cries so much already. If I take that away, he'll cry even more, and I don't know how I can stand it." My voice broke unexpectedly.

Seth pursed his mouth in sympathy. "He cries so much because he doesn't know how to comfort himself. He uses you as a pacifier."

With that, we heard a clatter and a wail behind us. While we'd focused on ordering and our conversation, a family with young children had been seated behind us, and the youngest girl had tried to climb her highchair and fallen off. We felt more annoyance than sympathy when we realized that she wasn't hurt, and her cries continued to clamor.

Seth and I looked at each other and had to laugh.

"Why is it the harder you try to escape, the faster it catches up with you?" I asked.

"Isn't that always the way?"

I turned his wrist to see the time on his watch. "And it's seven o'clock now. What are small children still doing out? Shouldn't they be home putting the finishing touches on the bedtime routine?"

Seth's voice grew serious. "You can never take the children with you on any of this."

"I haven't," I said, switching back to our earlier conversation and putting my hand on my heart. The child's cries were abating, but it seemed to be taking a long time.

Seth leaned back in his chair. "You met that Russian woman on the playground."

"She's from Belarus, not Russia." Of course, I'd been using Soviet names and territories interchangeably, as well.

He went on. "And you took them over to that creep Griffin's house."

"Okay, yeah," I admitted. "But, of course, I would never do anything like that again."

Chapter Nineteen

Sunday Afternoon

The funeral was on a Sunday, just like the afternoon of Lauren's party, and the weather was tailor-made with dark, lowering clouds that refused to rain. I didn't dare tell anyone, even Seth, that I was grateful we had something to do on the weekend, and that we could justify getting a babysitter. No one should be that glad to go to a funeral.

The funeral home was as sterile as the inside of a McMansion, but the director and his associate struck the right demeanor—somber and sympathetic, yet efficient, as we were herded into the viewing room.

I stayed at the back. Carmen had saved me from having to find Lauren the day she'd died, and I didn't want to see her body now.

In the hallway, as we waited to go into the room for the service, Rob nodded curtly when I murmured, "I'm so sorry," which could encapsulate a lot of things. He obviously would have preferred my absence, but unfortunately for him, I was part of the package deal. Rob seemed pleased to see Seth at least, and they clapped each other's backs. Everybody loved Seth, just like *Everybody Loves Raymond*. My half-joke to Seth was that I was the only one who really knew him. But he did have excellent social skills, more than any man I'd known and certainly better than me.

Standing behind Rob in the receiving line was Arlene. Her dark lipstick was intact, but black mascara dotted her cheeks. I hugged Arlene awkwardly, not only because I shied away from physical contact with people I didn't particularly like, but also because I was unsure whether Rob had told Arlene about our last conversation. He had denied saying anything to her about his wife's affair, but had he since revealed it to her? Or had Arlene overheard us talking?

Arlene was friendly, however, and insisted on giving me a run-down of the attendees. First, she pointed out Lauren's mother, who was surrounded by an entourage of older men and women who appeared to be her relatives. Seeing Lauren's mother weeping made my own throat close.

Oblivious to my emotional state, Arlene pointed again. "And that's Lauren's brother." A man about ten years younger than Lauren stood on the periphery against the cream-colored wall. I wondered, given the age difference, if they shared the same parents. A young, blonde woman stood beside Lauren's brother. Her black dress was more ap-propriate for a cocktail party than a funeral, and she wore pointy, four-inch heels. They were going to do a number on the wet soil at the burial.

I stepped out of the way as Barbara barreled over, and she and Ar-lene collided in a hug. Unlike all the other women present wearing dresses, Barbara wore slightly more formal versions of the usual black pants and top. The only time I'd ever seen her wearing a dress—and that was black, too—was at Seth's and my wedding.

"That's Lauren's father, Joel Schwartz." Barbara took up Arlene's run-down of the family as Arlene turned her attention to an older couple that had made their way past Rob on the receiving line.

Joel Schwartz was thin and wiry and walked with a slight limp, as if he'd been a runner until his knees gave out. His support system wasn't as extensive as his ex-wife's—just one older man, perhaps an uncle. I had the feeling Lauren's father had behaved badly at some point in the relationship, and that was why he was ostracized by the relatives on the mother's side.

"I met him at the wedding," Barbara continued. "He was with a Puerto Rican woman, and they danced the Salsa all night long." Barbara's head swayed, scanning the crowd. "I don't see her here."

At that point, the funeral director and his associates moved us into a sterile room for the service, and voices quietened to a whisper. I clutched the program, which had a photocopied picture of Lauren on its front. In the photograph, with a smile and without the heavy groove of a frown, Lauren looked much younger.

"When was this taken?" I asked Barbara.

She popped a hard candy in her mouth. "Before she met Rob."

Ah, that explained it.

She shoved the bag of candy at me. "Do you want one?"

"Thank you, no."

I must have looked a little pained because she made an excuse for eating candy at a service. "I have this tickle in my throat, and I don't want to cough, disturb everyone."

* * *

At the Shiva after the service, Barbara was first at the dining room table where the usual fare, bagels, rye bread, brisket, roast beef, lox, Nova, and cream cheese, was laid out. She tore off a slice of roast beef from a larger piece with her fingers and then left it on the serving plate, once again fondling food that others would eat.

As I stood in line, Griffin approached, already eating potato salad. "I thought you weren't going to tell anyone about me and Lauren," he said.

My cheeks warmed. I did like to keep my promises of confidentiality. That was part of my profession. But I had to tell Sgt. Reynolds my suspicions. Griffin had motive. Lauren had threatened to expose him.

He could lose his job and go to prison. Had they argued about that at her house, and he grabbed a nearby figurine in rage?

Griffin's red beard had grown wilder since I'd last seen him at his house. Now hair curled almost up to his eyes, and mayonnaise was captured in the snarl. "A lady police officer came to my boss and asked him to confirm if I was working the day Lauren died."

I smiled inwardly, picturing Sgt. Reynolds striding into the lab to corroborate his alibi. "She was from D.C. and pregnant, right?"

He nodded, his eyes shifting from left and right to make sure no one listened as he chewed.

"Then it wasn't federal," I said. "Your boss didn't find out about the insider information. That's your biggest worry. And I doubt if Sgt. Reynolds will turn you in. She's pretty focused on her cases." And she also hadn't appreciated the FBI and, by extension, other federal agencies.

I stepped forward as the line moved and picked up a paper plate and some plastic cutlery. "Excuse me."

Griffin still blocked my way. He couldn't even answer, his mouth too full of bagel dough.

"Obviously, your alibi held up." I didn't know that for a fact, of course.

He swallowed with difficulty as if he hadn't chewed his food enough. "I knew it would. I didn't kill her." He shoveled in more potato salad. "Although I'm not sad she's gone. It feels hypocritical even being here, but I thought the food would be good."

"There's your wife." I waved at Jodie who was standing at the other end of the table, spooning chips into a chunky-looking dip. I thought that would make him move out of the way. It didn't. Maybe making more accusations? "You didn't mention that you helped Rob get the funding from B.X. Martin for the Zemeron study." This was a guess on my part, which Griffin confirmed.

"That was all part of the deal Lauren arranged. Rob's just lucky he had her on his side."

Ironic, considering her affair.

"Hey, what happened to you at the zoo?"

I turned to see who'd spoken and saw that Meredith had gotten in line behind me. I wondered how long it had taken her to discover that day that I was no longer part of the group. So fed up, I hadn't bothered texting, but neither had she. I was honest. "Noah wouldn't go in the stroller, so I had to carry him, and I couldn't push the double stroller up the hill with him in my arms. And things kept falling out of the stroller and dropping. I couldn't keep up with you all."

She smiled as if she had granted me a favor. "Well, that's okay, my friends and I are meeting up again next Friday at the Mount Vernon School playground if you want to come."

"Where's that?"

"It's so funny you don't know where Del Ray is. I walk there from my house, so I wouldn't be able to give you good directions. All the people who were at the zoo—they'll be there."

I forced a smile, wondering at the extent of her cluelessness. Did she honestly think I had forged a connection with anyone that day? Or maybe that was beside the point. Did she just want to add to her collection of friends?

Of course, I would go. I was that desperate for social events and a way to amuse the children.

Meredith's eyes took in the living room. "It's so beautiful. Too bad Lauren didn't get to enjoy it."

"Did you know the builder died, too?"

"What? Like a heart attack?"

"Supposedly suicide."

She gasped and put her hand over her mouth.

"Did you ever meet him?" I asked.

She shook her head.

"What did Lauren say about him?" I wanted to see if Lauren had confided in Meredith.

"Not much—I think he did great work. It was just taking a long time."

"Isn't that always the case with renovation?"

"That's why I don't even want to start the kitchen renovation, even though I know it needs to be done. I don't want to live with everything torn apart for so long. Especially with two kids." She beamed at someone behind me and waved. "Oh, there's Rebecca!" She was done with our conversation.

I glanced around when she left and smiled inwardly, seeing that Barbara had pigeon-holed Tad against a wall, her broad back blocking him from view. Seth had made all kinds of muttered threats toward Tad on our way over here, the lunch still rankling with him: "That sleaze bag, Uncle Tad," and so forth. But I knew Seth wouldn't confront him.

I sidled over to Tad's wife, Liz, who was leaning over the dining room table, picking out food to put on her plate. Black polyester strained over her curves. Although she probably considered herself too heavy by the day's standards, she had a shapely figure.

I smiled a greeting. "Hi, Liz, I'm Cara Knight. I didn't get a chance to talk to you last time we were here. I had my children with me."

"I remember those days."

I picked up half a salt bagel and put it on my plate. I wasn't about to say, "Oh, I met your husband for lunch the other day." Instead, I started with, "How did you meet Lauren?"

"My husband is Chair of the Board at the D.C. Historical Preservation Office. He heard Lauren's application for the renovations she did here."

This didn't jive with what her husband had told me over lunch, that he and Lauren were neighbors, and that's how they'd met. "And you live right around here?"

"We're in Georgetown, but not close to here. More north—on Hutley Street."

Another contradiction. Her husband had said they were neighbors, implying that they had just happened upon each other.

I added a couple of brownies to my plate. I tried to restrain myself from eating goodies around the children; I didn't want to set a bad example. Having children had actually cured me of some of my junk food tendencies. When I saw them pawing through food, felt their sticky fingers staining my clothes, and had to wash the ice cream off their faces, it took the edge off any craving.

After finishing my food, I headed toward the bathroom to wash out the brownie fudge that was now gouged into my fingernails. Zach's girlfriend, dabbing a tissue to her eyes, emerged from it.

"Are you all right?" I asked.

She nodded, but her chin wobbled. Her eyes were red-rimmed, and the heavy make-up I'd seen around them was rubbed off. She looked better without it on, despite the tears.

I followed her into the family room. As beautifully decorated as it was, I no longer liked defined rooms with doors on them. In our downstairs, one area flowed into the next, and now anything else seemed constraining.

"You knew Lauren well?" I asked, thinking her grief stemmed from the obvious loss.

"Not really." She sank into a chair and perched at the end of it. "It's my boyfriend—Zach." Her face melted into tears. "He's such a shit."

"Where is he?"

"He went to find a liquor store."

I'd thought I'd imagined it at first, the sweet, fermented odor of alcohol when she'd exited the bathroom.

"It's so weird, no alcohol at a wake. I'm Irish, and it's all about the drinking. No offense if you're Jewish or anything."

"I'm not." I went over to an end table and switched on a lamp. I could imagine her, before she had sought refuge in the bathroom, alone in the dark. Never a good idea.

"Do you want to talk about it?" I asked, sitting across from her on the couch. The fabric was soft under my hands, and I smoothed out the velvet with my palms.

"He didn't even want me to come with him today," she warbled. "I'm supposed to be his girlfriend, and he's shutting me out."

"You're sad because he didn't want to include you in the funeral, which is a really important event, and all his family is here."

If I hadn't experienced it many, many times before, I would have been amazed—a simple statement, reflecting her feelings, was powerful. The floodgates released, and tears poured down her cheeks.

After a while, I commented, "People sometimes do strange things when they're grieving."

She rubbed at a raw-looking nose. "He didn't even get along with her."

"But she was still his sister and murdered, about the worst thing that can happen. He may even feel guilty."

"Why? He didn't do anything."

"Because they didn't get along, and now she was murdered," I said. "It might even feel like he made it happen."

"But he didn't."

"I know, it's not logical. It's just the way people think when they're upset."

She sat back in the chair, long legs stretched out. "Lauren was a bitch. I know you're not supposed to say that about someone who died, but she was. She had a Ph.D. and thought she was so important. She didn't think I was good enough for her brother, and she always called him 'lazy' and 'stupid.' She was a lot older than him, so he believed her.

"They have the same parents?" I asked.

"He was born right about the time the marriage ended. His dad left when Zach was a baby."

"How do you get along with his mother?" I leaned on the armrest, trying to look casual as I questioned her.

"I'm not Jewish." She rolled her eyes.

"I heard Lauren didn't get along with her mother either," I said.

"If you ask me, they're too much alike. But his mom thinks Zach can do no wrong. He always was her favorite." Smitten, she smiled.

"And what does your Zach do?"

"He dropped out of Rutgers, so he works for his dad now, manages one of his buildings where I live in Bradley."

"What's that like?" I played with the tassel of a pillow, raking my fingers through it.

"It's where I grew up. Not much going on."

"So, what do you do there?"

"I'm cocktailing." Her eyes reddened. "Even before all this, we weren't doing well. I'd just found out he'd cheated on me. It kind of runs in the family—cheating. That's why his dad's marriage went bust with his mom."

Lauren had adopted the pattern, too, apparently.

"And Zach couldn't sleep with just any slut." Her jaw clenched. "It had to be the daughter of one of his dad's business associates." After the flash of anger, her eyes filled with tears again. "But I don't want him to get in trouble." She hid her face behind the bedraggled tissue.

"Does his dad know about it?" I wondered aloud.

She sniffed. "I don't know what it's like around here, but up where we live—any real estate, you have to be like—" She broke off, wanting to talk about it, but not wanting to say.

"Connected?" I guessed.

"I guess we can't smoke in here, huh?" As I shook my head sadly, she kept talking. "You don't sleep with these guys' daughters, even if she does throw herself at you when you're drunk." She shook out her hands in an agitated gesture. "Look, I'm running my mouth. Zach will be so mad, but he shouldn't have left me here. He was so mean. He said he didn't want me to come with him, just wanted to be alone. Gee, thanks. I had to work last night, so I only got like three hours of sleep, and I'm hungover, but I came because I care about him. Then he leaves me in a house full of strangers. I mean, you seem nice, but no one else has given me the time of day."

"What will I be mad about?" Zach stood in the doorway, holding a brown-paper bag-wrapped bottle in his hand. He eyed his girlfriend's tear-stained face and flashed me a nasty look.

"Well, I'll leave you guys alone," I said and headed out the door.

"What did you tell her?" I heard behind me.

"Where have you been?" Seth said when I entered the dining room.

"Talking to Lauren's brother's girlfriend," I said, linking my arm with his. "I got some interesting information."

I could see Seth was trying to be all right with this. He said, "Misha's here. He wants to talk to you."

I was glad Misha realized that I had a husband who would miss me. After all, I was about to accuse him of being a hitman.

When I saw him, tall over the crowd, Misha gestured to the door. As I retrieved my coat from the closet, Seth programmed 9-1-1 on my phone. If there was a problem, I could hit send.

I tripped over the uneven sidewalk as Misha and I set off from the house. Apparently, I no longer knew how to walk alone without children. I remembered the day Lauren had died. I was weighed down with Noah and Alyssa, holding one in each arm and running back to the minivan, afraid that Lauren's perpetrator was nearby. Now the street seemed so civilized with its brick sidewalk and beautifully restored mansions. Well-dressed older couples wearing designer glasses strolled along with their Afghans and Malteses.

Neither Misha nor I spoke at first, and that was awkward, so I made small talk about how much Daria and Alyssa liked each other. It turned out that there was a sixteen-year-old boy in their home as well, Masha's son from her first marriage. Misha could have been the boy's grandfather. In the cold light, I could see he was at least twenty years older than Masha with balding grey hair.

"My son." He spoke in a measured, accented tone. "Anything Belarusian is bad. Anything from here is good. Belarus is old-fashioned, outdated. He won't speak Russian anymore, even though that's the only language we use."

"He's sixteen." I tried to keep my tone light. "He just wants to be like everyone else."

As if he didn't hear me, Misha said, "He says he'll run away, live with one of his friends. I say, 'Who would take you?'"

Not the most validating of responses, I thought, then pondered the stepson. If Sgt. Reynolds thought Carmen's son may have played a role in Lauren's death, why not this boy? He didn't want to return to Russia. Maybe he'd overheard his parents talking and discovered that Lauren held the keys to their stay. He found out where she lived and put pressure on her to help his family get visas. When she wouldn't acquiesce, he lost it and killed her. This was one of the best theories I'd come up with! "Do you want me to talk to him?" I asked.

"You?" He turned to me. "You're out to persecute us. What would you say to him?"

"I'm not out to persecute you. I'm trying to find out who killed Lauren."

"The police already know who did it. They've arrested the housekeeper. Why would you try to help her?" he asked.

"I'm a social worker, and I teach social work. I don't know if they have them where you're from, but we help people." Other countries varied considerably in the role of social workers. "That's why I could talk to your son. I used to be a therapist for a juvenile justice program."

"He is not a juvenile offender. He is a good boy. He gets good grades, plays basketball."

"I'm not saying he is. I'm saying that I know how to talk to teenage boys." I fingered the cell phone. The air was heavy with rain; yet it would not fall. My breath came fast at what I said next. "I overheard a conversation you had with Lauren when I was feeding my son in the spare bedroom at her party. It sounded like she would sponsor you for your visas, but you had to arrange something first."

As he remained silent, I involuntarily sniffed, trying to detect a trace of the malodorous compound of my attacker's breath. Coming up with nothing except the sharp tang of the chill air and fallen leaves, I glanced up at Misha. He seemed taller than the man who had crept up behind me, but my sense of vulnerability might have distorted my perception. He stared straight ahead as he talked, the white hairs of his beard stubble catching the light. "She said she knew a congressman who could ensure us a visa, but we had to pay her."

"Did you?" I asked as we strolled down the street.

"We were still in—what do you call it—the negotiation stage? That's what you must have overheard."

"She talked about your relatives being able to do something."

He shook his head. "That is not what we told her. She wanted to believe it. That is not— what do you say—that is not our problem what she believed."

"Still, if Lauren could get rid of her husband, it would have solved a lot of her problems." She could get out of the prenup, have the life insurance money, be with Lover Boy, and not be tied to the hit at all.

"But we weren't that desperate for her sponsorship." He turned up the collar of his coat to shield against a blast of wind. "What she was asking was ridiculous, and we have options, as you say, other than going back."

"I know the congressman Lauren was talking about that could help you. He has a Russian driver. What a coincidence, huh? And I was attacked by a Russian outside my place of work." I watched to catch his reaction.

He looked down at me. "Are you saying we did that? Then why would I be talking with you today? And if we did know this Russian driver, then wouldn't we have used him to get to the congressman to get our visas?"

Engrossed in the conversation and trying to figure out all the Russian connections, I didn't hear anything until footsteps registered right behind us. I gasped and turned to see that Misha had stopped and was facing an older man with spikey white hair and dressed in formal clothes.

"I've come to bring you back," the man said, speaking with a Russian accent.

Instead of answering, Misha swung his leg up and gave a roundhouse kick to the man's chest.

The man was propelled backward. He staggered but caught his balance and lunged forward. As the two men scuffled in earnest, I ran between two parked cars on the other side of the road. Fumbling in my pocket, I pressed the button on 9-1-1. Just like the morning after Lauren's death, suddenly no one walked the street, no dog walkers, no couples. I wanted a witness to this scene; the air was moist with unshed rain, and I felt like I was in a dream.

Peering out of my hiding spot, I winced as Misha kicked the other man's jaw with a crunch. The man fell backward on the sidewalk. He bellowed, revealing crooked, brown teeth as Misha sprinted down the street. I felt bad, but like gang violence, this seemed to have little to do with me, and my safest ploy was to get away.

When I looked back, I was almost at the door. The man had somehow gotten to his feet. After a few tentative steps, he ran off in the direction Misha had gone and disappeared before the police could get there.

Chapter Twenty

Monday Morning

Zach's girlfriend had said that Lauren's father was connected. Did Lauren die for something her father was involved in? Had she used her dad's connections?

Arlene was surprised when I asked for Joel Schwartz's cell phone number. "I wanted to give him my condolences," I said. She frowned but gave me the number.

When I called, I implied I was Lauren's friend and wanted to meet to talk about her. He responded to my invitation by saying, "Why don't you come here? Heck, I'm not doing anything, and a young woman hasn't come to my hotel room in a while."

"I'm not that young," I warned him. He couldn't be so crass as to come on to one of Lauren's "friends" after he'd just buried her, surely.

The motel off the highway in Springfield reminded me of places my family used to stay for summer vacations. I'd come up in the world since then.

Joel lay on the bed where he gave me the once over as I walked in. I had to teach my Monday afternoon Mental Disorders class after this, so I was wearing a skirt and boots. Yes, grief could take strange forms, but this was too much.

After I gave my condolences, he said, "Geez, you don't have to call me Mr. Schwartz. Joel's fine," and gestured that I could sit on the bed. I veered toward the one chair instead and placed my bag on my lap where it gaped unzipped. Both Barbara and I had open lines on our cell phones. I had made her side "mute" and had turned up the volume high so she could hear the conversation.

The T.V. was on loud to the usual Middle East disaster. When I used to make home visits, clients invariably had their T.V.'s playing. I would say, "Do you mind if I turn that off? I get distracted easily." How could anyone argue with you when you said it was about your distraction? I used the ploy now, and Joel Schwartz picked up the remote and obediently turned off the remote.

"You weren't at the funeral for very long," I said. "I was hoping to talk to you there."

He shook his head. "My ex-wife and I can't be in the same room."

"Not easy being around all the old family."

"Yeah." He clasped his hands behind his head.

"You decided to stay overnight?" I asked.

"My legs hurt when I'm cramped in the car like that." His eyes suddenly gleamed. "I need a massage."

I was working up to what to say, but now it was easy after that suggestive comment. "I don't know if you're aware, but I was at Lauren's house right after—" I paused. "I talked to the police, but I'm still wondering if something's off. Maybe you could answer some questions, help me get some closure?"

He hitched a shoulder which gave me permission to get into what I'd discovered.

Last Sunday evening, after putting the children to bed, I'd looked up the Historical Preservation Office. The website conveniently archived the board meeting proceedings. When I skimmed back through them to find Lauren's hearing, guess whose name I found first? Joel Schwartz. He'd appeared before Tad Gower's board on a property one block away from Lauren's.

"Lauren told me you now own property here. I suppose you wanted to check on that."

Part of the appeal of New Yorkers was their level of animation, and Joel couldn't hide his surprise. "How did you know Lauren again?"

"Through Arlene and my mother-in-law being friends." When I sensed his distaste, probably for Rob's mother, I added, "Lauren and I had talked about me subletting at her therapy practice."

That seemed to work better. "And your name is Cara?" He scratched his face. "Pretty good money in the shrink business, huh, Cara—when you can get it."

"But that was the problem, Lauren couldn't make enough that way, so she was exploring other avenues. One of them was the property with you and Kyle Harrigan."

He crossed his arms over his chest. "It was a great time to buy. Prices'll never be that low in Georgetown again. That house had been on the market for a year, and they accepted our low-ball offer."

"The house is in your name, but Lauren and Kyle were the ones paying for it."

This was a guess on my part, and, not surprisingly, he denied it. "Sorry, Cara, I don't buy a two-million-dollar property for somebody else." He ran his hand through his white, slicked-back hair. "I'm in it for the cash. Have you seen the place?" He put his arms back behind his head. "A big Victorian on a corner lot. Needs work, no doubt about that, but we can carve it up into little condos and charge up the ass for them."

"You said, 'we?'" I trailed off so he could answer.

"I'll work with a general contractor, sure. How else am I going to renovate it?"

"Aren't the rest of the houses in the area single-family houses? How can you just chop one into condos?"

"You just have to figure out how to preserve 'architectural details'—" He did the finger quotes in the air. "The cornices, the windows, door frames, the color of the paint, crap like that." He beamed and put up his hands to make a headline: "Right in the heart of Georgetown."

My heart beat fast as I anticipated what I would say next. "So, your daughter and the general contractor, Kyle Harrigan, came up with the money, but it's in your name. When Lauren—" I cleared my throat and paused. "Kyle realized he couldn't handle the payments. He mentioned fearing someone who was 'connected.'" Time for me to do my own air quotes. "He was afraid you would send people after him to collect."

At least that got Joel Schwartz off the bed. It had been downright creepy with him lying there. He tried to spring up but then winced and pushed off heavily with his arms.

He stood before me. I considered standing, but he'd crowded into the space and was afraid of dislodging the recording. "You don't think I've got enough to float this thing until it pays off?" he said.

I wondered whether I could overpower Joel if it came to it. He wasn't much taller than me and thin. Then again, male strength, even on an older man, might win out, despite my muscle-building from Noah and thrice-weekly Spin classes.

The only sound was the swish of traffic on the highway outside. I said, "Then why was it a secret about you owning the property?"

"It wasn't a secret. We just didn't want my ex-wife—her mother— to find out. It's bad enough she's always trying to get my son to tell her things, put him in the middle."

"You know your daughter was having an affair with Kyle?"

He turned and paced toward the closet. "I didn't ask, and she didn't tell. That was her business. But I knew she wasn't happy with Rob. He was a penny pincher, controlled the purse strings. That's not what she wanted. She wanted money of her own, and she was smart enough to get it."

"Who else was involved in getting this property rezoned? Don't you see, that may have been who murdered Lauren and Kyle?"

He came toward me. "I would never have put my baby in harm's way. Never." He sliced the air with an emphatic hand.

My mouth dry, I forced out the words. "You must have been surprised when you got those guys to go to Kyle Harrigan's house, and you found out he was dead?"

"You come to my hotel room to say crap like that to me?" He pointed an indignant thumb at his chest.

"Look at it this way—it lets you off the hook."

The lines of his face screwed up into a question.

"For Kyle's murder," I said.

"He committed suicide."

"How did you find out about his suicide?"

He stuttered for a moment, then said, "I called his office. They told me."

Ah hah, Kyle didn't have an office. He handled all his own calls. "Who talked to you?"

He shrugged. "Some woman."

"His wife?"

"I told you. I don't know. On and on, you women with your questions."

"Come on, Kyle's wife wouldn't have identified herself to tell a potential client caller that her husband had died?" And with the stigma of suicide, she wouldn't just volunteer this specific form of information to anyone who called. "He died suddenly," was the common parlance.

"Is Tad Gowers part of this?" I asked.

"Who the hell is he?"

"Seems like you would remember his name—he's the chair of the board you appeared before—the Historic Preservation Office."

He bowed his head. "Yeah, yeah, that guy."

"Did he take a bribe to pass through the changes you want to make to the building?"

"I'm not saying it happened, but where I'm from, it's just the cost of doing business. We build fifteen percent into the budget for all the palms you have to grease to get shit—I mean, stuff done." He smiled at his dirty mouth.

"But don't you see—it must have been him or someone else involved with the plans for the building that killed your daughter."

"You're a head shrinker, and you're this crazy?" He sat down on the long edge of the bed close to where my legs jutted out from the chair.

I pulled them back to reclaim my personal space.

"Anyway, it was that cleaning lady that killed her. Biggest mistake Lauren made was hiring her."

"Did you ever meet Carmen?" I asked. "Do you really think she was the type to kill someone?"

He splayed his fingers. "Who knows? Those people come from South America—they're desperate. She might have taken some money. Lauren found out."

"Rob didn't report anything missing other than the silver."

"Rob's got his head up his ass half the time. He was the one who made the money, but Lauren was way smarter. Why are you even involved in this? What do you want?"

"I was there that day," I said. "I want to know what really happened to Lauren. Don't you?" I paused, studying his face. "Or will you just go ahead with your plan, ignoring the fact that it might have gotten your daughter killed, and now her boyfriend's dead, too."

He stood again and loomed over me. "I've been in business a long time. No one's going to threaten me, including you."

I heard the muted thunk of a bottle dropping down from a vending machine outside. My stomach gurgled with nerves; here I was alone, accusing a man with possible Mafia ties. The evil smell of stale nicotine trapped in the fabric of the brown carpet and beige walls pervaded my nostrils as I went on. "Did your thugs kill her because you weren't paying up? Was it a warning?"

"You want a piece of the action, too, is that it?"

"Someone can hear us." I tried the code phrase that Barbara and I had agreed on.

He smiled. His teeth were stained from a lifetime of bad habits. "No one can hear us."

I tried to hold my ground, but eventually, shrank as he came closer. "Someone can hear us," I said more loudly, trying to stand.

Joel shoved me into the chair. "What are you doing?" I shrieked. My top, already stretched from Noah's unceasing grappling, was easy for Joel to pull away from my body, exposing the bra underneath. "Help, Barbara!" I shouted.

Joel's breathing was coming hard as I tried to push his hands away. So much for my relative youth winning over his male strength.

"I'm just—" he said, struggling and gasping. "Seeing if you're wired."

I had a great scream, which Seth had forbidden me to use for scary bugs because the high pitch rattled him. But I used it now, and the sheer force blasted Joel back.

At the same time, a knock on the door sounded, and my mother-in-law's voice yelled, "What the hell is going on here? Open this door right now. I've called the police."

"It's my mother-in-law," I said. "Let her in."

When Joel went to the door, she barreled through, clutching her black, fur-lined coat to her and holding a bag of potato chips. "I heard everything," she announced.

"I ain't doing shit. He hunched his shoulders in a disingenuous shrug. "I'm just a man trying to make an honest buck."

"Then why were you groping me?" I kept my arms folded across my chest. My legs were still too shaky to stand.

"I was just trying to see if you're wired. Why else would some young woman come to my hotel room? I could flatter myself, but hey, I know it's unlikely unless I was paying for it."

"If you were checking to see if I was wired, that makes you suspicious right there," I said. "You know what you're doing is illegal, and you're afraid the FBI is after you."

"You should be ashamed of yourself." Barbara popped a couple of chips in her mouth and chewed. She had obviously gotten nervous waiting and had resorted to stress eating. "She's the same age as your daughter. It's men like you why women my age don't stand a chance. Because you go after women half your age." She plopped onto the bed, and shoved the bag at me. "Do you want some?"

I put up a stop sign hand, listening in the distance—no sirens. "Tell you what, we can disappear before the police arrive," I said. "But here's the deal—Ann Harrigan gets no more visits."

"I'm not admitting nothing."

"You don't have to, just make sure it happens." I could stand now without toppling over. "Let's go, Barbara."

I hurried out the door and down the stairs, careful not to touch the peeling paint of the railing for fear of driving lead into my hands. I was at the car when I looked up and saw that Barbara was doing the child-like one foot down and then the other one to join it. "Hurry, Barbara, the police will be here any second." Or Joel Schwartz could summon his thugs. My gratitude at Barbara saving me was already giving way to the usual irritation.

She grinned at me and shook her head, mouthing, "I didn't call the police."

When we were finally in the minivan, I saw the bottle of diet cola in the cup holder. "That *was* you at the vending machine? You left your post for a soda?"

"Don't worry, I took the phone with me." She held up the crumpled bag of now empty chips. "I must not have had enough to eat this morning. My blood sugar dropped, and I started pouring with sweat. I had to get something to snack on. While I was at it, I decided to get a cold drink. But I'm going to need more than this little bag of chips. I saw a twenty-four-hour pancake house off the highway exit. Can we go there for lunch?"

As I started to reverse the van, she said, "You've got to sit down with me and tell me what's going on. I can't go on one of these stakeouts with you again until I have a better idea what I'm getting myself into. You know I have heart problems."

Chapter Twenty-One

Monday Morning

At the restaurant, Barbara and I sat at a booth in the front. She hadn't wanted to walk a step further, although I thought we'd do better in the back, where we wouldn't be overheard. Still, a couple of Latino families with small children and a foursome of older men in sweatsuits and baseball caps were the only other customers. She started to work through a stack of pancakes pooled with butter and syrup, two fried eggs, and bacon as I finished filling her in.

Over my banana pancakes and whipped cream, I said, "You have to promise not to tell Arlene any of this."

"I would never," Barbara said, her eyes wide and earnest, her hand to her heart. "Are you kidding? Arlene would probably have a heart attack—the boyfriend wasn't even Jewish." She piled butter and syrup saturated pancake into her mouth. After swallowing, she said, "No wonder Rob never seemed that upset about his wife's death. Arlene seemed sadder than him. I just thought that was because he was so unemotional, just like his father. Oh, it used to drive Arlene crazy." She swooped in for more pancake and chewed contemplatively. "How do you know Rob didn't do it? The night before he finds out about his wife's affair and then she dies the next morning?"

"He was at the doctor's—he showed me the receipt with the time and date stamp."

"And then the boyfriend commits suicide? What a tragedy!" She dribbled more syrup on her pancakes.

"It seems very suspicious that Kyle would die as well, so soon after Lauren was killed."

"Well, I would kill myself, too, if I was facing what he had to deal with. He spends all his money on a property with Lauren; he couldn't make the payments, and now he'd lost his soulmate in the bargain. He was looking at losing his business and maybe even his wife. Those are pretty good reasons."

I nodded, acknowledging that, as I made sure that sufficient whipped cream was represented on my next bite of pancake.

Barbara finally made the connection. "You think her boyfriend was killed?" She put down her fork and leaned in. "By who?"

"Not by Joel Schwartz. He wanted his money, and Kyle was worth more to him alive than dead. But maybe someone else who was involved in pulling off the real estate plan." I swigged some coffee to cut the sweetness of the pancake. "I'm sorry to break your heart, but that guy you were in love with—"

"Tad!" Her face lit up.

"There's a chance he's a part of all this. He lied to me about how he met Lauren. Why? And he was the one who presided at the hearing for Joel Schwartz's architectural changes. Maybe he was bribed. And he might have even been responsible for my attack. At the funeral, Seth saw Tad and Misha talking."

"So what—they know each other? I just can't believe that handsome man would do anything wrong."

I shrugged and ate from my dish.

"Is that good?" she asked.

I knew that was her way of saying she wanted some, so I relented but forestalled her from diving in with her fingers by putting some of the pancake on her plate.

She groaned. "Mmm, that's good. I'm going to get that next time."

We ate in silence for a while, and I tried to ignore the wide-screen T.V. playing at the front of the restaurant. Did twenty-four-hour news really go with digestion?

"I can't believe all the stuff you found out," Barbara said. "That beautiful blonde girl who's missing—Kristin Stockhauser—Lauren was her therapist?"

"According to Kutchin, Kristin was only pretending to be a client, going to all these different doctors to find out how easy it was for her to get medication."

She frowned. Even Barbara thought that was silly. "I've known women who've contested their prenups. They argue that their husbands made enough money when they were married to be entitled to a chunk of it." Barbara burped quietly, then said, "So what are we going to do next?"

I shook my head. "No way—too dangerous."

She sat up straighter. "I was never in danger."

"Hello—" I began to remind her of what had happened to me. But then I couldn't continue, shuddering at the thought of Joel Schwartz's hands on me. I pushed my plate away. Okay, it was empty, but even the remnants were now sickening.

"He was just searching for a wire." Barbara had an unfortunate tendency to minimize anything that happened to anyone else and maximize her herself.

"What's Seth going to say when he hears this guy tried to fondle me?"

"Don't tell him. I won't say anything."

Somehow, I did not like the idea of being complicit with Barbara against Seth. The phone rang just then, and of course, it was Seth. I broke my policy about talking on phones in restaurants and picked up. If I didn't, Seth would worry about what had happened to his mother and me at Joel Schwartz's motel. He had an all-day meeting with the defense attorneys on the fraud case. That was why I was stuck with Barbara rather than having him for muscle.

I filled him in on the latest, leaving out for now that Barbara had abandoned her post for snacks, as well as the fondling.

"I've got some news for you, too," he said. "On my way in, I made some phone calls. Those morons yesterday could have found out all this if they'd been willing to do a little work." He was alluding to my police report of the fight that had erupted between Misha and the other man who had come upon us in Georgetown.

The officers who had responded to the call had said, "So you're just a witness to all this? And these guys ran off? You're not hurt? Do you want us to file a report?"

"Yes," I'd said.

They didn't bother to conceal their sighs and had stonewalled mine and Seth's suggestions for how they could take this further.

"You already knew Misha was working for the World Bank," Seth began.

"Yes, his wife told me that."

"Well, his post there had ended. Since he was a representative from the Belarusian government, he was expected to return."

"His wife said they were trying to get a visa to stay here," I said.

"He couldn't get one."

"That's why I think Lauren might have asked them for money so she could work her connections to Kutchin, and he could pave a way for the visa. But then she died before it could happen." I sipped my coffee.

"It was news to the American embassy today that Misha was attacked in broad daylight. The theory is that a representative from the Belarusian government was sent to get Misha to return. When they tried to find Misha today, they discovered that he and his family were no longer at the town home they were renting. They've probably left the country."

"Misha's wife said they planned to go to Canada," I said. "Maybe that's where they went."

"There's another theory," Seth said. "That he was KGB, and he was defecting—and another person from the KGB was sent to go after him."

"What did he say?" asked Barbara when I'd hung up. When I filled her in, she said, "Seth was so smart to have figured out what happened to that man Misha." To her, it didn't matter how much I'd done, Seth would always emerge the hero. Barbara smiled and fidgeted in her bench seat. "Won't you let me question Tad Gowers?"

"Let's go," I said. "There's one more place I need to stop this afternoon."

* * *

When I parked outside Ann Harrigan's house, Barbara clutched her coat to her neck. "I'm not getting out of the car again. Too cold."

"You can't come in anyway." I started to climb out of the van. "And lock the door. The Mafia approached this woman. You don't know when they'll come back."

As I walked up to the front door of the Harrigan's ranch house, the wind blew through chimes at a neighbor's house. It was a melancholic sound. In the cold air, I smelled the cooking grease from the restaurant on my hair and clothes.

Ann didn't smile when she answered the door. Her eyes were red and raw. She took a quick scan of the street behind me and centered on the minivan. "Who's that?" she asked as Barbara's face turned to gawk through the van window at us.

"My mother-in-law."

"Why are you here? What if they see you?" She waved me inside where it was as cold as the outside air.

I folded my arms in front of me for warmth and dove in. "I wanted to tell you that I might have gotten to the bottom of it." As I explained, I saw the boxes in her living room. They sagged with the weight of their contents; the cardboard paper sides folded like accordions.

I finished with a brief recap: "Lauren's father might have needed the money from Kyle to pay the mortgage on the property in Georgetown. Now that his daughter was dead, he was looking to Kyle to take up the slack."

She gripped her forehead in panic mode. "But if you've talked to Lauren's dad, he knows I've told someone. Those guys said not to say anything."

"I told Joel Schwartz I wouldn't call law enforcement if he left you alone."

She clutched around her the frumpy sweater she seemed to be wearing for comfort. "I can't believe you've done this. I should never have told you anything."

"I told him you hadn't gone to the FBI."

"But he knew I'd told *you*." She darted to the window.

I followed behind more slowly, my heels not making a sound on the carpet. As I tried to come up with an argument that would convince her this was the best course of action, I peered out the pane. Barbara was now leaning back in the passenger seat as if the pancakes had induced a narcoleptic fit.

"What am I going to do?" Ann's skin on her face had flushed with a blotchy rash.

"Do you want to continue paying for a building in Georgetown?" I said. "They want to renovate it, and you know more than I do about how long that takes. Until it gets split up into condos Joel can sell, the mortgage will have to be paid." When that had no impact, I added, "And what about your children?"

"That's what I've been trying to do—protect them." Lines around her mouth deepened as if to bracket her statement. "What if they hurt the boys as punishment to me?"

"I'm sorry," I said. "I knew your hands were tied. I was trying to help."

She wrapped the cardigan around herself tighter. It was missing buttons, so she couldn't fasten it. "If it comes to it, I'll sell this house so I can just give them a lump sum and then get far away."

A house in Arlington would fetch a good sum, but not as much as a massive Victorian in Georgetown.

When she noticed me looking at the boxes, she said, "I've been going through Kyle's stuff." Tears brightened her eyes. "I found something."

"Related to the house in Georgetown?" I guessed. Or evidence of the affair.

"A suicide note."

My boots were too high to stand long, and her announcement made me step backward. "Do you mind if I sit down?" I asked and plopped onto the couch.

"In his top file drawer—a manila folder with my name on it. He said he didn't want the police or anyone else to read it, only me."

My fingers were cold against my face as I listened, my elbows on my lap. "He wrote the note?"

She nodded, almost defiantly. "I know his handwriting." A tight smile. "It's been the same chicken-scratch since high school. I'm the only person that can read it."

I itched to ask her what it said, but if Kyle hadn't wanted the police and the emergency workers seeing it, I'm pretty sure I was lumped into that same crowd. When she didn't offer it up, I said, "So you don't have any doubts?"

"None. What he had done was wrong. He knew it was wrong, and he couldn't live with himself."

I tried to think of a way to put it delicately but couldn't come up with anything better than, "You mean, illegal activity?"

"No," she said sharply. "The affair."

In my years of practice, I'd fortunately never had a client die by suicide. But now the self-blame set in. Despite my pressing hotline numbers and referrals on him, I might have been the only one with the knowledge that Kyle had been suicidal at one point. I hadn't wanted that sole responsibility for his welfare, but it didn't sound as if he had gone to anyone else. I had failed, no matter that he had stood me up at Panera's when I had arranged to meet him last. And then, when I had called him afterward, had I pressed him too hard?

I replayed his last words: he was going to get justice like he was going to confront someone. I'd been convinced that had led to his death. Now she was telling me that's not how it had happened.

"Was there anything else in the folder for you?" I asked. When she hesitated, I made a guess. "A stock certificate?"

"How did you know?"

"Lauren bought when the market was down to take advantage of a new formulation that may be coming out. If you sell right now, it might be worth even less. Hold on to it, if you can."

The irony didn't escape me—Zemeron might have caused suicidality and now Kyle had died of suicide.

"Kyle didn't know anything about stocks," Ann said.

There were likely a lot of things Kyle didn't know before he met Lauren.

Chapter Twenty-Two

Tuesday Afternoon

I had the children gathered around, ready to make an escape, when Barbara returned home, sinking into the nearest chair. "I'm exhausted," she announced.

"Where did you go—the hairdressers?" I asked.

Barbara's hair had been washed and blown out. She refused to wash her own hair. "Lunch."

"You're exhausted from lunch?" I said.

"Wait until I tell you with who."

"We're just about to leave to go to Gymboree, so come with us if you want to share."

"You're going to be so proud of me."

I shot her a dubious look. "Are you coming? Play time only lasts an hour and a half." This was the pinnacle of our afternoon, and I was not going to miss it.

"I've got to get out of this bra. Can you unstrap it for me?"

"Oh, help me, Mama," I protested. "We don't have time for this."

As she wrestled her coat off, she said, "You're going to love my story."

"Well, I'm going to have to love it at dinner at this rate, because we're leaving. I'm not missing Gymboree open play time for nothing." I suddenly gaped at her cleavage, which was far too long, like the gap between cow udders. "Please don't tell me you wore that today."

Thankfully, she pulled the sequined and brocaded top up but only to admire it. "On sale at Bloomingdale's—gorgeous. But not comfortable." She reached in and scratched her chest. "Let me just get changed and go to the bathroom."

I threw my head back and howled in frustration. For most people, this might involve a few minutes, but Barbara could stretch it into the next hour.

"When I get them strapped in, if you're not ready, I'm leaving." And just like with the kids, this was a vague threat, so I could feel I had some control over the situation.

I backed down the driveway, but that only hurt me. I had to watch Barbara make her excruciating path to the car.

I pulled away as she was still closing the door. She ignored her seat belt and sat back. "Remember how I took Tad Gowers's card?" She was smiling at the mention of his name. "Well, I called him."

"You did?" I couldn't help smiling myself.

"I told him I wanted to take him to lunch."

"Wow, that was very forward of you."

"It wasn't like a date. I said I wanted to talk to him about property— the best neighborhood to buy in if you were a woman of my age. I said, 'Pick a fancy place. It'll be my treat. I never get to go anywhere good because my son and his wife have two small kids.'"

We were stopped at the five-minute light at Edsall and Van Dorn, so I turned to her as she continued. "He suggested the Palm. Have you heard of it?"

"Like you said, we don't get out much."

"You and Seth really have to go there." Using dramatic hand gestures, she described the decor and lighting in tremendous detail.

As I shot off at the green light, she groaned. "And the menu—"

"Barbara, I can't sit through the whole lunch. What did he say?"

"We even held hands for a minute."

"What?" I sat up higher in my seat as I followed a trail of cars turning left at Pickett.

"I put my hand on his to make a point, and he held it."

"How long?"

"Like maybe a minute."

Knowing her tendency toward exaggeration, I revised it to twenty seconds.

Then she grunted. "But I bet he'd be the type to boss you around."

And by golly, if anyone was going to do any bossing, it would be her.

"Gymboree!" announced Alyssa. The brightly lit sign was like a mirage shimmering in the desert of depressing strip mall stores.

At the prospect of having to walk from the car into Gymboree, Barbara picked up the pace of her story. "I said to Tad—" she pulled out his name to ridiculous nasal lengths. "'The market's never going to be this low again. I should buy now. But where?'"

"The old helpless routine." I hopped out, unlatched Alyssa's seat belt, and walked around to Noah.

Barbara had managed to get her own door open at that point. She continued with her story but was sitting there as if she couldn't talk and move at the same time. "I can't handle a whole house—too big for just me. Tad mentioned Chevy Chase, but I said, 'What I hate is when you're in the middle of a bunch of apartments and condos. Even in a nice area like Chevy Chase, it turns into its own kind of ghetto. Isn't there an exclusive neighborhood where it's mostly single-family homes, but there's a little condo building tucked in?'"

I pulled a striped knit hat on Noah. He wouldn't always consent, but he looked adorable, the way it framed his face. He leapt into my arms. "You weren't laying it on a bit thick?" I said to Barbara.

"I insisted we order wine, so that he would be drinking."

"Good one."

Alyssa grabbed my hand and tugged. "Gymboree, Mommy."

"Come on, Gram, we're here." She had already eaten into fifteen minutes of playtime, and now we had little over an hour left.

"I'm coming, I'm coming," she said as irritably as if I had proposed that she walk home.

Since I had Noah in my arms, I couldn't hold the Gymboree entrance open for the three minutes it took her to reach the storefront herself. In fact, I had the children's coats and shoes off, had presented my card for stamping, and had washed the kids' hands with anti-bacterial soap before Barbara finally made it in.

I opened the gate to the play area, and Noah shot off. Good, maybe it was one of those days when he'd enjoy his time here. And not one of the days we spent breastfeeding in the corner. As much as I relied on this place for the structure it gave me, what was the point of spending so much on these classes when half the time, he became overwhelmed by the primary colors and the other children?

Alyssa ran after him. At least having Noah model boisterous play had showed Alyssa that she could actually climb around and explore. When she was as young as Noah, I would just perch her on top of things, like one of the stuffed animals we now posed at home.

Barbara was behind me, having produced a folding metal chair out of nowhere— her largest font of resourcefulness came from finding places to sit—and clanked it through the gate so noisily I realized I was supposed to go back and carry it for her.

As I plonked it down near a structure of giant plastic blocks that Noah was climbing up, I said, "So you and Tad were getting drunk together—"

"I only had about a half of glass. The only drink I like is Sangria— nice and sweet. I let him choose it, and boy, was that stuff expensive." She reached a hand up. "No, Noah. Too high. That's too high for you."

"He's fine," I said. I knew her parenting of Seth involved a danger-ous combination of both overprotectiveness in terms of any kind of physical risk and permissiveness in all things discipline.

Noah smiled devilishly and leaped into the air. Even my heart sailed with in fear for a brief moment, but then he landed on the play mat below. Alyssa poised at the top of the structure and looked down nerv-ously.

"Don't worry, darling, you can just climb back down to Grammy," Barbara said.

Alyssa jumped, and I clapped. "See, you can do it, too," I said. They both ran to do it again. As Barbara eyed them, I said, "They're all right. Finish telling your story."

She settled in with a pleased smile. "Okay, so then I started to rave about Georgetown."

"That wasn't too obvious?"

"Don't worry, I kind of eased into it. We talked about a lot of other areas first—Chevy Chase, Old Town, Shirlington, the Watergate, and I had poured him another glass of wine. And I'd told him my best friend from Miami was interested in moving up here, too."

"You didn't say it was Rob's mother, did you?"

"No, have faith in me, Cara. I didn't want him putting any of the connections together." She tapped her brain with her finger. "I knew what I was doing. And remember, I was wearing the killer outfit." She smiled at the memory.

"So, I said it would be good if my friend and I could live in the same building," Barbara went on, "You know, support each other. We both have health problems, and we're all alone."

At this point, I wanted to make a sad face and say, "Boo hoo," but I restrained myself. "What did he say to that?" I asked instead.

"He agreed that now was the time to buy, and he had a building in mind, but that it was just in the beginning stages of renovation. 'If you have time, like you say, then you can take advantage of the low prices now before the building is finished, and everyone sees how desirable it is.'"

Noah had bee-lined over to a monster tube and was starting to climb through it, but Alyssa, exhilarated by newfound jumping, remained on the plastic structure.

Barbara went on. "So, I said, 'Sounds fabulous. Do you have a brochure? Can you show me the building?'" Barbara smiled, pleased with herself. "Right there, he offered to drive by with me after lunch. It was a beautiful, classic Victorian, part of a gorgeous block of renovated mansions, such an exclusive neighborhood." Barbara clasped her hands together in glee. "He described the inside, and that sounded perfect, too. High ceilings, hardwood floors, crown molding, but also the latest features—granite countertops, Viking appliances, a sub-zero refrigerator." Caught up in her story, she replayed the next side of her conversation. "'How was the buyer able to make this happen?' But you know what—" She leaned forward and tapped my arm. "Tad had a good answer for that. The one building was a blight in the area. It needed renovation and had been on the market for a year, steadily getting more run-down. Having an eyesore next to theirs was bringing down the value of their own homes. They were glad somebody would put money into it."

I folded my arms in distrust at Tad's explanation. "Interesting that he had presented the process in this way because the D.C. zoning office and the housing commission, of which he was chair, were the ones to make this decision, not the next-door neighbors. I guess they could appear at a hearing or give their opinion in writing, but it wasn't up to them to bestow their approval, like he was portraying it."

Suddenly, I noticed Noah standing over what must have been a ten-month-old boy propped up by his mother. Uh oh. I never knew which way this would turn. It was like owning an unpredictable dog, one that would sometimes attack smaller animals, sometimes not. I rushed over to Noah's side, just as he bashed the smaller boy's head with his fist.

"I'm sorry, I'm sorry," I said and grabbed Noah. "No, no!"

Most mothers surprised me at how well they took Noah's bullying. I had been very protective of Alyssa from the wild, older boys I'd seen roaming around the play area, though none of them had ever touched her. But this mother gasped audibly and drew her child into her arms. "Are you okay, Jakie?" She held his forehead like he'd sprouted a sudden fever and said to Noah, "No, little boy. You don't do that to smaller children."

Noah stared at her defiantly.

"What happened?" Barbara shouted across the room. "Why's that woman yelling at Noah?"

My face flamed with embarrassment, particularly as Noah struggled out of my arms, as I tried to take him back to Barbara, so she would stop bellowing for the whole room to hear. I couldn't control Noah at all. What I should do, of course, was take him home, show him that he could no longer play if he was going to bully. But that would punish me and Alyssa more than him; I would have to try to amuse him at home again rather than here.

"I don't know what's wrong with that child," I said at Barbara's side as I watched Noah climb a monkey bar apparatus.

"Seth never acted like that. He was always so easy to manage."

"And I was one of those compliant children sitting in the corner with my dolls and books. But my mother has some rogue cousins with ADHD."

Barbara pointed. "Look at Alyssa." She was underneath a "house" made from a Gymboree parachute propped up on a wooden structure, playing with a blue spider puppet.

I smiled—that was more like it—before turning back to Barbara. "Did Tad end up showing you the place?"

"He said he didn't have time—he had another meeting, and at that point, we'd spent over an hour at lunch. But I wrote down the address." She rummaged through her bag and brought out a napkin with her large left-handed lopsided handwriting: 1919 Waterhouse Road. Sure enough, the building Lauren's father had bought.

"But let me tell you the best part," she said. "Right before he was about to leave, I told him, 'It would be so much nicer if you made the sales for my neighbor and me. I'll call her tonight and tell her about this great opportunity. Can't you be our real estate agent?" Re-enacting the conversation, she even batted her eyelashes.

I wished that Seth could have a sense of humor about Tad, but he became stony-faced when his name came up; otherwise, this would be the perfect story to tell him.

"Is this where you held hands?" I asked.

"No, but I did lean towards him."

I got the point that she had flashed cleavage. I wanted to turn my head to the side and quietly throw up, but she was going on with the story.

"So, Tad said, 'I can't represent you as the buyer, but I can represent the builder, and we can work from there. Of course, you're welcome to bring your own real estate agent to the table, but I'll make it as attractive as I can, and, without his commission, you can save right there.'"

Aside from Tad's blatant sexism for assuming the agent was a man, I tried to piece together what Barbara had uncovered. What he didn't reveal: as chair of the Historic Preservation Committee, he had ruled in

Joel Schwartz's favor to make the proposed changes to the building that would allow condos to be built.

"Did I do good?" she asked.

"This is fantastic." I raised my arm to give her a high five—I was so used to doing it with my children for pretty much anything—but she wasn't familiar with the gesture and awkwardly grasped my hand. "With both of us going to the FBI and telling them what we found out, they really can build a legitimate case against Joel Schwartz and Tad Gowers."

"I don't mind that Joel Schwartz is going to prison, but Tad?" she said. We had such a nice lunch."

"Yeah, because you had to pay for it."

Chapter Twenty-Three

Wednesday Evening

We were back in Shirlington, this time attempting a restaurant meal with the kids. Barbara had demanded Mexican food at Guapo's as her reward for "nailing Tad Gowers." I wasn't quite sure of the meaning of her phrasing.

"So, you liked the FBI agent I lined up this time?" Seth asked me.

After the failed Belarusian abduction Sunday night and my encounter with Joel Schwartz, Seth had worked his Department of Justice contacts for an agent on the Kristin Stockhausen case, arguing that I had enough information for probable cause.

Agent Jeff Strazinski resembled Nixon with his heavy black eyebrows and Mr. Potato Head-shaped skull, but looks were deceiving.

"Loved him" screamed Barbara. "Agent Jeff was the nicest man, and his wife just had a baby."

For once, Barbara and I shared an opinion.

When I met Agent Jeff in a cubicle that was smaller than my office, I had asked about Congressman Kutchin's limo driver, Vlad. "Maybe Kristin borrowed the limo and drove over to B.X. Martin for another meeting near there with Griffin Sewell.

"We don't have the exact day, but that should be easy enough to figure out. There's only a certain window," Agent Jeff said as if talking to himself and jotted something down on a legal pad. "We'll be all over this Griffin fellow, don't you worry."

"Do you think someone from the news is going to interview me?" Barbara now asked. "David Muir wouldn't be bad."

"They're going to investigate, so they probably don't want the media getting a hold of the story until they make an arrest." Seth scooped a chip into the salsa. "Didn't he tell you that?"

"Oh, gee, I didn't hear that part." Her hand plunged into the chip bowl. I concentrated on breaking a chip into small triangles so Noah, perched on my lap, could eat them without choking.

"Do you think they'll want me to wear a wire and talk to Tad again?" She leered at me. "If they do, I can't wear the same outfit."

This was supposed to be girl talk for the revealing top that had supposedly catapulted Tad Gowers into revealing too much information. I had strictly warned her off telling the FBI about her outfit. "They don't want to hear that stuff," Surprisingly, she had listened.

"Will I be on T.V. after this is over?" Barbara asked now. "Do I have time to get more Botox?"

The steaming platters of fajitas arrived, and the two steak ones were whisked in front of Seth and his mother. I directed the server to put the chicken fajitas in the middle of the table so Noah and Alyssa could share them. They didn't go for anything on the kid's menu. "You can sit in your booster now," I said to Noah.

He made a noise of protest and clung to me. In the struggle to place him in the seat, it got knocked to the floor, and the pink crocs fell off his feet. His mouth opened wide in a howl.

Seth and I exchanged the "uh oh" glance. "Come on, buddy," Seth said in a jocular tone. He got up to retrieve the seat. "Sit in the booster like a big boy. I'll get your shoes for you. Don't worry about it."

Seeing Noah's feet flailing in the air, Barbara said, "Where on earth are his socks? It's winter out there."

"My pocket." I patted my pants. "He wouldn't wear them."

She tried what my mother always did—to use the voice that had scared us as little kids into instant obedience. But Noah was oblivious to the voice of authority. He remained in my lap and now didn't want to eat the chicken meat I'd cut up for him. Barbara pushed rice at him, and even a raw piece of her meat, but this, not surprisingly, only made him cry harder.

There was nothing as frustrating as having a meal prepared for you that you couldn't eat. The melted cheese glistened on the enchiladas. Of course, they weren't like the ones in Texas, but the best thing in this area.

Seth often took the high road and walked Noah out so I could eat, recognizing that I bore the brunt of Noah's moods. But this wasn't one of those times. "I'm really hungry," he said.

I had mastered the art of leaving a public place with a crying child. Make eye contact with no one. You didn't want to see the hostile stares, but you also didn't want to see the sympathetic looks because then you might come undone.

"Miss." One of the waiter staff thrust a croc at me. "You dropped this."

I smiled weakly, and outside used the distraction technique. "Look at the tree. Look how pretty." I pointed at the giant Christmas tree planted at the center of the square near the fountain that was drained in winter. "Shall we go see Daddy and Grammy through the window?"

"No!"

I suspected that anything would get that response right then. He didn't know what he wanted, and I couldn't help him find that. I walked with him down the street and peered in the window of the restaurant.

Barbara was talking, her head ducked low like a turtle to her plate. Alyssa looked like a kitten next to her. I eyed my enchiladas. The cheese must be congealing. I sighed, knowing Guapo's didn't believe in microwaves.

I headed inside, and, threading my way through the crowd waiting to be seated, grabbed a handful of mints. I bit off a tiny piece of mint and fed it into his mouth. No matter how much I exhorted him to suck, he kept crunching on each piece I gave him.

I sidled up to the tortilla-making machine, which had caught Noah's interest. A T.V. was set up in the bar within my view playing the usual football. But then my eye caught the logo of B.X. Martin, and I moved closer to hear. A reporter stood in front of a grassy area backed up by trees now bare from leaves. He was saying, "…body found in wooded park behind B.X. Pharmaceutical Company in Reston. Possibly believed to be Kristin Stockhauser. . ."

I was surprised when the national news footage showed FBI agents leading Griffin away in handcuffs from the brick industrial building that was B.X. Martin. Not because Griffin was arrested—I had been the one to provide the civilian tip—but because I didn't feel more pleased with myself.

***

Seth, sitting next to me on the couch, after Barbara and the children were in bed, said, "It's amazing that you figured all this out," he said. "A national case."

With the backdrop of the Congressional dome, the T.V reporter, a boy-faced man in his fifties, said, pointing behind him, "Griffin Sewell had testified here in a congressional hearing for the Health Committee spearheaded by none other than Congressman Kutchin. The focus of the hearing was the medication Zemeron, a controversial drug used to treat attention deficit disorder in adults."

The scene switched to footage of Congressman Kutchin sitting in a high-backed leather chair leaning over a microphone in the hearing room. I didn't know whether it was the actual hearing in which Griffin had testified, but it looked good as a visual with Kristin Stockhauser seated next to Brad Miller among the other staffers behind Kutchin.

The reporter started a slow, casual stroll in front of the Capitol steps. "After the hearing, Griffin Sewell and Kristin Stockhauser were seen talking outside." He pointed downward as if to indicate "in this exact spot. What they talked about that day," the journalist continued, "Nobody knows, although it was that weekend her parents discovered her missing. Did Griffin Sewell have anything to do with her murder?"

Seth hopped from station to station, but all the news shows had basically the same version. There was only a little bit to add. It seemed that, according to Agent Jeff, to whom I talked briefly on the phone after we returned from Guapo's, Kutchin's driver Vladimir Yudin was only hired after the intern disappeared and Kutchin got death threats from the public. So maybe the attack on me had nothing to do with the driver, after all. That left Misha and his crowd as the likely suspects, and they were long gone. As the night wore on, the lawyers hashed it out some more. The defense attorneys stressed that no actual evidence tied Griffin Sewell to the death of Kristin Stockhauser; the prosecutors rebutted that cases were often tried—and won—on only circumstantial evidence. Cause of death was still unknown, as there was no trauma to her bones. Law enforcement commentators speculated that Kristin may have been poisoned; but the tissue in her body had decomposed, so there was no way of testing for this.

When Seth finally clicked off the remote, he said, "I think we've seen it all. Congratulations!"

"Don't you kind of feel sorry for Griffin?"

His eyes widened. "Feel sorry for him? He *killed* someone." "What you should feel is pride. The D.C. police couldn't solve the case in three months, and you wrapped it up single-handedly in a few weeks."

"But this wasn't even the murder I was trying to solve."

"Even more impressive." Seeing I wasn't convinced, he said, "Maybe he got a taste for killing. And he had motive. Laura had threatened to go to his boss and say he was revealing insider information."

"But that was an empty threat. Lauren would have gotten into trouble, too. And there was still the possibility this new medication might have produced the big pay-off."

He stood and pulled me up by my hand. "Come on, let's go to bed."

I followed, still talking. "Isn't this a bit like the last guy who was accused of the Anthrax killings? Everyone said how geeky and weird he was, but did that mean he had done it? And even before him, the FBI had another Anthrax suspect. They hounded him for years until they realized they had the wrong person. What if we all have it wrong now?"

Chapter Twenty-Four

Following Wednesday Afternoon

Always a site of grandeur, the Capitol Building looked particularly fetching with the sunset as a backdrop. The weather had been grey all day until now when the sun pushed up through the gloom, only to sink. Tense government workers in long black coats strode past, no more cheered than I by the prospect of Thanksgiving the next day. The Thanksgiving break loomed ahead, an endless stretch of time, trapped inside entertaining children. Seth and I would cope by chopping up the day in 45-minute segments and switching off duty.

And if I thought it was endless, what of Sylvia, Carmen's daughter, forced to celebrate with a foster family? And Orlando—what would he do without a mother, hang with the homies?

When I suggested we go downtown, Barbara brightened. "Can we stop by and say hi to Jeff?" The new FBI agent was also her new best friend.

"I'm sure he's busy," I said.

"How's that darling baby of his?"

"I don't know."

"So now he has two girls—is he going to try for a boy?"

"I don't ask personal questions like that."

She turned to me. "That's personal?"

The holiday had already started, and people were fleeing the city. But the traffic was also congested going in. That was D.C. for you. Our destination was the Capitol. In the time since the arrest of Griffin Sewell for Kristin Stockhauser's murder, I had left phone messages on Congressman Kutchin's office mailbox and e-mailed him. Earlier, I'd tried another call, and unbelievably, a young woman picked up the line and announced, "Congressman Ted Kutchin's office."

I guess on a day when few people were liable to call, that's when they answered their phones. When I asked if I could get an appointment, wondering how Grammy could manage both the kids if Kutchin granted one, the receptionist solved that problem. "Sorry, he's fully booked until four p.m."

"Is that when he's leaving for the day?"

"Yes, for the holiday."

As we set out for D.C., Noah descended into histrionics before we passed Seminary Road in Alexandria. I'd have felt bad for him if it wasn't so loud.

Grammy tried every trick in her book: "Grammy will get you an ice cream if you stop crying." "Be a big boy and stop crying." "Ah, shut up, you big baby!"

Grammy and I tried to converse to distract ourselves from the screaming. After I told her I wanted to ask the congressman about the man who had attacked me, she said, "He's not going to tell you the truth. Those politicians never do."

"I want to see if I can get a read on him." It was my true superpower, along with speed reading *Fox in Socks* aloud.

It was only when I circled for a parking space and was about to pull into one that I looked over and saw both Noah and Alyssa passed out, mouths open.

Barbara and I looked at each other. "You can't wake them now." Barbara was incapable of whispering.

I agreed though it was too late in the afternoon for naps. It might interfere with their sleep at bedtime. With young children, simple things like sleep had to be finessed. And all over, mothers were finessing their children through the routines of each day. Unsung heroes, all of them.

I studied the ambiguous directions of the parking sign. "I'm not sure this is a spot, after all." I needed a Venn diagram to understand where the three statements posted on the sign intersected. It was like a logic question from the Graduate Record Exam.

"Why do they make it so complicated around here?" she said.

"Good question. Welcome to the rat race."

"Just park here. We'll be fine," she said. "I'll stay with the darlings. Maybe I'll even take a snooze myself."

"Okay, but at least get in the driver's seat, so if someone tells you to move, you can without getting a ticket."

She waved in agreement with visible resentment at having to change seats.

I gave a final instruction. "Make sure to lock the doors."

"Got it." She gave a big thumbs up.

I followed the map I'd printed of the House Representatives' parking lot. It would be guarded—and a long shot—but I hoped to catch Kutchin's driver on the street outside. I couldn't get further in than that.

My breath was visible in the frosty air, and the sun hovered over the horizon line. My nerves still jangled: Noah's screaming and worry that this was my last chance to catch Kutchin. This was a madcap scheme but all I had with children in tow.

Part of the nerves was that I'd promised Seth that I wouldn't bring the children anywhere near my exploration of Lauren's murder.

But Grammy was with the kids, I rationalized. We were in the middle of tourist central, an area bustling with people, even in the cold and on the verge of Thanksgiving.

As soon as I thought of them, the phone in my hand suddenly went off. I saw that it was Barbara. Before she even spoke, I knew what was wrong: telephonic crying.

"You've got to come back," she bellowed. "They're both calling for you. I can't undo their seat belts."

I'd driven all the way to D.C., my ears still ringing, walked all the way over here, and was this close. After all that, now I would leave without any more information than when I had come.

But my children were crying and not only that but trapped in their car seats. When they got like this, no one but me could calm them. As it was, it would take a good ten minutes to hoof it back to the minivan. Ten minutes of screaming would feel like a lifetime to Barbara. I knew because I had been there.

As I scurried along, I mentally heard Noah's tortured wailing. Soon Barbara would lose patience and scream, "Shut up, you big baby!" I recognized that it was easier to feel sorry for Noah when I wasn't with him in the car.

Bright headlights shone from a car behind me. As I kept walking, the car pulled up alongside me.

"Dr. Knight." A man's voice called to me. It wasn't Kutchin's ringing tone or the driver's accent. But who down here would know my professional title?

It was the black SUV idling, the only car on the short one-way road. Brad Miller's plain face looked out over the rolled-down window. I peered in the back seat for the congressman, but with the faded light of dusk and the tinted windows, I could see nothing.

"I heard you wanted to talk to Congressman Kutchin?" Brad said. "He couldn't make it down and sent me instead. I'm privy to all his affairs." His tone was prim and self-important.

"I bet," I couldn't help retorting.

Brad bared his teeth in a version of a smile. "Where are you headed—the metro? I could drop you as we talk."

"I'm just there," I gestured in the general area of where I was parked, two streets away. It's actually easier to walk through the one-way streets." I knew that from circling the area repeatedly to find that spot. Plus, I'd promised Seth after the last time: no more getting into cars! I couldn't rationalize this one.

Brad's eyes went to his rear-view mirror. "Let me park this thing."

It wasn't a valid spot, but, if needed, Brad must have been able to whip out some documentation that said he was official. He stepped out of the car, wearing a suit like last time. "You certainly can't pin the murder of Kristin Stockhauser on Kutchin now. They've caught the guy—a chemist from B.X. Martin."

"Yes, I know. I was the one who told the FBI about Griffin Sewell."

For the first time, Brad seemed surprised by something I'd said.

"I just have a minute. I've got to pick up my children." I didn't explain that they were with their grandmother in the minivan two blocks over. "One night I was working late when your boss pulled up with his Russian driver at my place of work, and a week later, another Russian man attacked and threatened me. I want to find out if Kutchin sent him."

"You know Vlad is from the Ukraine, not Russia, right?"

"Oh," I said, embarrassed for stereotyping, a cardinal sin for social workers.

"We're devastated, of course, that Kristin's been found dead after all this time. But we couldn't do our work with this hanging over us. They actually wanted Ted to resign as chair of the Health Committee." Brad shook his head in amusement at the idea. "Since he refused, they asked him to keep a low profile. Everything he's done for the last three months has been colored by her." He looked toward the Capitol and its dramatic lighting.

Good for him that he saw it every day and never got tired of the view. As I studied him, clarity glimmered in the cold dusk air. "Kristin," the congressman said, was always trying to do something extra. He told me she was going to doctors, seeing how easy it was to get prescriptions and if providers would inform her about possible suicidal ideation."

"He told you that?" He said, tickled, leaning against the passenger door. "You know, I don't think Griffin Sewell killed her for anything to do with B.X. Martin and the medications they were selling. He was a perv, that's all. Her body was too decomposed from being in the woods to know if she was sexually assaulted."

I made a face that he might not have been able to see in the dim light.

"B.X. Martin isn't so bad," Brad mused. "Everyone always gets down on the pharmaceutical companies. But those medicines save lives."

"But that's not their objective. If people can't pay for their life-saving medication, they don't get it." This was a regular theme in the Mental Disorders class I taught, but I backed off on my lecture and changed tactics. "So, you're on the side of the pharmaceutical company. You had me there. I thought your ultimate loyalty was to the congressman." I paused, then kept feeling my way, looking for a way to hook him. "I know men like the congressman. You're the one who probably does all the work behind the scenes. And you don't get any of the credit."

I waited again, tapping down my eagerness to wrestle answers from him.

"How did you guess?" he finally said.

I swallowed, my heart fluttering. "I work in academia, remember? Another place, besides politics and law, where narcissists flock."

"I wanted to buy a building in Dupont Circle." Brad's gaze was off in the distance.

I had no sense of direction, particularly for D.C., where streets wound and curved, and it might have been toward Dupont Circle, a pricy section of Northwest D.C., near beautiful Embassy Row and lots of walkable trendy restaurants, yoga, and coffee shops.

"You went to the congressman for money?" I filled in the silence. The darkening light made my other senses keener, and I felt his surprise that I had nailed it.

Taking advantage of my bull's eye, I went on. "Kutchin was offended when you mentioned how much you did for him, where would he be without you? And, after all you did—covering up his affair."

He shook his head and laughed softly. "The congressman didn't have an affair with Kristin. He's always been faithful to his wife."

"Wow." I looked upward at the blue-grey of the sky. "Too much of a coincidence to believe that a congressman could have an affair with an intern; she ends up dead, and that those facts are unrelated. She was an attractive woman," I said.

"Yes, she was." His tone was wistful.

"And smart," I added. "Did you try to date her?"

He shook his head. "Her thing was Tinder."

"Tinder?" I recoiled—a hook-up app at best, a front for prostitution at worst. Yes, I waited late to get married, but at least it was before online dating. "She told you that?"

"Only later."

"Did you see her out somewhere with a guy from Tinder?" I was feeling my way again through the unspoken territory. I was getting close. A blast of wind came barreling down the tunnel created by the stretch of Mall. My teeth gave way to chattering. Maybe I was too close.

He nodded. "Reston."

"Reston?" She had to go that far to find a hot guy? Of course, that was also where B.X. Martin was headquartered. I didn't know much about the work on House committees, but representatives didn't march about conducting investigations. They read briefs and reports and questioned people at hearings. So, there would be no reason for Kutchin and his entourage to end up in Reston.

"Was this one of the *extra* things she did? Found one of the executives on Tinder and made a date with him? What did she find out? Was that why she was killed?" I realized I hadn't stopped pelting him with questions, which was never a good technique.

"I was the one who leaked it to the media," he said as if answering a question that I hadn't asked a few sentences ago.

I was genuinely confused. "Leaked what?" Then cold logic descended on me, and I said, "It would take the police and the public in an entirely different direction, away from—" I couldn't finish the sentence, but I saw what it meant and turned. "My children are crying. Their grandmother is looking after them. I've got to get my kids." About to bolt, I heard a click.

I downplayed to myself what the noise was. Just because you heard a car backfiring or firecrackers exploding didn't mean it was the sound of a gun firing. And just because you heard a click like a gun being cocked didn't mean it wasn't just the car door closing. Before I finished thinking about all these double negatives to protect myself from the knowledge of danger, the black shape of a gun appeared in Brad's hand.

"Get in the car," he ordered.

The night suddenly looked so beautiful—the incredible view of the Capitol, its majestic dome lighting up the night sky. Frightened tears jumped into my eyes. I wanted to run, take my chance of the gun firing into my back. If I got into the car, I would surely die anyway. But I couldn't lead him to the van where my children were. Better that I was murdered away from them where they couldn't see, where they wouldn't know. It was like I could hear Noah's screaming in the night air. Noah would sob his heart out for a mother that never came.

No, I had to come back to him and my sweet girl. I started talking, even though it felt like Novocain had dried up my mouth, and my lips were numb with fear. "You have a gun," was the only thing I could say. I avoided looking at it again and kept my eyes on his, but they were black pits.

"Vlad keeps it in the car."

"It'll come back to the congressman if you shoot me."

"As you can imagine, given the crime in D.C., it's not all that hard to pick up an unlicensed gun." His teeth gleamed in the dark. He wanted to talk; he wanted somebody to realize how clever he was. "I'm the one who hired him. His cousin owns a fleet of limos. He owes me the job."

"Then you were the one who had me attacked. Maybe not Vlad, but someone in his cousin's operation."

He smiled, basically admitting it. I was familiar with the type from academia—the narcissists who were part of every faculty; they didn't get the satisfaction they craved unless they lorded over someone how brilliant they were.

"When I saw that loser Griffin Sewell at the hearing, I knew he'd be perfect."

We used the term scapegoat in mental health circles, but I believe the Russians say, "useful idiot."

"The B.X. Martin execs and their lawyers tried to limit the time he was up there." He chuckled at the memory. "But he had to confirm that he was one of the creators of the compound. Then, he tried to explain the science behind it. Another disaster. I waited three months for the

D.C. police to snap to him as the villain. Thank you for finally taking the bait and telling the FBI."

I heard a siren far off but knew it wasn't for me. I saw Noah's face in my mind, eyes flowing with tears. I just wanted to hold him close, and never let him go. Why had I involved myself in all this, insisted on finding out the truth when I should have just stayed home with my baby and toddler?

"Were you and Kristin in on something together?" I had to keep asking questions.

"She thought she was so smart but wasn't in my league. I was having dinner with my contact at B.X. Martin. We only met in person. No cell phones, no email. Then she walks in with a man, some date from Tinder, I found out later. We had to pass her to leave, but I pretended not to see her."

"And the man you were with was oblivious. You couldn't tell him who she was. Because of what you were already planning." My insides started trembling.

"Like 45 minutes later, she called, and asked if she could use me as an excuse to get away from the guy. They had finished dinner, and she wanted to end the date. He'd picked her up from the metro, and she wondered if I could give her a ride home. We met in the parking lot. She showed me the picture she'd taken of the executive and me leaving the restaurant together. She figured out who it was. She'd been drinking with dinner and had cocktails before. If she was sober, she might have realized the risk she was putting herself in."

His gaze went to the distance as if re-living these last moments of her life. I saw where this was going. My muscles were so tense they ached. Should I run while his memories absorbed his attention?

"When we talked in my car, it was so easy to inject her with fentanyl." He smiled. "She never woke up again."

My heart ached at her fate. So young. And Grammy was right. She was so beautiful.

He shook his head. "It's time, Cara. You'll have to get in the car now."

As much as I tried to control my nerves, my teeth rattled audibly as I spoke. "And if I don't, you'll just shoot me here?"

"People do die by gunfire down here. In the shadow of the nation's Capital and all that. If I take your wallet, there'll be no questions."

Suddenly, jagged lights played over us, and I heard the roar of an engine. Our minivan was such a common make and color that we often parked next to one just like it in any given parking lot. But Barbara was behind the wheel, bearing down on the horn, doing her wackiest driving yet, lurching onto the curb. Metal crunched as she smashed into the SUV. I turned and ran toward the mall. I had to lead him away from Barbara and the children.

He was behind me. I looked back once to confirm that. I was in better shape than he was. I had that going for me. The spin classes. But he was taller and could cover more ground. And he had the gun.

"Cara! Cara, come back!" Barbara's voice resounded through the night, as did the sound of children's crying.

My breath was coming too hard, and fear clamped around my chest. I could not summon my voice to shout for help.

An explosion behind me was like a cannon going off. Among all these monuments, it was like I was trapped in some revolutionary war re-enactment. Tiny rocks pelted at me and stung my face. *He's shooting*, I realized, but I could still run.

BOOM! Gravel showered down on me again as the sound echoed into the empty space between monuments and museums. How could not even a single jogger be running this path—a dog walker?

I ducked behind a statue—a revolutionary war hero who smirked into the middle distance, indifferent to my plight. Seth knew the names and origins of all the statues. Surely, Barbara must have called him when I hadn't returned or answered her calls, but he would never make it through downtown D.C. traffic to save me.

The statue didn't provide enough cover from Brad, and I ran toward the U.S. Botanical Garden Conservatory, my back arched in anticipation of incredible pain. I needed him to shoot the glass, not me. Surely, the sound of national monuments being destroyed would raise someone.

Another shot fired out, its whine shooting past, exploding with deafening noise. As glass showered down, I dashed out of the way to avoid the shards, but still, my face stung. I rounded the corner, hoping that the falling glass would keep him back.

Glass crunched underfoot. I planned to run from Brad round and round the Botanical Garden like the carousel down the mall that Alyssa loved to ride, looking so tiny and sweet on the dragon she always chose.

I tripped, didn't know until I fell that it was a glass shard shaped in a half circle that had ensnared me. I raised my head. Brad came into view, panting. He trained the gun on me as I tried to scramble to my feet. The sound of the shot rang out, and I embraced the cold, moist grass.

"Suspect down!" shouted a female voice. "Need EMT at the U.S. Botanical Garden."

Chapter Twenty-Five

Thursday Afternoon

Seth and I were taking off our and the children's shoes in the foyer of what was now only Rob's house. The house still maintained its no-shoe standard even without Lauren. The Shiva had been a notable exception.

Seth murmured to me under his breath, "I would rather have stayed home and had chicken."

"I'm with you," I said, "but your mother wants the whole fix-ins, and she didn't want to cook." I had brought pumpkin cheesecake. I enjoyed baking more than making actual meals and never needed an excuse to eat cheesecake.

"I've decided I hate Victorians," he said. "They're too dark and closed in."

The style didn't appeal to me as much either with the events that now colored it.

As a crowd, we descended the hallway, joining Arlene and Rob in the living room. Barbara groaned. "Arlene, it smells so good—I can't wait to eat!"

Arlene stood near the couch, festive in a red and black ensemble of Chico's separates. She wore a dressy cardigan that could almost have been a jacket. Barbara had pulled on a checkered blouse over black stretch pants. On her feet were black shoes that were one up from sneakers. She claimed she couldn't bend to get them off, and if she did, she wouldn't make it back up.

I dressed as I did for work with a long skirt over leggings so I could make a quick change, trading tennis shoes for boots, if an opportunity arose to work out. Alyssa needed no excuse to wear a party dress and sparkly Mary Janes.

"Thanks so much for coming over." Arlene wore a vivid red lipstick. "We wanted to repay you for all your help during this difficult time—"

I stole a glance at Rob to see how he reacted to her statement. I'm so sure Rob was grateful for all I had done. Right.

"And we hoped that by hosting a celebration," Arlene went on, "we can get past all the sad events.

"Here, here," shouted Barbara.

Soon after, Rob and Seth decided to bond in masculine fashion over beer, and they set off in search of an open gas station to buy a six-pack.

Alyssa and Noah scampered up the stairs in search of Kitty. Alyssa had not forgotten who lived under the master bed. I plopped on the couch, already depleted from "the holiday break." Taking care of kids today was an anti-climax after yesterday's excitement, staying up and being questioned by all manner of law enforcement, then dreaming about being chased all night. Seth had told me that I should wake him up if I had any nightmares or couldn't sleep; he'd learned from me how to prevent PTSD from setting in: keep processing the trauma. But I didn't have the heart when he slept so soundly.

I heard Barbara regaling Arlene in the kitchen about her lunch with Tad. "You should have seen what I was wearing. I looked fantastic."

I padded in stocking feet to the kitchen and said, "Barbara, you're not supposed to tell anyone—it's an open FBI investigation."

"How did you know I was saying anything?"

"You're screaming—how could I not hear?"

"Who am I going to tell?" said Arlene, echoing what Barbara had said at our pancake breakfast. So much had been cleared up since then. Lauren and her father had conspired with Tad Gowers to change the codes and the historical detailing on the Georgetown building they had purchased. The FBI was also investigating Lauren's father's mob connections and how they linked to this case. They said they would protect Kyle's widow, Ann Harrigan, and her family against any possible repercussions, and I wondered if that included going into witness protection. I hadn't talked to Ann again, and I knew she'd be mad that I'd told the FBI about her involvement. Hopefully, the stock payout would provide some cushion for her new life without Kyle.

Although Congressman Kutchin had been vindicated of killing Kristin Stockhauser, it didn't reflect well that his Senior Aide was guilty of the crime, and people tended to think that Brad Miller had acted for the congressman. It didn't help that the gun that had shattered glass on the mall greenhouse was unlicensed and unmarked.

Griffin had been released from jail. I wondered if he would keep his job; after all, he had come up with new compounds for B.X. Martin rather than doing the copy-cat drug manufacture that most of the pharmaceutical companies relied on. The FBI might have overlooked the insider information he'd provided Lauren in exchange for making the case on Brad and the other federal violations that were part of this case.

Everything was being cleared up except for one thing—Lauren's murder.

The FBI was confident that her death was connected to the intern's, even though I'd told them that Brad had denied it while admitting to everything else. Since they were still trying to make the case, Carmen remained in jail.

"What can I do to help?" I asked Arlene now.

"You can chop vegetables for the salad." Arlene pointed to a cutting board where a couple of tomatoes lolled nearby. A salad seemed like overkill for Thanksgiving, but okay. I grabbed the knife and set to work.

"I can't believe all this happened last night," Arlene told Barbara as she stirred a pot of instant stuffing. "You must be exhausted. Are you sure you're up for this?"

I turned to look at Arlene to figure out what she meant—Barbara not eating Thanksgiving dinner? Was she kidding?

"I'm okay," Barbara said bravely.

Arlene put the lid on the saucepan. "After we finish here, we should sit down and watch the news—it must be the big story today." Not a surprise: how much time could the media spend on Black Friday after all?

"And we haven't even had a chance to watch any of it because the kids' shows are always playing when the T.V. is on." Barbara flashed me a doleful gaze.

"Seth's recording some of the news shows," I said, "but the kids can't hear all that stuff anyway. Murder and poison, bodies decomposing, skeleton remains, a shoot-out with suspects."

"What happened to that congressional aid anyway?" Arlene asked.

"He's at George Washington Hospital, out of ICU now." I sliced the tomato and thought of Brad's blood. I didn't think I'd be eating the salad.

"Man, you were lucky that Park Police officer heard the shots," said Barbara, lifting the lid off the stuffing pot and plunging her fingers in to grab a ball of stuffing.

"I *was* lucky that my strategy paid off. I hoped glass raining down from the conservatory of the Botanical Garden would get some attention."

Her mouth full, Barbara asked, "When do you get to meet her?"

"*The Washington Post* is interviewing us together on Monday morning," I said.

"I wonder if you'll end up on T.V.?" Barbara licked her fingers greedily.

"Imagine running around the Mall being shot at." Arlene shook her head.

Just as the conversation had veered toward me, Barbara dragged it back to herself. "I didn't mean to crash into the congressman's car, you know. I was having a low blood sugar attack. I was so worried and upset when you wouldn't answer your phone, and the babies were screaming their heads off for their mommy. I tried calling Seth, and he said for me to pick him up so we could look for her. In the meantime, he was going to make calls to the Capitol police and Kutchin's office." She smiled. "Seth always knows what to do."

I had to admit his competence was an appealing trait, but he would hate the doting from his mother.

"He gave me directions, but I became mixed up with all those one-ways," Barbara said. "I was talking to Seth on the phone, shaking and sweating from the low blood sugar, and I lost control of the wheel when I saw Cara standing there with that man."

"But you didn't know it was me," I reminded her.

"Well, no, not at first. That little darling, Alyssa, said, 'Mommy, Mommy,' which she and Noah had been saying over and over again. I was so sick of it. But it *was* Mommy. Just when I got it, I wrecked the car."

"What about the kids?" Arlene put her hand to her chest. "Were they all right?"

"Sure, I'd tried getting them out when they were crying, but those darn car seats are too complicated." Barbara popped a piece of carrot in her mouth.

Suddenly, something dropped upstairs. "Cara, where are the children?" Arlene asked.

"I'm sorry, I'll check on them." I put down the knife and jogged off.

When I went upstairs, I found them in the guest room, where Noah had pulled out the nightstand drawer. Luckily, it hadn't served as a receptacle for junk—Lauren and now Arlene were too tidy for that—and only a few things had spilled out onto the floor beside the bed. As I knelt to pick them up, Noah took this as an invitation to leap on my back.

I grimaced at Lauren's face, looking up at me from the memorial service program and scooped up that and the bits of paper. They were boarding passes, I noted, and my eye caught the date on the first one—October seventeenth—the day of Lauren's murder. My heart pounded, and my face grew hot at the realization of what this meant.

"Everything okay up here?" Arlene stood in the doorway.

My heart sunk to my stomach, and I felt sick. "Yes, I mean, well, Noah pulled this drawer out, but I'm sure I can—" Noah slid off my back as I shoved the papers inside the drawer and tried to jam it into the nightstand. Spatial orientation was not my strong suit in the best circumstances, but now I was hopeless with trembling fingers. The drawer collapsed again with what seemed like a thunderous noise. "Kids, let's go downstairs. This isn't a place to play, and Daddy can have a look at it when he gets back, which should be any second now."

The children, as usual, ignored me, but Arlene's voice brooked no nonsense. "Alyssa, Noah, go to your Grammy now."

Alyssa backed out from under the bed, where she'd tried to coax the cat out of its hiding place. Noah hurtled his way past Arlene, who stepped aside. As Alyssa threw one last longing gaze at Kitty under the bed, I moved to follow.

Arlene blocked my way. "Not you, Cara."

"I have to be with my children."

"They're fine with Barbara. She can take care of them."

As wrong as it felt to bodily move an older woman, I had reached out my arms to do so when she pulled a gun from the pocket of her cardigan. The bedspread was a metallic grey, and the gun seemed to match.

"If you make a move toward me, I swear to God, I'll shoot you." She cocked it, ready to fire.

I backed away from her, putting me further from the door. "What are you doing?"

"Oh, please, don't try to play innocent. I know what you saw, and you know what it means. Why have you persisted in all this—trying to figure out what happened to Lauren? You weren't friends. She was too unpleasant to have friends. Were you jealous? Is that it?"

"Jealous of what?"

She flung her arm out. "This house for starters. That crummy area you live in—the view of the parking lot behind you. Everybody wants this."

My ears picked up a sound. It was the T.V. blasting. Good, that would keep the kids downstairs. "A loveless marriage?" I said. "Everyone wants that?"

"Rob loved Lauren."

"But she didn't love him. She married him for money. She was having an affair with the builder."

"And no one would have found out if you hadn't kept on and on."

"When Rob told you about the affair that night, did he ask you to come, or did you do it alone?"

Her face had a limited range of expression because of the facelift. "He never knew I was here. I just wanted to talk to Lauren and try to get her to see sense. She couldn't break up their marriage. They'd only been together two years. She hadn't given it a chance. I brought a lovely housewarming present with me." She smiled in memory.

"The figurine? And you dumped it at the airport when you took the flight back. Lucky for you, they thought it was Carmen or her son because she tried to escape to El Salvador a couple of days after that."

The dim wattage of the table lamp didn't give off much light, and the black hole of the gun barrel seemed to loom as Arlene said, "I never meant to pin it on Carmen. I thought they would think it was a random burglary."

"A burglar who only took the silver you gave for a wedding present?"

"Lauren always made it clear that she didn't appreciate the silver, just like the housewarming gift. I said, 'What do you mean you don't like it? It fits in perfectly here.'"

"So, you hit her on the head with the statuette when she turned around?" Perhaps Lauren had fallen after the first hit, but then I suspected that Arlene must have bludgeoned her a few more times to kill her. It wasn't that easy to die from a blow to the head. "Does Rob know?"

"No, he thinks I'm wonderful like all boys think their mothers are."

Whoa. I decided to switch tactics. "The thing is, whatever you did, I don't blame you. You're right, Lauren was unpleasant. And you don't even know the worst of it. She was planning a hit on Rob. Did he tell you that? She had struck a deal with the Russians to do it. And if that didn't work out, she was planning to divorce Rob once the terms of the prenup were over. She had already bought property with her boyfriend and was planning how to develop it."

"I know, I know. Barbara told me the whole sordid story. Lauren did deserve it. I came in on the 6:00 a.m. flight. I was back in Miami before Barbara even woke up. I called her from the airport when I arrived and pretended to be at home, inviting Barbara to lunch to establish an alibi in Miami. But it never came to that."

Downstairs, I could hear the children calling out to Grammy. My heart hurt like a hand had reached inside and squeezed my valve. Is that what it would feel like if I were shot? I couldn't get air in my lungs to get the words out. "But you must have regretted it." My throat closed, and I swallowed before speaking again. "After you found out Lauren was pregnant. All you ever wanted was to be a grandmother."

Her face distorted like a paper mask that had been balled into a fist and then let go.

Seeing weakness, I rushed on. "Turn yourself in—you have a good defense. You were distraught about what Rob had told you, exhausted from staying up all night, the early flight. You have untreated OCD. And chances are, Rob's not the father of the child. He was getting fertility treatment."

She sucked her breath in sharply, and I realized she hadn't known this. He hadn't confided everything.

"I knew they were having a hard time getting pregnant," she said. "I figured it was her—too old."

The smell of turkey wafting up from below was a surreal background to what she was saying.

"So, you're telling me not to be upset—it was probably the boyfriend's child. At this point, I'm so desperate for grandchildren I wouldn't care. I want one to hold."

"Then how could you do anything to hurt me when I have children?" I asked. "You know my children; you've told me how beautiful they are."

Arlene's eyes narrowed. "With you out of the way, Barbara would be even more involved, and I would be there with her."

"Do you think Barbara could be friends with you after that?"

"She needs me more than I need her."

That I could believe.

"I've killed two people," she said. "Do you think I'd have a hard time with another one?"

Chilled, I tried for a tone of bravado. "My body would be a little harder to explain."

"It was a terrible accident. Ever since Lauren's murder, I was nervous to be in the house. I talked Rob into getting a gun. The children found it in the nightstand drawer. When you picked it up, it accidentally fired."

I swayed at how plausible that sounded. I had to keep her talking. If she was anything like Barbara, she would have no upper body strength, and continuing to level that gun at me would take some effort.

"What if Rob is arrested?" I restrained my desperation and kept talking. "There's a great case against him. He found out his wife had an affair, and she was planning to get rid of him one way or the other. She had bought stocks and property with her boyfriend and must have used Rob's money to do it."

She smiled, her lips caked in red matte. "That's why I hired him a great lawyer, who Seth suggested by the way."

Suddenly, Barbara's voice carried up to us. "Arlene, what should we do about the turkey? You don't want to overcook it."

"Take it out of the oven!" Arlene screeched back.

After all this, was Barbara going to sit down and have Thanksgiving dinner with me bleeding upstairs? I swallowed and went on. "And you would have let Rob go through a jury trial? Would you ever have come forward?"

"But it never came to that. All this was for Rob, not for me. All I've ever done is for Rob. When Rob's father was going to leave, I didn't care—as long as he paid alimony and child support. But Rob—how was he going to live with the shame of his father leaving us for another woman and her children? No, I couldn't let that happen."

"You killed him instead." My tone was hushed in horror.

"He already had health problems. A bad heart."

"You're a nurse," I murmured. "You knew how to do it so no one would suspect."

"He had high blood pressure. He didn't like to take his high blood pressure medicine because it affected his 'performance.'" She rolled her eyes. "I didn't care—I'd long ago lost interest in him that way—but I suppose it mattered to lover boy and his new girlfriend." She gestured with the gun toward the bureau, and I glanced over. "I was beautiful then."

A black and white picture of Arlene and a man who must have been her husband was one of an array of pictures. I hadn't remembered it being there during "the tour" the night of Lauren's party. Perhaps since Lauren had died, Arlene had moved in her pictures. I could see from the photograph that Arlene was all glam like a nineteen-fifties movie star with dark lipstick and rolled hair. Her husband was bald, with a hook nose and wide grin.

Barbara's voice again. "It's too heavy for me to lift. Get Cara to do it."

I pleaded with Barbara inwardly, *Come upstairs. See what's going on. Stop your friend from making this terrible mistake.* But I knew she would never walk up a set of stairs if it wasn't necessary.

"We'll be down in a minute!" Arlene screeched back.

I listened, and then, hearing no other noise than the T.V., let out my breath. "The autopsy on him didn't reveal anything?"

"Nope—natural causes." She pursed her lips in satisfaction. "And between the life insurance and the fact that my husband never spent a dime—and never let me do so either—Rob and I have been taken care of ever since."

I heard a thump on the stairs, but Arlene kept talking, oblivious.

"Rob went to Harvard undergrad, Yale medical school, no loans. He never had to work, just concentrate on becoming a doctor, like I'd always dreamed for him."

I talked fast to cover up the sound of Barbara thudding up the stairs like a mummy emerging from its tomb. Arlene, like Barbara, must have been a little hard of hearing and too vain to wear hearing aids. "That's what made you so mad about Lauren's infidelity. It was like your husband leaving you all over again."

"It was all for Rob, not for me."

"Are you happy? He married a woman exactly like you."

She flinched.

That had gotten her like nothing else, so I continued, "She controlled and dominated Rob like you did with his father. And Rob's like his father. He wouldn't let Lauren have more than fifty dollars a week, and she had to shop at discount places and show him her receipts. I'm sure you know how much bitterness and resentment that breeds."

"I have no choice but to shoot you. You've already impressed upon me how little money means to you, so I won't try to offer you any to keep quiet." She pressed her lips together, determined.

I heard Barbara's wheezy breathing in the hallway before Arlene did.

Arlene whirled as Barbara walked into view of the bedroom door, saying, "Cara, the turkey's going to get dried—"

"Don't get in the middle of this, Barbara," Arlene interrupted. "It's between Cara and me."

Barbara's eyes widened at the sight of the gun in Arlene's hand. I realized then that Barbara was chewing on something, and she swallowed. Barbara's arm came up, and a turkey drumstick hurtled through the air.

When it struck Arlene in the face, she screamed. With her distracted, I bounded over the bed and knocked the gun from her hand.

Epilogue

My Thanksgiving Day stint at the Washington D.C. main police station was a corrective experience. This time, unlike the day of Lauren's death, I was no longer alone to chase my children around and protect them against the inevitable germs of criminals. Instead, we were on a three adult (Seth, Barbara, and me)-to-two children ratio. This was ideal in my book—always try to outnumber the children. And since everything was closed on Thanksgiving Day, the police department wasn't a bad play area. Staff were few, so we weren't disturbing anyone, and running around those cubicles was darn fun. Alyssa and Noah couldn't have cared less about Thanksgiving dinner; they had vending machine snacks.

Sergeant Nelson was a big crank because he had to leave his football game or whatever people did on Thanksgiving other than eat. He offered no apology for me being right in the end, although he did share that Sergeant Reynolds had given birth a couple of days before—another girl. "Now she's got three of 'em." And he had to smile at the flying turkey leg that had distracted Arlene, even as Seth and I made faces at each other; the level of detail and drama of Barbara's story as drawn out as her climb up Rob's stairs.

"I just had this feeling." Barbara pulled a long face. "Something was calling to me." She swept her hand up, gaze following.

I rolled my eyes at Seth at her dramatic re-enactment. We knew she'd only forced herself upstairs because of her horror of eating overcooked turkey. She preferred her food dripping and raw.

"It's not easy for me," Barbara continued. "You know—my knees. And then, once I saw the look in Arlene's eyes, I could tell she'd finally lost it." She turned to me. "I told you she needed medication."

"But earlier—" Sergeant Nelson flipped through a page. "You mentioned that she was your best friend. You were best friends with an EDP?"

When Barbara looked blank, I supplied, "Emotionally Disturbed Person." No person-first language for the police.

Barbara put on her sad bull-dog expression. "Well, ever since my husband died, it's been so lonely. Arlene was the only person who stuck by me. She had lost her husband, too, so we had a lot in common." She was brought up short by her own statement. "But now you're saying that she admitted to killing Howard. He was cheap, but he didn't deserve to go like that."

"Ma'am, let's get back to your statement."

Barbara didn't balk under Sergeant Nelson's sharp tone or quicken her pace in the least. "So, there I was, standing in the hallway. Cara had obviously accused Arlene of something." She said to me, "Why you did it then with me and the grandbabies downstairs, I don't know."

"I accidentally spied the plane ticket receipt, and you know she never gets rid of anything," I reminded her. "Arlene could tell I'd figured it out."

As if I hadn't spoken, Barbara groaned. "All I could think about was those precious darlings watching *Maisy Mouse*. I had to do something before she killed us all. The only weapon I had—" She nodded grimly. "The turkey leg."

Sergeant Nelson didn't ask why she carried a turkey leg in her hand at that particular time. She'd explained to us earlier, "I needed to see if the turkey was done. There's nothing worse than overcooked turkey."

Barbara said, "I hated to think of the grease getting on that beautiful bedspread, but I had to do it. And I got her right in the eye." She cackled triumphantly, and we had to laugh at this part of the story just as we had each time she told it.

Barbara smiled slyly at the police detective, and she may have even batted her eyelashes. "Do I get a medal for solving two crimes?"

Okay, I gave her credit for the arrest of Tad Gowers on city corruption, but two crimes?

A little later, as we sat in molded plastic chairs waiting for Sergeant Nelson to print out our statements, Barbara shook her head sadly. "All that food Arlene cooked, and she'll never be able to eat it. I'll have to move up to Washington. There's no one for me in Miami now." Barbara opened her bag of chips and popped one in her mouth. After chewing in contemplation, she said, "Surely, they'll give Arlene a break on her sentence—she's almost seventy."

"She deserves everything she gets," Seth said. "She's a cold-blooded murderer. She'd killed twice already, and she wouldn't have hesitated to kill again…" Spying Sergeant Nelson heading toward us, Seth jumped up eagerly. He did not have my basis of comparison and considered the time we had spent at the police department nothing short of hellish.

Sergeant Nelson handed us our statements. "Okay, folks, read these over, sign them, and you'll be free to go home." He seemed slightly more cheerful now that it was almost over.

"And you'll get Carmen released?" I asked.

"Yes, ma'am."

While we'd waited, I had worked the channels at the County Department of Human Services, so Carmen could pick Sylvia up from foster care that night. I trusted that Carmen knew how to get word to her son that she was now out of jail. Hopefully, he would return home, too.

"Hey, guys," I called to Alyssa and Noah. "We're leaving."

As we waited for them to emerge from the divider, Seth said, "I still can't believe I was out buying beer when your life was in danger." He had been kicking himself routinely for the last several hours. "We went from place to place, and everything was closed."

Barbara put her arm around me. "Don't worry, Seth. We did just fine without you. Let's go find a restaurant that does Thanksgiving—it's on me."

About the Author

Jacque Rosman (Jacqueline Corcoran) lives outside Washington D.C. with her husband, two children, two cats, and a rescue chihuahua. She is the author of *A Surrealist Affair*. *Murder In Georgetown* is the first in the Academic Mom Mystery Series.

Upcoming New Release!

JACQUE ROSMAN'S

Murder Off U Street
The Academic Mom Mystery Series
Book Two

Dr. Cara Knight hand-picked student Emily Vinter for the internship at Metro DC Police Victim Services, but the assignment brings out Emily's dark side, and she's fired for meddling in the investigation of an apparent suicide. When Cara discovers Emily's body under similar circumstances, can she discover the truth, with the aid of her interfering mother-in-law, before more young women in the U Street district befall the same fate?

Murder Off U Street is the thrilling second book in The Academic Mom Mysteries!

For more information
visit: www.SpeakingVolumes.us

Upcoming New Release!

BY
GERI SPIELER

Regina of Warsaw
Regina of Warsaw Series
Book 1

**"The Story of a Young Woman Who Rebels Against Violence of
Early 20th Century Poland"**

Regina Anuszewicz looked forward to visiting her sister in Bialystok for a late afternoon stroll along the Bialy River. It was June 1906, and it should have been an exciting time to stay overnight in the women's boarding house. However, a violent pogrom blasted those plans as a rage of violence shook the town and Regina's hopes. Stormtroopers swarmed the streets and homes, stomping up to her sister's boarding house, forcing Regina to hide inside the wardrobe, barely able to breathe as she heard screams and people begging for their lives. The trauma of that day shaped Regina's life and every decision she made as she moved through the days and years, coloring her approach to every event that took her from Poland to the United States and the four children she sought to protect.

**For more information
visit: www.SpeakingVolumes.us**